Archibald Clavering Gunter, Fergus Redmond

A Florida enchantment

Archibald Clavering Gunter, Fergus Redmond

A Florida enchantment

ISBN/EAN: 9783743304888

Manufactured in Europe, USA, Canada, Australia, Japa

Cover: Foto ©Andreas Hilbeck / pixelio.de

Manufactured and distributed by brebook publishing software
(www.brebook.com)

Archibald Clavering Gunter, Fergus Redmond

A Florida enchantment

ARCHIBALD CLAVERING GUNTER'S
Celebrated Novels.

MR. BARNES OF NEW YORK.

MR. POTTER OF TEXAS.

THAT FRENCHMAN!

MISS NOBODY OF NOWHERE.

Story for Children of All Ages.

SMALL BOYS IN BIG BOOTS.

ILLUSTRATED.

CONTENTS.

BOOK I.

THE METAMORPHOSIS OF MISS LILLIAN TRAVERS.

BOOK II.

THE BOYHOOD OF LILLY TRAVERS.

6   CONTENTS.

A FLORIDA ENCHANTMENT.

BOOK I.

THE METAMORPHOSIS OF MISS LILLIAN TRAVERS.

CHAPTER I.

THE PURCHASE AT VEDDER'S.

"YES, right there!—The one between the rattle-snake's fangs and the alligator's skin."

"Oh! the little black box," remarks the sales-woman.

"Yes—the ebony casket," says Miss Lillian Travers to the woman who presides behind the counter in that portion of Vedder's extraordinary museum, which is devoted to commerce in the form of disposing of Florida curiosities and horrors, to Northern tourists. These crowd the place now, for it is the beginning of February of the year 1891, and already many have escaped from wintry winds and snowy blasts, to throng St. Augustine, bask in its sun, and drink in the mild orange-scented breezes, that prevail the first four months of the year, to make this place a paradise to lovers of tropic scenes and nursers of failing lungs.

"This thing?" exclaims the woman in an astonished tone of voice, for she has been expecting a liberal order in sharks' jaws, manatee-skins, and bead-work, from her customer, and is rather surprised at the young lady's selection.

"Yes," rejoins Lilly Travers hurriedly; "how much is it?"

"Ain't no price marked on it—but five dollars'll do!"

"I'll take it!"

"Five dollars for *that!*" cries a bright, laughing voice in Miss Travers' shell-like ear. This is from pretty Bessie Horton, who being a resident of St. Augustine, is showing Lillian the sights of the town. "Five dollars for an old moth-eaten, cobweb-covered black box, without any key to its lock!"

"Hush!" whispers the New York girl, to her lively companion. "That's the reason I want it; it hasn't been opened for a long time—there may be something in it." Then she turns to the woman who is about to wrap up her purchase, and says: "Do you know where that thing came from?"

"No," replies the saleslady; "it's been on that shelf ever since I came here. I told Mr. Vedder that I didn't think it was any good keeping it there, as nobody would buy it; but he said, 'This is the shop to sell odds and ends! Always find a customer for everything, some time or other.'"

"Can I see Mr. Vedder?" inquires Miss Lilly eagerly.

" Oh, he's gone out for the afternoon ; he's over on Anastasia Island, hunting rattlesnakes—our stock's pretty low."

Here their conversation is broken in upon by a juvenile, high-keyed voice crying to the ebbing and flowing crowd: "Walk in now, ladies and gents. The animals in the back yard—the 'gators in the water trough—and the snakes in the snake-room. Our new diamond-back rattler is about to eat a squirrel. Please walk in to the feed, and don't faint if the moccasin hisses!"

This harangue calls forth from various ladies stifled exclamations of horror, emphasized by vivacious feminine shudders. But Lillian Travers takes Vedder's boy aside and says nervously to him :

" What do you make such horrid remarks for? One would think you like to frighten people."

" So I does," grins the youth solemnly, " when the old man's out. Wouldn't you like me to show you our stuffed rattler? It's the largest in the world— it's twelve feet long and as big as a boa constrictor."

" No," replies the young lady with a little stifled cry; " but I would like you to tell me if you know where this little black box came from?" She has the article in her hand.

"Oh," answers the boy, " that was taken out of the sand on 'Stasia Island, a couple of miles below the light-house—about five years ago. I was a kid at the time." He is only about fifteen as he makes the remark. " And it's been lying up there ever since." He points to the dusty shelf.

" No one has opened it ? "

"No one, as I knows on. We ain't had any time to bother, as there warn't no key. Perhaps dey don't want it sold."

"It is already sold!" cries Miss Travers excitedly. "I have bought it! Don't you dare try and take it from me! I—I have paid for it!" which she has already done, and clinging to her prize, she rushes out into Bay Street, as if fearing she may be pursued, and her treasure taken from her.

"Why did you pay five dollars for such a worthless thing?—and you are really frightened that they will take it away from you," laughs pretty Bessie Horton, as she follows her companion.

"Don't you see," answers Lilly hurriedly, as she walks along the unpaved street, drawing in the fresh breeze that is blowing from the open waters of the Atlantic, over Matanzas Inlet, as if she enjoyed it. "Don't you see, Bessie, that this is perhaps a duplicate of the ebony cabinet on Aunt Constantia's parlor table, which is considered one of our family heirlooms? That's the reason I paid five dollars for it."

"Yes—I remember I've seen it on Miss Connie's table," acquiesces Bessie.

"I would have paid fifty, if they had had the sense to ask me," continues the possessor of the box eagerly,—for Miss Lilly Travers, when she is twenty-five will come into a very pretty New York fortune. At present she is considered twenty-one by her friends, and hardly looks even that age as she trips gracefully along with cheeks reddened in the sea-breeze that is tossing her delicate laces and mousse-line de soie about her lithe and charming figure and giving passing glimpses of a pair of pretty feet and charming ankles perfectly booted and hosed.

But if her figure, which, though tall, is exquisitely graceful and feminine, is alluring to the eye, Lillian Travers' face is even more so. Though an American, there is almost a foreign piquancy in her laughing lips and sparkling eyes. These last are dark, grand and scintillating, but at times of wondrous softness and tenderness,—indicating that when this young lady loves she loves deeply, passionately —even jealously. The whole effect of her countenance would be softly feminine, were it not for a Grecian nose, as delicately chiselled as that of a classic statue, but with a peculiar dilation of the nostril that gives to it whenever her pride is deeply wounded a haughty, even aggressive, firmness.

She is in direct contrast to the pretty Southern girl who trips beside her trying to keep step with the longer and firmer stride of her Northern companion; for Miss Bessie Horton is a plump little blonde, with golden hair and violet eyes and a rounded figure whose graceful outlines and exquisite contours go straight to the masculine eye and enslave the masculine heart. She has the soft, cooing speech that is peculiar to Southern women, and is a member of an old Florida family who make their home at St. Augustine, her father owning considerable orange lands and phosphate properties in the southern portion of that State.

Miss Travers, on the contrary, is an importation direct from New York. Her father had been a Wall Street banker, though her mother was a

member of the Oglethorpe family, one of the best
known in Florida, descendants from the grand old
governor of colonial times.   At present she is
visiting her aunt, Miss Constantia Oglethorpe, a
maiden of some fifty-five summers and winters, who
lives near the shell-road in a pretty villa that, sur-
rounded by orange-trees, palms, and cacti, faces the
blue waters of Matanzas Inlet.

Upon this lovely piece of water the girls are gazing as they pass along Bay Street and enjoy its
picturesque beauty.   Faced as this street is by old
buildings on one side, that give it an air of anti-
quity and romance, enlivened by its crowds of white-
sleeved, bare-armed boatmen at each of the little
wharves that run out into the limpid waves—embellished by its Northern tourists and a few Southern
planters and orange growers—dotted by shining
negroes and yellow-skinned mulatto boys; and
fringed on the other by the rippling waters of the
bay, which are made lively by sail and fishing boats
and bright yachts whose white wings have brought
them from the far North in search of perpetual
summer ; under the azure sky and soft warm sun it
is like the Riviera in April, though no mountains
are back of it to give it grandeur, nor antique pal-
aces to lend it romance.   Out on the blue ripples is
a steam pleasure ship whose millionnaire owner has
fled from winter to seek abstraction from business
in pursuit of game and fish on Southern rivers, or
beautiful women in the gardens of the Ponce de
Leon or balconies of the Córdova.

Lillian Travers thinks the sparkling scene very
beautiful after New York snow and cries enthusi-

astically, "Isn't this worth thirty-two hours in a rail-road train, Bess?"

"Oh! just look at that steam yacht; can you read its name? G-a-d-a—the—the Gadabout!—what a funny name—but what a darling boat! Her owner must be very rich—and I hope young," cooes Bessie, her blue eyes devouring the graceful craft lying at anchor some hundred yards from the shore.

"Rich, but not young," remarks Miss Travers sententiously. "I know Mr. Remington quite well. You can see for yourself.—He's landing now." She points to a naphtha launch which is depositing its passengers upon a little wharf nearly opposite the two young ladies.

"Oh, the gentleman papa is going to sell the phosphate lands to," cries Miss Bessie; for her father, Major Calhoun Benham Horton, has given up any animosity he may have felt toward North-erners at the close of the war, in the delight of sell-ing them phosphate properties; the Southern eye being as quick to see and the Southern hand as deft to catch the almighty dollar as those of their per-haps shrewder but no more eager brothers of Con-necticut and Massachusetts.

As she says this, a gentleman is passing through the crowd of boatmen that gather round him eagerly offering their craft for the various pur-poses of pleasure, fishing and excursion, about the inlet. Arriving at terra firma the yachtsman sees the two young ladies, and, taking off his hat po-litely to Miss Travers, whom he knows very well, is introduced to Miss Bessie.

A moment after the Southern girl whispers to the
Northern one : " You were quite right ; he *is* too
old for anything except giving me a sail on his
yacht." For Stockton Remington is a man who is
sixty and has spent two-thirds of his life in fighting
for a fortune in Wall Street, and his face shows
signs of the struggle.

"This is an unexpected pleasure," he remarks,
" my dear Miss Travers. I had supposed you could
not run away from New York gayeties."

" Oh," replies Lillian lightly, " when Lent begins,
New York functions cease, and I come to Florida.—
I arrived on the ' special ' last evening."

" Ah, in search of fun ?" remarks Mr. Remington.

" Perhaps," answers the young lady, though her
countenance grows serious as she utters the word.

" Bound for the centre of town ? "

" Yes. I have just been to Vedder's and made a
purchase, and am now in search of a locksmith,"
says Miss Travers smiling.

" A locksmith ?" exclaims the gentleman, astounded—" a locksmith to unlock the alligator's jaws ? "

"Oh no ; I have just bought this little black box,
and want to find out what is inside of it," returns
Lillian, holding up the article for inspection.

" May I carry it for you ? "

" Not for worlds—its contents may be very precious," laughs Miss Travers.

"The article does not look very promising," remarks Remington examining it—" I hardly think
you'll get your money's worth."

" Oh yes, I will ! " answers Lilly gayly.

" Of what ? "

" Curiosity—romance—whatever's inside it "—
returns the girl, and they pass up Cathedral Street,
chatting on the various subjects peculiar to the
time and place. At the corner of St. George Street
Miss Travers says : " We must bid you good-by,
Mr. Remington, for the locksmith's."

" You are not stopping at any of the hotels, Miss
Travers ? " queries the yachtsman. " I must know
your address. The Gadabout is lonely ! You must
make up a sailing party for me soon."

" No ;—with my aunt, Miss Oglethorpe, just off
the shell-road, where I shall be delighted to see
you."

" I shall undoubtedly drive on the shell-road," responds Mr. Remington gallantly. " At present I
am on my way to the Ponce de Leon to see Mrs.
Lovejoy."

" Stella Lovejoy ? " asks Lilly eagerly, with a shade
of apprehension in her voice, which has been laughing a moment before.

" Certainly, the pretty widow. She came down
on the Gadabout as my guest and as chaperon for
my party, with Mr. Wilkes and Miss Key of Balti-
more. Now, having grown tired of sea-life, the
whole crowd have deserted my ship for more roomy
quarters at the Ponce de Leon. There's gratitude
for you ! " answers the yachtsman with a grin.

" Mr. Wilkes," cries Miss Bessie suddenly,—" Mr.
Charley Wilkes ? "

" Yes."

" Why, he is the young man to whom father
sold the orange grove on Indian River. He comes

here every winter. He isn't a New-Yorker,—he's a Floridian. He's too consumptive to be a New-Yorker!" laughs the Southern girl. Then she says with a pretty pout: " Of course he is devoted to the beautiful widow."

" He was, on the yacht," replies the gentleman sententiously; "but on shore"—here he chuckles slyly and remarks impressively—" there is a doctor."

" A doctor! Who?" asks Miss Travers suddenly, turning to Remington who notes with astonishment that the young lady's eyes have somehow grown quite sad.

" Oh, I never tell secrets," the New-Yorker says pointedly.—Then as if to cut off further questions, he raises his hat, and remarks suggestively, " Shall I give your regards to Mrs. Lovejoy?"

" Certainly," replies Lillian in a set tone of voice, as Remington turns towards the Ponce de Leon, wondering what the deuce affects Miss Travers, who is believed in New York society to be heartless, as she has never given her heart away to any of its beaux or social lions, though many have sought it— for her beauty is great and her fortune will be large when she is twenty-five.

" And now, the locksmith's," laughs Miss Bessie. " I am dying to see what is in the ebony box."

" Ah! the locksmith's," ejaculates Lilly, as if she had suddenly remembered something—an absent-minded mood that remains with her until they reach the artisan's place of business.

After a few moments' examination and some minutes employed in fitting a key to its wards, the workman remarks: " The lock is rather rusty."

"Rusty! I should think so," cries Bessie. "It perhaps has not been opened for a hundred years."

"It works as if it hadn't been opened for a thousand," replies the artisan; but after deluging the wards with oil and working the key about in the lock with his vise-like hands for some little time the bolts finally yield to his strong fingers and spring back. He is about to open the lid, when Miss Travers, who has been gazing at him in a preoccupied manner, suddenly gives a gasp, seizes the box and astonishes both the locksmith and Miss Bessie as she exclaims: "Not now! There may be a secret inside it—a secret for which I paid five dollars. Please do the box up in paper; I'll take it home with me for examination there."

"And I am not going to see what is inside that box *now?* If they are jewels—I shall expect a present," pouts Bessie with curious eyes, for the girl has been letting her imagination run riot on the contents of the old casket and would not be surprised if it disclosed the wealth of Golconda in diamonds and rubies.

"Not until we get to my aunt's, anyway—and then perhaps I shall want the secret all to myself," returns Lilly, who has apparently awakened to what is passing around her and thrown off any cloud that may have been on her mind. "Then, perhaps, if you are a good girl——"

"Oh, I'll be very good," laughs Bessie; "with a secret ahead of me, I am always to be relied upon. Suppose we go to the Ponce de Leon and listen to the band; it makes me feel romantic and poetic these sunny mornings."

2

So chatting together, the two girls walk straight
to the Alameda and are soon standing in Old Spain
where Miss Lillian Travers gets one of the shocks
of her life.

CHAPTER II.

THE PEEPING EVE OF THE PONCE DE LEON.

THE young ladies are between the two great
hotels of St. Augustine—the Cordova, with its
Moorish windows, square turrets and narrow arches,
and the Ponce de Leon, whose Spanish-domed
towers and sloping tiled roofs in the architecture
of Seville or Valencia are embowered in its gardens
of orange and palm and flowering shrubs. Immediately facing them is the square of the Alcazár
with its ceaseless fountain and tropical plants; beyond, the Villa Zorayda looking like some Grana-
dan villa from which the Emirs of the Moorish
Kingdom issued five hundred years ago to sack
Andalusian villages and carry off the maids of fair
Castile to Eastern harems.

Through this scene of the Old World passes the
Alameda which is all of the modern; its asphalt
pavement, covered with prancing steeds and liveried
equipages; its stone sidewalks peopled with brilliantly dressed men and women displaying the
toilets of Paris and New York.

Arch this scene with a bright blue sky, without a
single cloud; light it up by a tropic sun, temper its
heat by a sea-breeze that gently moves and rustles

the foliage of the luxuriant vegetation; brighten this all with lovely American women—make it musical by the light laughter of people who live but for pleasure, mingled with the soft melodies of a brilliant band playing one of Verdi's love songs, and you have what the two young ladies look upon this morning in St. Augustine,—this old town of the Spanish conquistadores, now rebuilt and revivified by a modern conqueror of finance and oil.

After a short pause of contemplative enjoyment, Miss Bessie, to whom the scene is much more familiar than to Miss Travers, hurries her companion along, stopping occasionally to greet a passing friend, Lilly also recognizing one or two Northern visitors.

A moment after Miss Bessie says: "Oh my! Here's papa."

And Miss Travers finds herself warmly greeted by an old-time Southern gentleman of semi-military manner and semi-planter dress;—for Major Calhoun Benham Horton prides himself upon always remembering that he once held a commission in the Confederate Army signed by Jefferson Davis. He bows to the young lady with punctilious politeness and welcomes her to St. Augustine and Southern hospitality with the grace of a modern Bayard.

" Egad!" he remarks; " Miss Lillian, those Northern roses on your cheeks look so charming, that if I were—ahem!—slightly younger, I should certainly think of giving Bess a stepmother."

At this Miss Bessie gives a little pout and mutters—" You'd better not—not even Lilly!" Then wishing to turn the conversation—for Miss Horton lives in horror of her father in his gallantry to the fair sex giving her a stepmother to rule her—she says: " Have you seen Mr. Remington? He's just come ashore from his steam yacht."

" No. Is Remington here?" asks the major, hurriedly. Then he continues: " I must see him at once. Those phosphate lands he wrote me about are almost disposed of to an English company, and if he does not move in a hurry, Johnny Bull will for once in his life get ahead of the Yankees."

" Mr. Remington is probably in the Ponce," remarks Miss Travers; and the three stroll into the court-yard of that beautiful building, where the major cries out *sans cérémonie* to a dark-colored gentleman in gorgeous yellow livery, knee breeches and silk stockings, " Here, boy, chairs for the ladies ! "—and darts for the office, or the billiard-room, or the bar, or some other place usually frequented by masculine humanity, in search of the Northern capitalist. A moment after the two girls are provided with camp-stools, Miss Travers' quarter of a dollar soothing the colored servant's vanity that has been deeply wounded by the major's " Boy!" Then they listen to the music of the band from the loggia, and look over the lovely garden with its gushing fountain—hemmed in on all sides by these modern buildings of old-fashioned Spanish architecture, making it look like the *patio* of some great Chilean house or Mexican *hacienda*.

The soft Southern air and dreamy melodies bring contemplation to Miss Travers. She sits looking at the little ebony box which the locksmith has done up in paper, as it lies on her lap, and indulges

in a few minutes of brown study. Miss Bessie has
probably less on her mind, and keeps her bright eyes
pretty well occupied noting robes and millinery;
directing, however, a few veiled glances at such of
the masculine portion of the assemblage, as find
favor in her sight—there being plenty of men to
choose from scattered about in costumes varying
between the bright flannels of the tennis-court and
the sombre black broadcloth of gentlemen from the
prairies.

After a few minutes of this, Miss Travers is suddenly roused by Bessie's hand upon her arm and
Bessie's whisper in her ear, " Hush. Don't look up
too quickly—don't appear to notice her—but see,
that girl on the veranda of the second story of the
hotel. I have been watching her for five minutes,
and her face has expressed love, hatred, jealousy,
despair,—and she's just lovely in all of them."

"Who is she?—Ah!" ejaculates Miss Travers.
For her eyes are resting upon a very beautiful girl,
who, partly screened from observation by the heavy
columns of the Spanish arches of the balcony that
faces the court-yard, on the main building of the
Ponce de Leon, is glancing diagonally across the
garden into one of the open windows of the left
wing of the building.

"See," whispers Bessie. " A moment before, her
eyes had love in them; now they have despair.
What a gallant he must be to agitate her so!"

" He—who ? "

" The man she is looking at, of course!" cries
Bessie.

For at this moment the young lady they are discussing leans against the pillar of the veranda as if overcome by some cruel emotion.

" I wonder who she is," babbles Bessie. " She must be awfully in love with him."

" In love with him ! "

" Yes ; of course—the gentleman that girl adores— Suppose we run up to that balcony and take a peep ourselves."

" Do you think it would be precisely fair ? " remarks Miss Travers.

" Yes—if he's handsome ! Come on ! You know I cannot go alone, but together we can wander up nonchalantly and carelessly. He must be a lovely fellow, to produce such potent emotions. Quick, or it will be over."

Thus adjured, after a careless refusal or two, Miss Lilly, who is a woman and also curious, follows Bessie into the hotel, and a few minutes after they are on the balcony, chatting in apparent carelessness.

The rustle of their dresses—perhaps the sound of their voices—reaches the object of their solicitude, who has been gazing intently upon a little Moorish balcony that communicates with one of the suites of apartments in the right wing of the building. The moment she sees them, her face by a mighty effort becomes placid, calm—perhaps even careless ; and a second or two after she saunters off the veranda into the rotunda, humming in apparent nonchalance the air the band is playing.

" A wonderful actress," whispers Bess enthusiastically. " Perhaps she may be a real one. Now, let us see this Romeo who was the cause of her passion, jealousy and despair."

The next instant she is standing in the young lady's place gazing upon the same veranda, and beside her is Lillian Travers with passion, jealousy and despair also in her heart, leaning against the selfsame column and uttering the same sad despairing sighs of the former watcher.

Fortunately Bessie is too occupied to notice her companion's agitation. "Isn't he lovely," she ejaculates ; "and isn't she a stunner?" For upon the little balcony to which she devotes her attention, is seated a beautiful woman opposite a very handsome man.

The lady is perhaps five and twenty and looks her age, but no more. As the graceful yet mature developments of her figure are outlined by the clinging yet flowing drapery of a beautiful semi-tropical morning toilet, they seem perfection in their careless pose and languid ease. One pretty foot in light, silken hose, and dainty slipper is tapping nervously the veranda. One white hand ornamented, not covered, with rings and bracelets is resting pensively upon the arm of the chair in which she lounges. The other, which cannot be seen, may be—probably is— in the grasp of the gentleman seated beside her. Her eyes, which are of a brilliant, metallic steel blue, are glancing vivaciously at him, and her rosy lips, parted in smiles, show the white pearls between them as she apparently utters a word or two to the cavalier beside her.

He, however, is doing most of the talking— undoubtedly earnestly, probably passionately ; his gestures being those of devotion and persuasion, and his eyes having in them a reckless fire. He is

nearly six feet tall, of slight yet handsome propor-
tions, and has a kind of off-hand insouciance in his
attitude, as if he felt he had his battle well in hand.
His forehead is high and would be noble were it not
contradicted by his other features; for his eyes,
though beautiful, are careless, reckless, insincere;
his nose, though dominating, is not delicate, and his
handsome mouth, under his long drooping mustache
shows passion rather than love; a face that would
scarcely be true to wife, maid or widow—certainly
not to wife. His figure and bearing are of that
manly recklessness, jovial good humor and dashing,
devil-may-care coolness—perhaps impudence—that
makes deadly war upon female hearts,—the face of an
Adam whom Eves will love and run after for all time,
and who for all time will betray his despairing Eves.

"Isn't Fred lovely," cries Bess, after drinking in
this scene with open eyes. "You'll meet him at the
hop to-morrow night, Dr. Frederick Cassadene.
Isn't he beautiful! Why don't you answer me?
Are you so love-struck that you've lost your voice?"
and she turns round, but to her astonishment discovers that she is alone; that Lillian Travers has
silently deserted her. At this she muses to herself:
"I wonder what is the matter with Lilly;" then
gives a sort of stifled, frightened gasp: "Can she be
smitten like that other girl?" and so meditatively
finds her way to the court-yard below, with its
laughing crowd, dreamy music, bright sun and
happy faces.

But nowhere can she find her companion of the
morning, for Lillian Travers, staggering and stunned
with misery, has faltered through the palm-swept

alleys of the Ponce de Leon and crossed the crowded Alameda into the more lonely plaza of the Alcazár, where only the hum of voices from the crowd comes floating to *her*. The music of the distant band seems a requiem of hopes never to be realized—of love that perchance has passed away,—and she sinks on a bench screened by a spreading oleander, where the splashing fountain murmurs in her ears the despairing refrain : " He whom I loved and trusted —who was to have been my husband—has forgotten me ! "

She writhes under this thought, and mutters— " Fred—Fred—Fred !" as if to call her careless lover back to her." Then pride comes to her, and self-esteem tells her that if Mrs. Stella Lovejoy, whom she has easily recognized as a New York acquaintance of hers, is a rich and beautiful widow, she Lillian Travers is a rich and beautiful girl—and she says reassuringly to herself : " Of course, it was a professional call—I should remember my fiancé is a doctor.—A woman who gives her heart should give her faith."—Next she cries out in feminine logic, " Who was that horrid jealous girl who was spying upon him ?—I'll—I'll make Fred give me a satis- factory explanation as to *her*—I'll—He must have got my note by this time, he must know I'm in St. Augustine.—He'll be at my aunt's this afternoon I must hurry home and dress—I'll try and show him I'm not jealous—jealousy seems despicable in a man's eyes.—There was no man gazing in agony from that veranda at Stella Lovejoy,—then says desperately, " Oh, if I could love like a man !" rising from her seat to go in search of Bessie.

But turning her eyes toward the Ponce de Leon she catches sight of that young lady deeply engaged with Mr. Wilkes, and this gives her mind another wrench—"Even that creature," she thinks contemptuously, for Wilkes is not a noble looking biped, "is a man, and has forgotten Mrs. Lovejoy in Bess's bright eyes. And yet Remington said he had been cut out of the beautiful widow's affections by a doctor."—Here her heart gives a throb of agony and she cries savagely, "What doctor?—My doctor Fred?—if it should be——" and clinches her pretty fist—then sniffs at the fountain and mutters, "What horrid sulphur water!—This place is not healthy!" and almost tottering to the Alameda calls a carriage and gasps, "Miss Oglethorpe's place—Sunny Grove —Quick!"

So, getting in, she is driven to her aunt's home in so gloomy, meditative and sighing a mood that she entirely forgets the box that lies carelessly upon her lap. An abstraction that does not argue well for Doctor Fred when he makes his afternoon call upon his pretty fiancée; as Miss Lillian Travers had but an hour ago a very lively curiosity as to its contents.

CHAPTER III.

THE WIDOW'S FLUTTERING PULSE.

HER indifference to the object lying in her lap is not surprising; for Lillian Travers is running over in her mind the events of the last six months. The

orphan daughter of a New York banker, she has
no near relatives, save the lady to whose house she
is driving, and though her own mistress has not
been, until the last few days, the mistress of her
own fortune; for her father, having a mortal dread
of his beautiful child's wealth making her the prey
of some matrimonial fortune-hunter, had provided
in his will that all his property, both real and personal, should remain in trust for his daughter and
her descendants, only the income from it to be
used for their support and maintenance.

If, however, Miss Travers remained unwed until
her twenty-fifth year, the property should then pass
into her sole possession and unlimited control; the
testator apparently thinking that Lillian's wisdom
at that age would protect her from an unwise marriage.

This provision had for some time after her
father's death apparently been unnecessary, Miss
Travers' heart being invincible to masculine ad-
vances; until the preceding summer, chancing to
spend a few days at the Grand Union, Saratoga, she
had met Dr. Frederick Cassadene, who was acting
as the physician at that celebrated hotel.

Called in to see her professionally, to treat some
passing ailment, his prescriptions had been beneficial
to her health, but his charms of manner and conversation had been fatal to her heart. It was a case
of love at first sight on her side—probably on his;
for this medical gentleman's attachments to pretty
women were not so permanent as ardent.

Under these circumstances Lilly's visit to Saratoga had been extended to the end of the season,

and when she left that watering place, Doctor Fred's engagement ring sparkled on her white hand.

During the first of the winter the Doctor had followed her to New York and pressed her for an early marriage, stating very candidly that his means were only the uncertain income derived from a practice in Saratoga during the summer months, and an equally precarious attendance upon invalids in St. Augustine during the winter exodus of Northern tourists to that celebrated resort. This exposé of his financial inequality with the New York heiress had been made with seeming ingenuousness but with great ingenuity; for Doctor Cassadene knew that Lillian loved him well enough to take him, rich or poor, and be only happy that her wealth could add to the prosperity of the man she adored.

At his request Miss Travers had immediately informed him of the peculiarity of her father's will, and had been delighted at the generosity of his reply; for he had implored her to marry him immediately, saying that he loved her too well to postpone the happiness of being her husband for the pleasure of being rich.

She loved him more than ever as she answered, " Had we not better wait until I am twenty-five? —then I can lavish upon you the principal, not the interest, of my fortune, Fred."

"Fancy the horror of waiting four years!" he had muttered. Whereupon she had given him a roguish smile and remarked demurely, " Perhaps the four years will run around sooner than you think. Wait until next spring; then if you wish to marry me immediately, you may have my hand as you have my heart now."

A few days after this promise, the Doctor had departed for St. Augustine, carrying the kisses of his beautiful fiancée upon his lips, and two months later, Lilly Travers had suddenly taken the— "Florida Special" to visit her aunt, following the man she loved, with a great gladness in her heart and a rapturous surprise for him in her mind.

Perhaps it is this that causes her to murmur as she drives up the pretty avenue of orange trees, " Fred, if you knew the revelation I have in store for you, the confession I have to make to you—you would be waiting for me on that porch—now ! "

As she says this, she steps out of the carriage and is welcomed by her aunt, Miss Constantia Oglethorpe, with the soft words and tender kisses an old lady gives to a young one who is very near her heart. They sit down to lunch and Miss Connie remarks, " You did not eat anything for breakfast, Lil, and have no appetite now—perhaps this letter may improve it,"—and smilingly produces a little note that Lilly, clutching with a cry of joy, tears quickly open.

With hasty perusal comes sunshine and content.

She says : " Auntie, he is coming this afternoon at three. He reproaches me for not telegraphing him. Then he could have met me at the train."

" Ah ! " replies Miss Constantia ; " then I shall soon see the Doctor Fred of your letters, Lilly. Bessie Horton knows him slightly and says he's very handsome—and you told me the same, I believe, last night."—Here the aunt gives a roguish glance at the niece, for these two are great chums and confidants, and Miss Connie has had Lilly's secret in her keeping almost from the time it was a secret.

A moment after, Lilly cries impulsively: "And to think that I doubted "—she checks herself.

"To think that you doubted what?"

"Oh, nothing," says the girl, reddening; then remarks suddenly, as if to turn the conversation, "Aunt Connie, tell me the story of that old ebony casket—the little one in your parlor—the family heirloom.—It has a romantic history, has it not?"

To which Miss Constantia replies: "There is nothing peculiar connected with *that* casket, though I believe there is a very extraordinary story linked with the other one!"

"The other casket! What *other* casket?"

"Why, there was once a duplicate of the one in the parlor," replies Miss Connie, smiling at her niece's eagerness. "Both of them belonged to my grandfather, old Captain Hauser Oglethorpe."

"Ah! the great sea-dog of our family, the one whose picture I am looking at," says Lilly, glancing at the portrait of a bronzed and wind-battered tar whose wicked face seems to leer into hers from a gilt frame on the opposite wall of the dining room.— She can't stand the gaze of this man on canvas, and her drooping eyes fall upon the little bundle she has brought home with her, which is standing upon the side-board.

"Yes," continues her aunt, who, like most old ladies, is always eager to tell a story of the past. "During the war of 1812, when my grandfather and your great-grandfather returned from a voyage to Africa, where I believe, my dear"—here she laughs a little—"he had been for a cargo of slaves, though that is omitted in the family annals, he was pursued by a British sloop-of-war, the *Falcon*, and his vessel, the *Firefly*, was wrecked about a mile or two below the lighthouse over there"—she points to the one that towers above Anastasia Island.

"A mile or two below the lighthouse over there," exclaims Lilly with an excited start, the boy's remarks at Vedder's in regard to her purchase flying into her mind.

"Yes," continues Miss Constantia, unheeding the interruption; "his sufferings during the shipwreck and gale were such that his mind was shattered. As a child I can remember old Grandpa Hauser, and he was then a gibbering idiot, in his dotage and nearly ninety years of age. He was always crying and pointing to that island, and saying that in the other casket, lost forever beneath the ocean, was what would make him very rich and some woman very happy."

"Some woman very happy!" ejaculates Lillian. "Why, all women are happy—any woman that is in love—any woman who is loved."

"Ah! you are certain of that, my dear?" remarks her aunt, a sad light of the past coming into her eyes. "Don't be too sure. The poor old imbecile had some curious ideas, however, for he said 'it would make that woman a man'!"

"Make the woman a MAN! What an absurd idea!" And Miss Lilly giggles merrily.

"Yes, it is an atrocious thought—one in which

only a strong-minded woman would indulge," says Constantia sternly.

"I wonder how I would look as a boy," cries her niece, rising and strutting about; for Fred's letter has made her vivaciously happy.

"Dumpy," remarks Connie sententiously.

"Dumpy! I—dumpy? Why, I am quite tall— five feet six and one-half inches."

"That is very well for a girl," replies Constantia, "but I'll warrant you would not think Doctor Fred tall with that number of feet and inches."

This puts another idea into the young lady's head and she mutters to herself, "Then, if I were a man, I could not love a man,—I could not love Fred. Awful!" Next she gives a playful little shudder, glances at her watch and exclaims, "Half-past two. I must run up and dress for him. Doctor Fred does not like to be kept waiting. Physicians love a punctual patient."

"Or sweetheart," suggests Constantia.

This is drowned by Lilly's joyous laugh as she runs up to her room, and cries to her mulatto maid, "Jane—you've only twenty-five minutes to make me good-looking," forgetting, in her anxiety to achieve an effective toilet, the purchase that had occupied so much of her thoughts during the early morning.

"Bless yo heart, yo's a Venus already. What more dos yo want—I knows what's de matter wid yo. Doc Fred's coming, Honey—I felt jus' the same when my Gus was here last night "—says her saffron-hued attendant who is very *épris* with a colored gentleman of Sixth Avenue, New York, who is at present acting as the second waiter of the Ponce

de Leon and one of the glories of its dining
room.

"Nevertheless Venus will indulge in a new
dress!" replies Lilly and places herself under Jane's
deft hands with such good results that when half
an hour afterwards Dr. Fred Cassadene springs from
a carriage and enters Miss Connie's parlor he thinks
he does see a Venus, and ejaculates to himself—
"Great Powers! I'd forgotten how lovely Lilly
was!" In truth Lilly Travers might cause rapture
to any masculine heart as she floats towards him,
some bright shimmering gauzy dress clinging to and
draping her graceful figure, a love light in her young
eyes and tender kisses on her rosy lips.

Over this beautiful vision the reckless young doctor goes into a lover's transport, forgetting that a
beautiful patient is impatiently awaiting another
professional visit from him at the Ponce de Leon
Hotel. For Fred Cassadene generally loved best in
his careless way the woman whose eyes he was
gazing into. After a few minutes of mutual rapture,
the conversation passes from the romantic to the
every-day concerns of life, that affect lovers as well
as other people. Then, this gentleman, who has
learned to read a woman's mind much more accurately than he diagnoses a patient's disease, noting
that his sweetheart's manner is a trifle embarrassed,
thinks to himself, "If she suspects I'll set myself
right before she opens the battle," and cries lightly:
"Ha ha! you've a secret, Lilly."

"Yes; two," says the girl, emphasizing this remark with both a pout and a blush, as if one were
pleasant and the other not so agreeable to her.

" Humph ! you'll tell 'em to me of course. No secrets from your loving Fred—who has none from you." And Mr. Assurance looks severely upon Miss Innocence who blushes nervously.

" Then let us go into the garden ! " mutters Lilly. " I don't want to be at home to anybody but you, Fred, on this our first meeting for nearly two long months ! "

" Yes—it did seem an awful time to me here in St. Augustine," returns the gentleman as he follows her into one of the orange alleys that leads to a summer house overlooking the blue waves of Matanzas Inlet —" But for you in gay New York, the balls, parties, opera—Eh, naughty Lilly ! " and he makes his sweetheart happy by giving the pink shell she calls her ear a dainty pinch.

" Pooh ! I didn't go to any ! Not a function this season," whispers the girl with a blush. " You would not have been there—and I was unhappy as I thought of you in lonely St. Augustine."

" Of course—*very* lonely St. Augustine ; there were few visitors here until the last week, but then——" here Fred checks himself suddenly.

" But for the last week you've done pretty well," laughs Lilly. Then she says sadly, perhaps pointedly : " The Gadabout arrived here a week ago ? " and gives a little sigh.

" Oh—ah ! That's where the land lies," thinks this medical Machiavelli and remarks, " Yes, that yacht brought me a patient—a friend of yours : Mrs. Lovejoy "—and hoping to carry the war into Africa continues rapidly : " But your secrets, *ma belle ?*—You needn't fear confession—you have a merciful judge—

your beauty shall plead in mitigation of your follies. You've been indulging in a little flirtation—eh?"

At this his sweetheart cries, "Oh, Fred—for shame!" in indignant tones and wounded voice—and with flashing eyes, confronts him—hitting him harder than she guesses as she says, "Do you think so meanly of me as to suppose I could flirt with any man with your engagement ring upon my finger?" and flashes the diamond in his face to make him ashamed of himself—for a moment—his impulses good or bad seldom last longer.

He cries quickly, "Forgive me—don't cry and break my heart"—for tears of wounded pride are in the girl's eyes," then utters impetuously, "Don't cry, and I'll never make you weep again!" and means every word he says as he looks at his beautiful sweetheart.

"Very well," she whispers, glowing under his attentions.

"You forgive me?"

"Of course—I could forgive you much more than that! I have forgiven much more to-day!"

"To-day—how have I offended?" He looks carelessly innocent as he puts the question.

"Ask your own heart?"

"My heart tells me nothing but that I love you!"

"You are sure?"

"Sure as that I love you!"

"Then you have something to forgive me," whispers Lilly, made radiant by his declaration, and she tells him the incident she had witnessed in the morning at the Ponce de Leon. Next, being very

happy to get the thing off her mind she laughs,
" And I was *so* jealous, Fred."

This gives her lover an opening.

He suddenly thinks any jealous tendency in his
sweetheart must be crushed or he will have an uncomfortable time between his beautiful fiancée and
the lovely widow. With this idea in his head he
says, " Jealous, Lilly ! " in a wounded tone that
makes her start, and then pronounces judicially the
following oration : " You must learn not to be jealous, you must understand that a medical man has
certain duties.—I presume after we are married you
will be uneasy if I go to the club—if I stay out
late of nights when my patients call me away. But,
Lilly, this will not do for the wife of a practising
physician—you must learn to control yourself as a
man would. You must have a man's faith. Men
are never jealous."

At this extraordinary statement the girl gasps,
" Men *never* jealous ? "

" At least very seldom. Did you see any man on
that balcony at the Ponce gazing in anguish at Mrs.
Lovejoy ? " he asks with a smile. " And yet I presume some men think her handsome—one man has
loved her."

" Who ? " ejaculates Lilly in sudden anxiety.
" Her husband ! " replies Fred in careless nonchalance
—" she's a widow, she must have had a husband."

" Oh, Fred ! How curiously you do put things ! "
murmurs Miss Travers with a sigh of relief. Then
she whispers, a beautiful blush flashing over her
mobile features and a soft tender light coming into
her eyes, though she turns them away from his

glance and droops her head—" I've something else to tell you, my own—something I came all the way from New York to tell you—I've got all my property!"

She is interrupted here by an astounded "What?" from the doctor; but continues excitedly, "Yes—all —bonds, securities, money in bank—real estate!" Then blushes and hides her head upon his shoulder and whispers, "You remember what you asked me in New York. There's nothing to stop our— " she goes on desperately, "our marriage now!"

"Impossible!" cries Fred in an astonished voice, for he hardly can believe her. "Your father's will said you couldn't come into possession till you were twenty-five—and you're only twenty-one and don't look that."

But here a greater surprise comes to him—perhaps a shock; his sweetheart gives him a glance of feminine reproach and mutters, "Men can never take a hint!"

"A hint of what?"

"A hint of anything sensible. Don't you know a girl never likes to tell her *full* age to her lover "— cries Lilly desperately. "Oh, how hard you make it! A week ago I was—" She cuts the awful sentence short by hiding her face again on the astounded Frederick's shoulder.

But he finishes the sentence for her by ejaculating, "You—you were twenty-five, by Jupiter!"

"Y-e-s!" This is a sigh from under his chin where Lilly's head is.

"Ah, now I understand," he goes on after a second's pause—" that was the meaning of your smiles and laughter when I groaned ' Four years was a long time to wait '—when you mocked my impatience by—— "

But she interrupts him, crying, " Don't reproach me—I only thought you would be delighted by the surprise—I—— "

" And you deceived the man you love? "

And Fred would be very stern with her, but the girl having gotten over her confession regains her spirits and laughs, " That wasn't very difficult—look at me!   I don't appear more than twenty-one; do I?"

Then glancing at her the doctor is appeased.   He cries, " My Heaven !   How beautiful you are—my own, my promised wife !" and seizes her to his breast, as her tender arms close round him and she pleads to him with kisses.

After a series of confidences and raptures, and almost naming the wedding day, Cassadene with medical prudence and lover's care says—" I must keep you from the evening fog—where's your wrap, Lil?—You don't know our Florida evenings "—then looking at his watch cries, " Nearly six o'clock,—what will my patients think?—I must be going," and Lilly, hanging on his arm as happy as any girl the sun is shining on, strolls towards the house.

" Won't you come in and see my aunt? " suggests the young lady.

" Not now—what'll my patients do? "

" Of course you'll come this evening ! "

" Well, I should rather think so," says Fred, with a little squeeze which makes his sweetheart very happy.

"What time?"

"How will eight do?"

"So late?"

"Well, half-past seven—you'll have your tea over by that time."

"Yes, and something ready to show you—I'd forgotten all about it—it's a curiosity," and she tells him of her purchase at Vedder's—then asks, "Are you an antiquarian?"

"I'd be anything to sit beside you," cries Fred.—"No, your aunt can't see us"—for they are at the gate now, and he is anxious for a kiss.

"There! No more till the evening." And with a little laugh Lilly escapes from him and drawing up her white skirts to clear the plants covered with evening dew, runs lightly along the path, making a lovely but fleeting picture of floating robes and twinkling feet and exquisite ankles and blushing face upon which her lover gazes with admiring eyes and mutters—

"By Jove! how charming! and mine too! All mine—youth, beauty and fortune. Lucky boy, Doctor Freddie!" Then whistling a merry air, he turns his steps toward the centre of St. Augustine, for he loves Lilly Travers very dearly, and is happy in his love, just at this moment.

A few minutes after, as he passes the San Marco, the lights of which are already twinkling in the dusk of the evening, Doctor Fred thinks impatiently, "By George! it's a pity I had not known of Lilly's coming into her fortune, before! This complication with Mrs. Lovejoy may be inconvenient, if she should discover"—he gives a long, con-

templative whistle, but a moment after mutters to
himself: "I've had two girls on the string before—
I guess I can handle this pair, even though both are
heiresses, and one is a widow!" and with this
steps briskly on to the Ponce de Leon, where his
servant, waiting for him in his office, informs him
that Mrs. Lovejoy is very ill.

"How do you know that?" he asks hastily.

"She has sent for you three times within the
hour, sir."

"Oh, is that all?" he says, with a relieved smile,
and strides up to the magnificent suite of apartments on the second floor, occupied by the rich
New York widow, to find her playing invalid in a
coquettish tea-gown, evidently donned for his conquest and undoing. Here he's received with playful
words of reproach at his professional neglect, but
with such alluring smiles and captivating graces that
Fred Cassadene very shortly forgets the physician
in the gallant and loses from his capricious mind
all thought of the beautiful girl with whom he has
just been discussing their wedding day, and thinks
only of the beautiful blue eyes that are gazing into
his, and the lovely pulse that he has felt half a
dozen times to see if it fluttered, and found it fluttering every time. But, if any one had accused him
of treachery to his fiancée, even at this moment, he
would have denied it indignantly, for Fred Cassadene's nature is perfectly irresponsible. Though
come to man's estate, in matters of the heart he is
still a grown-up boy, and has a boy's knack of loving
all pretty women—the one nearest to him, the best.

CHAPTER IV.

" FOR WOMEN WHO SUFFER ! "

MISS LILLY comes in, her face covered with smiles of happy hope.

" Aunt Connie," she says playfully, " Doctor Fred did not have time to be introduced to you this afternoon. He had so much to tell *me*."

" So it seems," replies the old lady grimly, for in matters of etiquette she is as punctilious as a Spanish grandee and thinks herself slighted in her future nephew-in-law having visited her house without going through the ceremony of presentation to its mistress.

" But he will be 'here again this evening, and then you will be able to judge how handsome he is," mutters Lilly apologetically.

" Oh, I have already seen him."

" Indeed !—Where ? " queries the niece.

" Walking up the path with you this afternoon," answers the aunt rather savagely. " Then I discovered I knew Doctor Cassadene very well by sight, though not by name. I recognized him as a gentleman I had often seen driving about St. Augustine, during the last two months. My attention had been called to him by the beaut——" the old lady checks herself suddenly and cries, " But come in to tea, Lilly, at once."

" By the beautiful what ? " asks Miss Travers eagerly.

" Which do you like best, tea or coffee ? " says the aunt, as they seat themselves at the table.

"With whom did you see Doctor Fred driving?"

"With his patients, I presume," is Miss Connie's unsatisfactory response. "Tea or coffee?"

"Tea!" replies Lilly desperately, knowing she will get no further information until she has informed her relative on this point.

A few minutes after she tries to turn the conversation to the matter once more, but to her chagrin, Constantia deftly refuses the subject, apparently having made up her mind to discuss Doctor Cassadene no further with her niece, at present.

So the meal runs along, Lilly dividing her attention between old Hauser Oglethorpe's picture, which still leers at her from its frame, the clock on the mantel-piece, and her purchase, which is yet on the sideboard, in exactly the same state in which she has brought it home from Vedder's Museum. The clock, however, receives most of her attention.

It is now striking seven, and Lilly's thoughts are turning to the half hour when Doctor Fred will again be by her side, when a rap is heard upon the hall door, and one of the servants answering it, ushers in a messenger boy, who carries a magnificent bunch of roses, and a note, in a well-known handwriting.

"For me!" cries Lilly, seizing both note and bouquet, at the same moment. "Look, auntie, lovely roses from Doctor Fred! Isn't he a darling boy?" and smells the perfumed buds in so caressing a manner, that Miss Connie says significantly, "Don't mistake the gift for the giver!"

But even as she does so, pauses in her laugh, for Lilly, having torn open the envelope and glanced over the note, gives a cry of disappointment, then pouts, and there are tears in her eyes, for she is reading the following:

PONCE DE LEON HOTEL.
ST. AUGUSTINE, FLORIDA.
February 1st, 1891.

MY DARLING LILLY :

· Horror of horrors! I'm just called to attend a desperate case of snake-bite, about four miles from here, out on the Tocoi road. I must leave immediately, as the snake was a rattler, or moccasin, and every instant is important.

I send with this an invitation to the hop at the Ponce to-morrow evening, to which of course I will take you.

Also send a bunch of flowers, all my love and ten thousand kisses.

Yours forever,

FRED.

P. S.   I'll give you the kisses in person to-morrow, with interest.

"What is the matter?" asks Miss Connie, for Lilly's face is now almost despairing.

"This," cries the girl, impulsively holding the letter before her aunt's eyes. But suddenly withdrawing it she remarks: "I'll paraphrase it, dear Connie. He is called suddenly away, to attend a patient on the Tocoi road, who has been bitten by a snake. Of course he had to leave instantly."

"Of course!" responds Miss Connie dryly.

"But the dear fellow will be here to-morrow morning to make his apologies,—and by the by, he has sent me an invitation to the hop at the Ponce de Leon," continues Miss Travers as if making excuses for her absent lover.

"Any answer?" interrupts the messenger boy, who has been gazing open-eyed at Lilly's beautiful face and stunning gown.

"No," replies that young lady hastily; but as

the lad turns to go, she suddenly cries " Stay ! " and
sitting at her desk, writes one of the sweetest,
loveliest, dearest notes a girl has ever penned to
her lover. One that would make that reprobate
blush with shame, if he could read it, but Dr. Frederick Cassadene has other occupation this evening.

This being despatched, and the boy made happy
by a liberal fee, Lilly, after reading the note over
again, curiously enough gets the blues. She tries
the piano and sings a pretty love melody, and that
brings tears into her eyes.

She wanders about the house, and fidgets her
aunt, who has just become interested in a new
novel, until that long-suffering female looks up and
says : " What's the matter with you ? "

" Noth—nothing ! "

" Yes, there is ! Since you came here last night,
you are not the comfortable girl you used to be a
year ago."

" Yes, I am. I'm very comfortable—I—Aunt
Connie ! why do you tease me so ? Don't you
see I have got enough to worry me ? " and tears
trickle down her fair cheeks.

" Now I know what's the matter with you ! " cries
Connie sternly. " You are jealous ! "

" I—jealous ! What, makes you think that ? "
mutters Lilly indignantly, though nervously.

" If you are not jealous, why did you try to pump
me about the people Doctor Cassadene rode with,
before you came here—Eh ? " growls Miss Constantia.

" Did I do that ? " This is attempted surprise
by the sufferer.

"Yes, you did at tea, twice—no, *three* times!"

"Well, whom did he ride with?" cries the girl anxiously—almost savagely.

"There! you're bothering me about it again. I suppose you are jealous of the beautiful widow who has been at the Ponce de Leon for the last week!"

"Stella Lovejoy!" cries Lilly suddenly.

"Ha—ah! you have said it!" remarks the old diplomat with a knowing smile.

"And so have you! She was the person you saw Fred driving with, before I came here!" gasps Lilly, growing very pale.

"Yes," replies Constantia, shortly. Then seeing what a terrible effect this revelation has upon her niece, she goes on: " Haven't you faith in Fred?"

"Lots!" cries Lilly enthusiastically, and then more slowly: "He—he needs lots." This last with a little sniffle in her voice.

Whereupon Miss Connie astonishes her niece by ejaculating: "So does every man!" then says oracularly: "As a woman who has profited by sixty years of heart-breaking spinsterhood, I tell you, Lilly, don't remain single, as I am! Marry and believe!"

"Everything?"

"Everything," returns Miss Elder Spinster. "If your husband says he has been detained until two in the morning by business, *swallow* it! If he declares that he has been at his club until three—don't ask him *which* Club! If he swears he was locked out and struggled to get into the front door all night, DON'T DOUBT IT! Have the faith of the martyrs—believe in miracles! It is the only way to be a happy wife!"

"Have the faith of the martyrs!" gasps Lilly. Then she mutters : "You think all women are martyrs?"—a kind of horror coming into her beautiful eyes.

"Most wives are!" remarks Miss Connie sententiously.

"What wretches men must be!" is Lilly's shuddering answer to this awful statement.

"Not at all! They are what nature made them —selfish animals, and as nature has been very kind to them," remarks her aunt with a grim smile, "they do the best for themselves, and have a pretty good time in *this* world. Ours will come in the *next*, my dear!"

At which her niece astonished her, for she cries: "I can't wait! I have too impatient a disposition. I—I believe I'd like to be a man, aunt!"

Whereupon the aged spinster raises up her hands in horror, and ejaculates: "Thank heaven! you are of a nobler nature than our tyrant, man. Love your Doctor Fred, but love him blindly, and— please—please let me read my novel!"

With that, she takes her precious book with her, and departs, leaving Lilly muttering to herself: "Love Doctor Fred—love him blindly! If he rides with that widow again, I shall hate Doctor Fred and hate him blindly!" then cries, "No, no—" in horror at the thought. "I love him, for I am jealous. It is awful!—awful! If I could but remember Aunt Connie's instructions and Fred's advice—if I could only love in the selfish, careless way men do, and be happy!" As she says this, her eyes fall upon the picture of old Hauser Oglethorpe, for the foregoing conversation has taken place in the dining room. The small cunning cruel eyes of the canvas seem to grin and leer at, and mock her.

This makes her remember the purchase of the morning, and she thinks, " I'll drive Fred out of my mind, and become at least placid, by investigating the contents of the little box," and so picks it up.

But as she does so, her eyes are turned once more to the picture on the wall, and now it seems to have a broad grin upon its countenance, and she mutters to herself, "Absurd ! My nerves are running away with me ! The idea of a picture grinning !" Then shaking her finger at it, she forces herself to say : " I'll not open this in face of you, sir," and passes, box in hand, to the parlor.

Here, sitting down near the little table that holds the old ebony casket, the family heirloom, she receives another shock ; for as she takes off the wrapper from the one purchased at Vedder's, she perceives that barring sea water and the stains of exposure to weather, the two are identical, and drops the one she has in her hands, with a start, beside its duplicate.

At this moment the voice of her maid, who comes in with a tray covered with tea-things and sandwiches gives her confidence.

Jane says to her, " Honey, ef yo's goin' to sit up late, I thought a cup of tea would be refreshin' to yo'. Yo' aunt has gone to bed with her novel, so I was afeared yo'd be lonely."

" Tea is just what I want, Jane," returns her mistress. "You can put it on the stand over there, and I shall not require you any further this evening.

So, if Mr. Gustavus Duncan makes his appearance,
after his duties are over at the Ponce de Leon, you
need not hesitate to give him your undivided attention."

" Yes, I 'spects Gus is comin' over, but I've heard
strange 'ports 'bout him roun' town to-day, an' ef
he don't give an explanashun of hisself, he'll heah
somethin' startling!" remarks Jane, with a savage
sort of snarl, as she retires from the room.

" Ho! ho, she's happy too!" mutters Lilly, sti-
fling a nasty little laugh that is not pleasant, coming from one who is young and should be happy.

As she says this, she drinks hurriedly a cup of
tea, which is much too scalding to please her, and
cries vivaciously, " That settles my nerves! Now I
am equal to my antiquarian investigation!"

Then picking up the ebony casket, once more, she
looks at it meditatively, and thinks, " If this should
be the one old Hauser told about—the one that
would make him rich—the one that would make a
woman a man!" next gasps, " What an absurd
idea—uncanny—weird—awful!"

But curiosity is always potent in woman, and Lilly
puts the little key she has obtained from the locksmith into the old wards, and clicks back the lock
of the box in a hurried, nervous, desperate way, and
so lifting up the lid, within is a little package, done
neatly up in brown paper, and sealed.

After a moment she lifts it out and it seems wonderfully heavy, if entirely manuscript.

The outside of the packet bears an inscription,
and reading the time-stained characters carefully,
she gives a little shriek, and drops the affair as it

were red hot into her lap with a shudder, for she has read :

"*To be conveyed to my family, by the finder, un-opened!* HAUSER OGLETHORPE."

The signature is that of her great-grandfather—whose picture has been grinning at her in the dining-room—the old sea-dog and slaver, Hauser Oglethorpe himself.

After a pause to calm her nerves and thinking excitedly, "Can it be that I am to know the secret my ancestor spoke about, or was it as Aunt Connie thinks but the jabbering of a senile imbecile?" Lilly's curiosity again dominates her and breaking the seals she opens the packet. Its contents are two documents, both stained by age—one short, apparently a memorandum, the other of much greater length, and carefully wrapped up in them a little glass vial, its stopper sealed with wax—within it she can easily perceive four amber-colored beads or seeds, each one about the size of a small grape. Their glazed outlines have a peculiar phosphorescent gleam about which the lamplight plays, giving them the varying hues of the rainbow. As she turns the vial in her hand these seem to leap about and play with one another as if instinct with life and vitality. Upon the bottle which holds them has been pasted a slip of paper which bears this curious—perhaps uncanny inscription :

FOR WOMEN WHO SUFFER. HA! HA! HA!

CHAPTER V.

THE MARVELLOUS RECORD OF HAUSER OGLE-THORPE.

"FOR women who suffer," quotes Lilly—with a bewitching little shudder, and turns to the perusal of the first and smaller document.

This has apparently been hurriedly written. Its paper is yellow with time and stained with sea water, and is covered with a peculiar, cramped hand-writing. This she manages to decipher, but only by taking the utmost care, and even then very slowly. It reads:

October 15th, in the Year of Our Lord 1813.

Being pursued by the English sloop of war, *Falcon*, and in danger of wreckage and losing my ship off the coast of Florida,—I, Hauser Oglethorpe, of the Parish of St. Mark, Carolina Plantations, in order to increase the worldly goods of my kindred and make them rich, give to them the following marvellous statement written at my leisure on board ship, fearing some such fate as has come upon me. It will not be believed, but it is the Devil's own truth, so help me Beelzebub!

I have not much more time for writing, as that accursed British sea tramp has already opened fire upon us unarmed slavers with his long thirty-two, for which may they all go to Davy Jones' locker and their infernal souls go to the place I am bound for! . . . . .

The paper finishes with two or three imprecations so horrible in their blasphemous intensity that the

girl drops it with a gasp ; but fired by curiosity,
after a little time picks up and deciphers the longer
document which is headed :

*Record of my Marvellous Discovery of the Tree of
Sexual Change.*

and drops it with a cry of mocking unbelief. But
gazing at the document again gives a little gasp of
wonder—for it continues in a kind of weird presti-
digitation :

THAT'S WHAT I KNEW YOU'D DO—YOU'D DROP
THE PAPER AND SAY IT WAS AN INFERNAL SAILOR'S
YARN. READ TO THE END—THEN TRY A SEED !

On this voyage to the West Coast of Africa,
after being driven by contrary winds to take refuge
between Quorra, or the mouth of the Niger River,
and Bonny, on an excursion after both white and
black ivory, I was compelled by the presence of an
accursed British frigate to slip my cables in the
night. I sailed N. by W. about 150 miles, taking
refuge from the observation of my enemy between
the islands that stud the lower part of this coast,
and the main land, in anchorage too shallow to permit entry by the frigate, and confident that I and
my crew of fifty sturdy Yankee tars could give account of any boats that they might send against me.

The longitude of this place is about 5° E. and
latitude 7° 35' N. and I soon succeeded in obtaining
a cargo of slaves from a barracoon in charge of a
couple of Portuguese, paying, however, a good price
for them in beads, muskets and ammunition. Chancing to notice one of the coffles of slaves as they came
on board, to my astonishment I perceived they were

all men—a most unusual circumstance ; ana on questioning one of my Portuguese factors, I was told the
astounding story that they came from A TRIBE OF
NATIVES WHO WERE ALL MEN.

Not believing such bosh, I shouted, "One thousand pounds of ivory against a hundred niggers that
story is a marine's yarn!" Judge of my astonishment when my wager was promptly taken up.

To settle this, the Portuguese trader and I made
a journey to the village of the tribe, located where
the hills come down to join the lowlands, one day's
march in the interior. May I be cat-hauled if I
hadn't lost my bet! The tribe were all men—beyond peradventure!

On investigation I found they recruited their
ranks by capturing women from the surrounding
tribes, and these women, extraordinary to tell, soon
after entering the village became men also—every
man jack of them—or every woman jack of them—
whichever you like to put it.

Quassi, the chief of this singular gang, was a
wily nigger. I tried to get his wondrous secret
out of him, but he only muttered that spirits would
punish him if he told ; for these sacrilegious brutes
have an extraordinary superstition that evil will come
to them if they reveal the mighty secret they possess.

But it was a mighty secret I had determined to
know. I made Quassi drunk—then plied him with
questions, but he only jabbered, ' Who wants to be
woman when can be man !'

Disappointed in milder means, by the use of the
all-potent fire-water, I inveigled Quassi to the coast,
the creature going with me very simply, thinking

me his friend; and carrying him on board my ship, I *ordered* him to tell me his secret, but in the surly manner of these dogged blacks he muttered that misfortune would come to him if he did.

I told him misfortune would come to him if he didn't, and turning him over to my boatswain, an athletic Spaniard with the temper of Old Nick, I ordered him four round dozen at the gang-way with the cat-o'-nine-tails, and a brine dip afterwards. Under the persuasion of my athletic warrant officer the wretch gave up his secret. There was a tree, he sobbed, the seeds of which changed men to women, and *vice versa*, women to men. No man ever ate one, but all the women of his tribe did.

I ordered him to take me to this wonderful tree, at which the wretch cried out he would be cursed forever by his Obi if he did,—but another two dozen at the gang-way persuaded him to do my bidding.

Next day we set out—I, my boatswain, and four stalwart seamen—in my gig, carrying with us a week's provisions; for Quassi in his gibbering way had made known to me it was a three days' journey to the object of my desires. The surly savage I carried manacled with me in the stern of my boat. As we left the ship I clapped a pistol to his head and told him as he loved his life not to betray me.

Under my boatswain's persuasions, he guided us to a two days' journey up the coast, to where the cliffs come down to the sea, and then began to tremble and pray to his gods, as nearly as I could make out, in his lingo, to forgive him what he was doing. I clapped the pistol to his head and persuaded him again, and under his direction my gig was turned **for** the cliffs, which seemed to have no opening, being covered with heavy verdure, tropical plants, and great trees the branches of which came down to the water to meet the mangroves growing in the shallow places.

Parting the branches of one of these trees that grew to the water's edge and forcing the boat in, under Quassi's guidance, a narrow cleft was discovered, cut straight through the solid cliffs, that rose above us hundreds of feet. Though the water was deep, the opening was so narrow, that as we entered this defile, the sun was cut off above us, the water grew dark to the view and the blackness of night came over us. There was scarce room for the play of the oars in my gig between the rocks, and a strong current setting out to sea made our progress very slow. Bats, disturbed by us, flapped their wings over our heads ; serpents, coiled upon the branches of the trees that grew out from the sides of the cliff, hissed at us as we passed beneath them. To encourage my men, who wanted to turn back, I went into the bow of the boat, conning it myself through the passage, and after four hours of hard labor, the sunlight came to us again ;—we had passed through the cleft of overhanging rocks, and found a lagoon opening before us in weird loveliness.

Its shallow waters, made black by African mud, ended in swamps on every side save that on which we entered it. These were bordered by cane-brakes filled with serpents and crocodiles—and the heavy forests beyond resounded with the jabberings of monkeys diversified and made terrible by the roars of lions and cries of elephants.

About two miles from us the sun—even now sinking behind the mountain tops—rested on a beautiful island, which Quassi pointed out as the end of our journey, and sunk on his knees and jabbered petitions to his deities to forgive him for disclosing the sacred secrets of his tribe.

Inspired by the news, my men gave way readily and the boat surged through the calm waters, once in a while colliding with a crocodile, for all the beasts and reptiles and fishes about here knew so little of man that they did not fear him. Under the stalwart strokes of my crew, before the sun had sunk, we reached the island, which was but one hundred feet long by half that width, and upon it for the first time I saw the

"TREE OF SEXUAL CHANGE,"

the most beautiful plant upon which the sun has ever shone—the most curious that ever human eyes have gazed upon. Its long stems rise to the height of fifty feet, covered with graceful leaves of a supernatural green and crimson blossoms of such marvellous beauty and size that our eyes could hardly be withdrawn from their loveliness. Even the perfume of its flowers had a wondrous effect. As we breathed we seemed to become effeminate and our natures milder, and even our cruel Spanish boatswain became softer in his language and less savage in his blasphemy.

This tree, Quassi informed me, blossomed and seeded but once in a thousand moons—the sacred periods of its harvest being carefully kept by the Obi men of his tribe.

At these times carefully watched for through succeeding years—a party of picked men came from the village in canoes to harvest the precious seeds, and these were then kept guarded in the tribe's obi-house for the use of future generations until the tree bloomed again,—one thousand moons thereafter,

While listening to his yarn I was inspecting the tree, and cried : " Here's luck ; we've struck the time of harvest—once in a thousand moons ; " for the pods were ripe and opening, and dropping over the ground the amber-colored seeds.

At this announcement, my crew—all of them having discovered the secret on our journey—gave a cheer, and into Quassi's eyes came a cruel, cunning gleam that spoke of vengeance for the boatswain's cat-o'-nine-tails that had scored his old back with many a sore welt and burning blister. Had I not been too much interested in the tree—fool that I was—I would have noticed his gleaming eyeballs, that had become red by suffering, and the hideous grin that showed his white teeth, and would have known what they meant.

Securing the boat, the crew landed, bringing Quassi with them, and we stood upon the shore—myself, five white men and one grinning negro, and before us was the tree, in whose wondrous power we as yet scarcely believed but soon would know.

" Blow my eyes ! " cried Bill Jones, a strapping sailor who pulled bow oar in my gig. " One of them little things turn *me* into a woman ? " And before I could stop him—he had bolted one of the amber seeds and stood looking at us astonished, his eyes rolling, half in fear half in amazement. Then he suddenly uttered a bashful cry and hid himself behind the foliage as if timid and ashamed; while we gazed open-mouthed upon him,—for his screams were no more those of the hoarse sailor, but those of a shrill-voiced woman, and he simpered and giggled and looked at us in coquetry. Then his maiden antics made us laugh until the tears rolled down our cheeks, for Bill Jones was by no means a prim-mannered prude—in fact, so inspired the rest of us men with curiosity that, idiots that we were, we all did eat a seed, save the Spanish boatswain, who swore nothing would make him become a woman, especially when there would be five fat, lusty and healthy wenches on the same lone island as himself.

And soon we all became women, and thought ourselves beautiful and had wench's airs, graces, feelings—and walked down to see our reflections in the limpid water and ask ourselves if we were not lovely. And after that we five did look lovingly upon the boatswain, for he was the only white man among us,—and so grew jealous of each other, and fought with each other, that the boatswain might be our own best fellow, scratching and tearing each other's hair,—while he, our lord and master, looked on and laughed, crying in a jocular way: "Go it, Poll! Scratch her, Sue! Ho ho! This is a rare harem for the boatswain of the *Firefly*—I have as many wenches as an Arab sheik!"

Upon this scene Quassi looked with grins of pleasure, hoping, as I afterwards knew, in his cunning African mind, that the boatswain would eat a seed, so he could conquer all of us; for the four sailors and myself, having become women, were timid and would not encounter man in battle.—

The boatswain also liking the situation vastly, used his power over us and forbade us to eat the seeds, so that we might become men again and his equals and masters.

Thus we might have continued there forever, had not I, in preparing his evening meal for the savage boatswain, with whom I had fallen deeply in love and of whom I was much afraid, in gathering wood for the fire accidentally picked up one of the seeds; and curiosity coming upon me, a woman, I had eaten it, and found myself once more a man, and as such the Spaniard's captain.

Striding up to him as he sat languishing under the attentions of two handsome girls—one of whom had been the coxswain of my boat and the other pulled the bow oar—I commanded him to hold each of the four women while I administered a seed to them.

Recognizing that I was myself again and as such his commanding officer, he did my bidding, though sulkily, and a few minutes after my crew of stalwart men, under my orders, was quickly loading the boat with several bags full of the precious seeds we gathered hastily from the wondrous Tree of Sexual Change.

But rapid as had been our labors, the night had come upon us more quickly. Safe navigation of the lagoon in the darkness was impossible,—we must wait upon this island until the morning. Then the men, made superstitious by the astounding properties of this unnatural tree, grew timid at the thought and built a huge bonfire so that light might give them courage; and I ordered them to construct a pyre round the Tree of Sexual Change, to be lighted as we left the island, for I feared other adventurers and discoverers and wanted a monopoly of the wondrous seeds so that women would beg me for them, and queens and princesses cringe to me the gruff old sailor and the treasures of the earth be poured upon me by beauties who longed to be beauties no more—only simple men.

I served out extra rations of rum at six bells; then taking our bite of hard tack and salt horse, we all lay down to sleep together. But I could not close my eyes, which was fortunate, otherwise I would not have been writing this.

As nearly as I could make it out, about three o'clock in the morning, old Quassi became restless in his irons (for we still kept him securely bound and chained), and his restlessness made me suspicious. Looking at him by the flickering light of the camp-fire, I could see that he was listening intently. I opened my ears also, but heard nothing, savage senses beating civilized senses. He apparently heard something which pleased him, because he began to chuckle to himself and grin and chant and laugh in an uncanny manner,—and listening again I heard a sound that made me start up and wake my men;—and cry, "The splash of paddles on the lagoon—the savages!"

Another second and the crew had silently manned the boat,—but on looking round for Quassi he had disappeared. Ironed as he was, the old man had wriggled himself into the thicket, and we had no time to search for him, for the paddles of the canoes sounded very near.

So tossing a brand from the fire into the pile of light wood that we had built about the sacred tree I gave my orders in a whisper and we moved away into the darkness;—and just in time, for we had not gone a cable's length when we saw by the light of the burning Tree of Sexual Change, that, blazing up, illuminated the weird scene, ten canoes glide up to the island shore.

Then I guessed what had made the old man grin when he saw the tree was ripe for harvest.—He knew that that night a party from his tribe, headed by their Obi men, would come to harvest after a thousand moons of waiting the precious seeds.

As the wild niggers sprung on shore I heard a voice shriek to them in their lingo, and by their answering yell of hideous dismay and rage knew that Quassi had told them their gods had been insulted, the secret of their tribe ravaged from them and their Obi tree polluted and destroyed—and shuddered as I thought of their revenge.

My men, hardened ruffians as they were, trembled as they heard the awful wail and hideous screams as they pulled away, I setting the course as nearly as possible to the entrance of the lagoon by the red glow from the burning tree that cast its light to show us to its avengers whose eyes are like those cats at night, the darkness of their forests developing nocturnal vision.

So they were after us! My gig—a quick racing boat—flew through the waters, jostling many a sleeping crocodile and narrowly missing a hippopotamus that was tossing the water from his ugly snout. But strong as we rowed, the savages paddled their light canoes more strongly. "Throw over everything," I whispered, "except the precious seeds. They will make our fortune forever if we carry them away." Then overboard went everything except our arms, one small keg of biscuit and our water cask. Thus lightened, the savages overtook us more slowly, though they were almost fatally near, when Bill Jones, the bow man, screamed out, "We are at the cliff, Cap'n—I think I see the opening! By Jove! we've struck it right."

Then the men made the ash blades of their oars bend with a mighty sweep, and a shock nearly threw me out of the boat; for in the darkness we had mistaken the passage and dashed against the solid cliff.

The next instant we were all struggling in the water and arrows from the savages flying among us, their war clubs striking us—the light from the most marvellous of God's plants that we had impiously fired lighting up the lake to show us to our enemies. Being an expert swimmer, I took a long dive and turned towards the marshy shores of the lagoon, where I made a landing and found myself followed by the Spanish boatswain, who swam like a fish, and Bill Jones, the active bow oar of my gig. To my astonishment, the boatswain carried one of the smaller sacks of the precious seeds in his hand. He had clenched it even under the arrows of the savages and the waves of the crocodile-haunted lagoon.

Silently we pressed through the swamp, its sickening miasma mingling with the early morning air, for the sun was just rising,—and sneaked through the thick jungle, the cries of our pursuers showing they had found our trail.

Still we struggled on, the sun coming up to burn us; when, just as we were about to reach the higher ground and leave the swamp slime behind us, Jones shrieked out a horrid cry, 'My God, Cap'n, he's bit me!' And looking back I saw a dying sailor, and beside him one of those awful serpents of West African marshes and damp ground, the river-jack, the bite of which is death.

To remain meant capture and death for us also; and the boatswain and myself hurried along, turning our steps toward the sea, which now could not be more than a mile or two away from us, though we had a range of hills to climb before we would reach it. Ere we lost sight of our dying comrade, the savages, headed by old Quassi, came up to him, and looking backwards I shuddered as I saw the vindictive nigger finish Jones' agony by a smash from a war club and then bound on with a whoop of joy in pursuit of me and the Spanish boatswain in vengeance for his tortured body and his outraged deities.

Through a dense forest of trees filled with monkeys, whose horrid jabberings as we passed beneath them gave signal to our enemies of the path we followed, we struggled along, running where the ground permitted, but most times clambering through dense underbrush, yet all the time struggling onward.

Then the murmuring of the distant sea brought hope to us, and the boatswain muttered: "We've pulled through the trip—with seeds enough to make us nabobs."

But even as this left his lips the wood resounded
with a mighty roar, a yellow, tawny beast flew
through the air and struck the Spaniard to the
ground with its big claws, and the white fangs of a
lioness whose two cubs were playing in the pathway
sunk themselves into the neck of the sailor as he
uttered his death shriek.

The bag of precious seeds was torn to pieces in
this awful struggle of man and beast, and the amber
pellets tossed hither and thither were trampled into
the black mould and swampy undergrowth. Almost
struggling with the lioness myself, in my desperation I quickly gathered what I could of the sacred
seeds, for Quassi and his gang were now upon me.
They were only four ; but four of these magic things
were enough if I could escape !

The lioness was barring the pathway to my pursuers, and snarling in their faces, they did not dare
to dispute the way with her, and so with gasps of
joy I hurried to the beach, which by a blessed fore-
thought I had ordered to be patrolled by a boat
under the command of my second officer.

He soon saw my signal, and by the next day I
was on board my ship, minus the crew of my gig
and the Spanish boatswain, but having in my pocket
the four wondrous seeds in the little vial I have
marked "For Women Who Suffer," which mean to
me four fortunes ; for rich women as well as poor
ones suffer the pangs of their weak, down-trodden
sex, and I can sell them to the princesses and queens
of the world.

Within half an hour of getting on shipboard—
our cargo being all below the hatches—we weighed

anchor and put to sea; for Quassi's whole tribe would soon be upon us to avenge the insult to their gods in the destruction of the tree that blooms once in a thousand moons to make such women as are blest by eating of its seeds masculine and happy.

This story will not be believed by the average man, or average woman, either, but to these facts I swear as I am now a living man and was for one short hour a woman and very beautiful and very vain.

HAUSER OGLETHORPE,
of the Parish of St. Mark, Carolina Plantations.

Given on the 27th day of August, Anno Domini 1813, upon the American Bark *Firefly*.

CHAPTER VI.

"WHY NOT?"

As Lillian finishes the manuscript, which she has read eagerly—intently; pausing at times to shudder at the old man's cruelty, disclosed by its pages, she exclaims: "Hauser Oglethorpe a woman—and very beautiful!" and thinking of the old sea-dog's leering picture in the dining-room, a harsh and strained laugh comes from between her pretty lips.

This is succeeded by a pause of contemplation when she suddenly ejaculates, "What a Rider Haggardish story! I feel like the veritable 'SHE' herself;" the record having made a strange impression on her.

She tries to shake it off exclaiming, "Pooh! one would think I believe this likely sea yarn!"

Then the shining amber seeds catching her eye

she seizes the vial, wraps it up in the manuscript; and placing the package in her pocket, looks out through the open windows upon the moonlight that is falling upon the waters of Matanzas Inlet with its banks shadowed by moss-bearded oaks and cypress, and thinks, " Had I better tell this to Aunt Connie? It will put the old lady in a marvellous state of excitement." Next impressed by the weird moon-light effects of the landscape she murmurs, " This country with its wondrous flowers that blossom when we should have snow, its cypress trees and reptile-haunted swamps, seems to me uncanny, also," and gives a little shudder and sneers : " I feel creepy myself."

Suddenly she mutters, " This story is too much for my nerves!" and would turn away and run upstairs to her aunt's bedroom and break in upon that lady's fascinating novel and tell her that she has a more wondrous tale than is often seen between yellow-backs,—when she hears the sound of excited conversation on the veranda outside, and Jane's voice comes to her in agitated tones : " Oh, laws a' massy, dis am awful ! Oh! oh! oh! " and in deeper answer is returned : " It's gospel ; take my camp-meetin' oath, it's gospel, Jane ! "

To which her handmaid returns excitedly : " Oh ! my poor young missus ! "

Throwing open the French windows that lead to the veranda, Lilly looks quickly out, her face filled with feminine anxiety, and whispers : " What's the matter? Is it burglars ? "

Burglars from her earliest childhood have been one of Lilly's bugaboos.

5

" No, miss, it ain't burglars, it's only Gus!" is the
reply. In the moonlight she sees the mulatto girl,
in a state of great excitement, listening with open
mouth and open eyes to some extraordinary news
that her lover, Gustavus Duncan, has brought from
the Ponce de Leon.

" No, ma'm, it isn't burglars," says that gentleman; " dar's been a terr'ble accident down on de bay."

" An accident?" cries Lilly, and steps out on to
the veranda to hear all about it.

"Yes, Miss Travers; dar's been an accident, as I
befo' explained to you,—on Mr. Remington's steam
yacht, de Runabout."

" Nothing's happened, I hope, to Mr. Remington," says Lilly quickly.

" No, miss; Mr. Remington he's all right. But
it's de widder."

" The widow—Mrs. Stella Lovejoy?"

" Yes;— a boat takin' her to de yacht was
drowned."

" A boat drowned!" gasps Lilly astounded at this
extraordinary statement.   Then she says slowly,
" and Stella was drowned also?" and there are tears
in her eyes as she thinks of the beautiful woman she
has seen in health and loveliness only this morning.

" No, Miss Travers; she was saved by de gallantry of a gent," remarks Gustavus, with a wave of
his hand similar to that with which he indicates a
chair to a guest of the Ponce de Leon.

" The noble fellow!" cries Lilly enthusiastically.

"Yes; de Doc', he plumped right in after her like
a porpoise, an' pulled her out," adds Gus excitedly.

But here Jane suddenly lifts up her voice and

yells: "Doan' yo' tell her, Gus. Yo' 'll break her heart. You doan' know what yo' 's doin'."

But this makes Lilly very eager—perhaps anxious. She mutters: "Doc'?—what doc'?"

"Doctah Fred Cassadene," answers Gus—and the secret is out. The young lady grows very pale and places a little trembling hand on the railing of the veranda to steady herself as she whispers: "Fred there!—" Then she cries out suddenly: "No! he was with a patient on the Tocoi Road. Impossible! He was called away to a desperate case of snake-bite."

"Snake-bite? Ha ha—ho ho!—he he!"—This is a hideous chuckle from between Gus's white teeth.

"Doan' you tell her—you'll break her heart; doan' you tell her," shrieks Jane.

"He shall tell me *now!*" cries her mistress in an awful voice, and striding up to the disconcerted second man in the dining-room of the Ponce de Leon, Lilly says sternly—"I want all your news. Don't dare prevaricate!"

"Well—" answers Gus in a sheepish manner —"well, de Doc' was goin' on a moonlight sail with de widder."

"And the — the snake-bite — what of that?" gasps the girl, a sudden dread coming into her countenance.

"Dar wan't no snake-bite. De widder ain't got no snake-bite. Doc' Fred was wid her at dinner an' took her off right from de table to de boat."

"You are sure?"

"Sartin! Didn't I stan' behin' 'em at dinner to-day, and wasn't dey talkin' all de time 'bout de boat-ride dey was going to have—and how de moonlight was becoming to widders. Lawd bless yo'! dar w'an't no case of snake-bite."

"Oh Lawdy! what's de matter with yo', Miss Lilly?" breaks in Jane suddenly upon the harangue, for the girl's face has become an awful one. She has put her hand to her heart, and is reeling and staggering. Then she suddenly cries: "There *was* a case of snake-bite!—the snake has bitten me!"

The next instant she bursts into a jeering laugh, for her words have struck terror to her sable auditors, and Jane has bounded upon a chair for refuge, and is screaming: "Oh massy! Is it a rattler?" And Gus crying: "A snake on the veranda! Oh, Lawdy! Lawdy!" has sprung over the railing, and chancing to land in a thorn bush is now shrieking, "I'se been stung too!" A moment after, the girl stops these demonstrations. She says in a set, hard voice, "The snake was a metaphor! Don't either of you dare to tell what has happened to-night!" then staggers, and would fall, did she not clutch the curtains of the window; though to Jane's proffered assistance and words of love, she mutters "No! don't dare to come near me to-night! Go to your lover and tell him to say no word of this—especially to Doctor Cassadene!"

So passing to her chamber she crosses the dining-room, and as she does so beholds the picture of old Hauser Oglethorpe, which now seems to literally laugh and chuckle at her, and this brings to her mind what she carries in her pocket, and she cries to him: "For women who suffer!" and laughs back at the canvas man; for at this moment, jealousy, despair, and the agony of knowing that the man she loves has lied to her and deceived her for the smiles of another—has made this poor stricken creature almost insane.

Then getting to her bedroom she sinks upon a chair, and thinks: "How can I endure the agony of this night?—My God!—I must have some drug to destroy thought—for a little while!"

As she does so, she feels the vial in her pocket press against the woodwork upon which she is sitting, and drawing out the manuscript and tossing it on one side, by the mellow light of her lamp, which has been lit for her coming, she gazes at the sparkling seeds that dance and flash, roll over and play, and juggle with one another in the yellow beams, and sighs—"If this would only take away my jealous woman's heart —to make me cold—indifferent—selfish—as men, our masters, who torture us by making us love them!"

Then, breaking the sealing wax that surrounds the glass stopper, she uncorks the bottle, from which a faint, delicious odor comes, and sits looking at the seeds and conning over in her mind the marvelous story of the old slaver, and quotes poor Quassi, "Who would be woman when can be man?" An astounded look comes into her eyes, and she mutters, "My Heaven, if this wondrous tale is true! If I took one and became a man, what kind would I become? an 'out and outer,' a 'throughbred,' to play with women—to break their hearts, to make their love and truth a curse to them—like Fred does me?"

Here her agony becoming too potent, she staggers to her feet and totters about the room wring-
ing her hands and gasping, "What is life without
him—and I a woman? Were I a man, I should
love him no more! If I remain in my own sex,
he will come to me, and again cajole me and take
my feeble female heart into his grasp, to juggle
with, until I forget his treachery—and love him
again and so suffer on and on so long as I live.
NEVER!!! What do I care! These seeds may
give me death—but what is life without him?"

With this—a kind of ecstasy comes into her beautiful eyes and she cries "*If it should be true!*"—and
desperately, as if not daring to contemplate what
she is doing, seizes between two white fingers, one
of the amber-colored seeds, and opening a pair of
as rosy lips as were ever kissed by man, she gasps
in awful voice, "WHY NOT?" and tosses the "seed-
of-sexual-change" into her mouth.

Its effect is horrible—appalling—it seems to be
alive—to have wings and fly down her throat, giving her tonsils an awful twinge as it passes them,
and springs straight to the centres of her brain.
She reels and sinks upon the sofa and lies there half
dazed, half stunned—electric thrills run through
her and make her muscles tingle and throb and even
her bones to creak under their subtle waves—and
sensations indescribable and unknown to her leave
the ether about her and become part of herself—and
others pass away from her to give them room.—
After a time her mind appears to suddenly become
more logical than it had been before, and her nerves
to grow stronger, and have more toughness to defy

A FLORIDA ENCHANTMENT. 71

sensation. She feels sleepy, not as if affected by a narcotic, but simply as if her mind were easy and content, and burdened by no despairing jealousy, because she loves herself better than anything else on earth.

She mutters " I think I'll turn in !" and hastily undresses—no longer with dainty care and careful folding of garments—but with reckless untidy haste, tossing her boots to one corner of the room, her stockings to another, firing her garters on the mantelpiece, and throwing the other articles of her apparel in reckless disorder over floor and furniture.

Then she springs into bed, with a dashing bound, and rolling herself up in the clothes says, " By Jove, that's the first time in my life I didn't squint under the bed, for burglars !—Burglars be blowed," and her lovely eyes look astonished at this remark.

A minute afterwards her breath becomes long drawn and regular, and sleep comes upon her, but anyone standing by her and looking at her glorious wavy dark brown locks that cover her pillow would have heard her coral lips murmur, " I'll bet Fred had a bang-up time to-night—with that fetching little widow ! "

A very quaint and curious speech to come from the lips of a jealous maiden about her lover and her rival.

*   *   *   *   *

The next morning Jane entering her mistress's chamber somewhat later than usual, finds her difficult to awake—an unusual thing, for Lilly's slumbers are always of the lightest.

Then an astonished expression comes on Jane's

face and she mutters: " Laws a massy! ef she ain't
snorin'.—Reckon she must have been up all night
in a jealous spasm. She looked like Lady Macbeth
a doin' de cake walkin' ack last night, when she
heard of Doc' Fred's inconsequency!"

So on tiptoe, this dusky African maiden, who
loves her mistress with the faithful love of a dog,
trips from the room, fearing her footfalls will
awaken Lilly Travers to thought and suffering.

An hour afterwards she comes in again to find
Miss Lilly is still. snoring. Becoming alarmed, the
girl shakes the sleeping figure, and presently Lilly's
eyes open and gaze upon her with slow reluctance.

" Why doan' yo' get up, Miss Lilly? It's almos'
ten o'clock."

For this attention she is greeted with two very
savage snarls—which astonish her, for Lilly is usually
a very sweet-tempered girl, even when her slumbers
are disturbed.

" Yo'se been snorin' too—though I never heard
yo' do dat befo'! Please get up, Miss Lilly!" says
the persevering handmaid.

Then her mistress's voice comes to her: "Confound you! You tell a story—I don't snore!"

" Laws! Miss Lilly! talkin' that way. What
ails yo' this mornin'? But yo' did snore, I declares."

" Well, I don't believe a word of it!" is the reply.
" Now go and fix my bath."

" And yo' voice is so hoarse and coarse, yo'd better
let me fix yo' a warm one, yo'se taken a bad
cole. Dis Florida night air can't be trusted," remarks Jane in considerate tones.

" No warm baths!" says the girl sharply; then
she shocks her servant again, for she remarks briskly,
" You think I'm a spring chicken?"

" Oh, Lawd; how curious you does talk!"

" Perhaps I do," answers Lilly, with a contemplative smile; " I feel a little peculiar this morning.
I—I believe I have had some extraordinary dream
in the night. I cannot remember it exactly."
After knitting her brows in thought for a second
or two, she cries out in sudden excitement: "Oh,
yes I do! Jane, I'll tell you all about it;—it's a
corker! Jane, I dreamed last night I became a
man! What do you think of that? There's a
funny vision for you," says Lilly, and gives a pleasant laugh.

" Yes, indeedy?" answers Jane; " I'd like to be
one myself. That Gus is driving me to desperation,
he is,"—and would go on with melancholy account
of her wrongs, did not the smile on her mistress's
face at this moment become a horrified giggle, and
Miss Travers, with an astounded, " Well, I'll be
hanged——" sink down among the bed-clothes,
rolling over in them as if to conceal herself from
view.

For this young lady, chancing in a lazy way to
fold her arms over her bosom, has suddenly discovered, in place of the usual rounded billowy softness,
a massive masculine chest that would do honor to
a Yale rusher;—and recollection, astonishment,
horror and trepidation have fallen upon her.

" Massy! what's de matter with you, Miss Lilly?"
cries her attendant—" sayin' cuss words, too! Is
yo' out of yo' head?" for poor Lilly at this moment

is gasping and uttering yelps of surprised astonishment and panic terror.

After a little Miss Travers recollects that she is
still alive anyway and becomes somewhat calmer.
She cries: "Get out of the room!" in a voice of
such deep contralto that she is astounded at the
noise she makes.

"An' fix yo' bath?"

"Yes; anything—fix my bath." And her attendant having withdrawn reluctantly from the apartment with exclamations of astonished concern,
Lillian Travers gives one desperate bound from the
bed and staggering in a dazed way to her bureau,
picks up the paper she had tossed away the night
before. There it is—old Hauser's wondrous tale,
in his cramped characters; and before her stands
the vial with its three little miraculous seeds dancing in the yellow sunlight to give proof that it's no
hallucination of her wandering mind.

She gives one look at the mirror, staring in it to
see if her face betrays aught of the great physical
change which has somehow come upon her. No;
her features are the same—only wondrously excited and astonished, and containing a threat of
coarseness in the near future, for a bolder light
seems to gleam in the staring, questioning eyes that
look upon her as she gasps, "Great God! can it be
possible? I am a man!" and sinks down upon
her knees, a prey to the most singular and varied
sensations that ever rent a human frame. For
at last she knows the truth! and it stuns as well as
horrifies her. At times she thinks another soul is
inside of her and her true spirit has wandered into

space—but so perfect a recollection of the Lillian
Travers of yesterday and of every preceding event in
Miss Travers' life comes home to her so clearly that
she knows she is the same spirit, though *man* instead
of *woman*.

After the first horror of this knowledge there comes
an exalted sense of supremacy, a feeling that the
world is now hers from which to choose her amusement and her career in life, and this gives promise to
her—excited and nervous as she still is—of a happy
future. She turns an inward gaze upon herself, she
is apparently well, strong, and certainly hungry—and
sits in a kind of dreamy contentment gazing vacu-
ously about her.

"Yo'r bath is ready, Miss Lilly," remarks Jane
and calls her from herself.

"I'm so hungry I think I'll take my breakfast
first," says the putative Miss Travers, for the first
time in her life discovering what a masculine appetite really is. And Jane departing on her errand, her
mistress takes advantage of her absence to put very
safely away the vial with its three precious seeds and
the curious record of old Hauser.

This is hardly done when Jane steps briskly in
with the breakfast.

"Ah! That coffee smells good.—Jane, you're a
brick!"

"Miss Lilly, is yo' crazy?" cries out the maid to this
repetition of the curious language that has caused
her so much astonishment during the morning.
"'Cause if you is, I want to get out ob heah."

"Neither crazy nor sick, Jane, but better than I
have ever been before," remarks her mistress orac-

ularly. " By the by, don't you tell aunt any confounded nonsense about what I have said to you
this morning. Here's fifty cents for you," and she
tosses her attendant a coin, thinking, like most other
men, that money is stronger than sentiment.

Then donning a *robe de chambre* she sits down to
the smoking breakfast, which Jane has placed on a
small table, and does justice to it in a way that makes
her handmaiden open her dusky eyes.

After a little Miss Travers says, " Jane, get out."

"Get out? what fo'?" asks her maid, astonished.

" I'm going to dress !"

" Of course, I always helps you!"

" But you are going to do so no more. Your fuss-
ing would make me wild. Get out!"

And so Jane departs wondering what crank has
come upon her young missus. The next instant
Lilly begins her toilet, communing with herself that
great caution and self-command must temper her
conscious possession of manhood. Of femininity,
a small amount yet remains, else she would be peril-
ously near immediate exposure. From the immediate revelation of her marvellous transformation she
still has sufficient womanhood to shrink aghast.
The little Lillian Travers left in her thinks, " Only
for to-day I will be a man, to see what it is like—
and then go back to my old self again.—And love
him—" but here suddenly her new nature bursts
forth. " Never! I'm in for a good thing, and I'll
clinch to it!" for her peace of mind shows her that
if, as a woman, she was entirely engrossed in Fred
Cassadene, as a man she is entirely absorbed in self—a
much more comfortable and contented state of feeling.

But the business of the day is before her, and with a don't-care gesture, she throws off the many difficulties of the thorny path into which she has entered and begins rapidly dressing ; a sudden and acute curiosity having come to her to test how it will feel to wander about the streets and enjoy her new sex.

Her toilet is not an easy one, and she anathematizes the tight corset that trammels her lithe movements ; and she finds it necessary to make use of certain artifices to give to her figure even a portion of the beautiful, rounded outlines that had made it graceful and lovely the day before.

Just as this is completed, Jane comes in suddenly and says :

" Mrs. Stella Lovejoy and Miss Bessie Horton has jes' been heah ; but I tole 'em yo' wasn't well."

" Well ? I never was better in my life. The girls haven't gone away, have they ? you numbskull ! " cries Lillie anxiously and savagely.

" They's jes' goin'. I—I didn't 'spose you'd want to see de beautiful widow," gasps Jane apologetically, remembering the incidents of the night before.

" Beautiful widows are just in my line, Janey ! Skip down-stairs and tell the girls to stop at once —I'll be with them in a minute."

" Yo's out ob yo' head—I neber saw yo' speak so befo', Miss Lilly," cries her astounded handmaiden.

·" No, but you will from now on "—then pausing at her own rashness, Lilly suddenly says : " Jane, I have concluded to throw off care and forget Doctor Fred and be happy without him.—Fly down and tell the girls to remain one second.—Stay, I'll catch them myself!" and Lilly strides down hastily to the parlor to receive and inflict new and wondrous sensations.

BOOK II.

The Boyhood of Lilly Travers.

CHAPTER VII.

"Ah! Naughty Boy—What Shall I Christen You?"

SHE swoops down-stairs, but her long, trailing skirts have become awkward to her, who yesterday in these same clinging garments, was the poetry of motion, and grace itself. Giving her trailing jupe, which at this moment gets under her feet, almost throwing her down, a very vicious and masculine yank, Lilly enters the parlor, from which through the half open door, comes the staid voice of Constantia, mingled with the more vivacious tones of Stella Lovejoy, and the delicious Southern babble of Bessie Horton.

"I hardly think she's got over the effect of her railroad journey," remarks her relative, apparently apologizing for her niece's laziness.

"Why, she was as bright as an oriole," murmurs Miss Bessie, "when we went to Vedder's yesterday morning."

"I have counted on Miss Travers for our hop

to-night," says the widow. "You don't think she
will disappoint me?"

"Hardly!" mutters Constantia grimly, turning her
glasses upon Mrs. Lovejoy, and thinking: "No
wonder Lilly is jealous of *her*." As she says nonchalantly: "'My niece has only got the blues."

"Not this morning, aunty" cries Lilly, breaking
in upon this scene. Then giving Miss Connie a
loving but careless kiss of relationship, Miss Travers
lifts up her eyes, and gives an astonished gasp as
she gazes upon Stella Lovejoy and Bessie Horton,
for it is the first time she has ever seen the wondrous loveliness of women with masculine eyes.

The two are in delicious contrast: Bessie looking
like a lovely wild flower in the light muslin dress of
girlhood—Stella in some fleecy creation of Worth's
that makes her exquisitely developed figure a series
of curves of beauty, as she rises languidly to receive
Lilly's greeting.

"The blues of which your aunt accuses you, seem
to have changed into a cold. You're very hoarse,
my dear," remarks the beautiful Stella.

"Not half as hoarse as you should be, from your
moonlight ducking last night. Doctor Fred pulled
you out in great shape, I hear.—Rather romantic, I
imagine," remarks Lilly, in easy enjoyment of Mrs.
Lovejoy's embarrassment at her adventure being
known to her rival, for as such she regards Miss
Travers—especially as she thinks uneasily, "She is
not jealous, therefore she feels sure of her position
with Cassadene."

"Oh, you know of our unfortunate accident,"
murmurs Stella, and she extends her hand to Lilly

and then to stop further discussion of the moonlight episode nonchalantly holds up a luscious rosy mouth to be kissed, for she is one of those women who always kiss other women.

A pair of dark brown eyes gaze into the radiant blue ones;—the invitation is accepted suddenly, ardently!—Lilly's coral lips press those of the beautiful widow;—a thrill—an ecstasy—an electric shock! Stella's lovely face becomes rosy with sudden blushes; she turns away and sinks into her chair, uttering a kind of lingering, longing sigh. ·

As for Lilly, though somewhat prepared, the sensation she experiences is much more potently soft, tender and exquisite than she expected. This first kiss of man to woman.

Her hand seems to linger longingly, perhaps caressingly, on the widow's rounded shoulder, as she turns away towards Bessie, who has cried in girlish enthusiasm : "My turn next!" For these two having known each other from childhood, kiss at sight in the careless, easy way peculiar to girls.

At first Miss Travers seems inclined to disregard this demand. She turns away as if about to sit down, but Bessie's face is thrust before hers and a wounded voice is in her ear, muttering—"It was my turn first—you sha'n't slight me altogether."

Fighting to subdue the tender feelings that are in her, Miss Travers grants the plump little blonde's demand, and apparently produces a great sensation on that young lady, for she ecstatically cries: " Just one more !" and gives the tall brunette another salute that comes from the very bottom of her heart and goes on enthusiastically, " Lilly, you are

6

the best kisser I ever saw—boys or girls!" then
suddenly pauses—for Miss Connie's voice is heard
in reproving tones " Bess! "

Whereupon the maiden stammers, " No, I don't
mean that ! Of course I don't ! I don't know what I
am talking about ! " and sits down covered with rosy
blushes.

The laugh attendant upon this serves to conceal
the putative Miss Travers' emotions which are like
those of a Romeo after Juliet's first kiss—for if
Stella's salute has caused rapture, Bessie's sweet
lips red and dewy as two morning rosebuds have
brought ecstasy.   .

She sinks into a chair, muttering " Darling Bessie! "
and hardly heeds the conversation, which has fallen
upon the ordinary woman's topics of the day.
Bessie running on vivaciously about the lovely time
she expects at the hop this evening, and Aunt Connie giving Lilly a receipt for colds that has been
transmitted to her from the dark ages.

But all this time, Stella's lovely eyes, though she
forces them to wander about the room, return
always to Lilly, an inquiring and wondering look in
them.   Once or twice their glances meet, and though
the widow's droop under the bolder looks of the
young lady, Lilly gets uneasy herself and wonders
in a nervous feminine manner, " Can she suspect? "
But masculine logic coming to her aid, she thinks,
" Pooh! Suspect a miracle? As a little girl I went
to school with her ! "

Then her eyes turn to Bessie, and she says to
herself: " The dear little girl! Funny I never
thought her so lovely before ! " for Bessie as she sits

prattling away, an unknown happiness in her heart, one pretty foot and ankle carelessly peeping from under her dress, makes a very lovely picture to masculine eyes, though she does not know that they are upon her.

Shortly after this, Miss Connie produces a sensation. She says suddenly: "Lilly, I shall insist upon your calling in a doctor!"

"A doctor—for what?"

"For your cold. It is awful. Your voice is hoarser than I have ever known it."

"Perhaps you had better send for Doctor Cassadene. He must have finished his case of snake-bite by this time," remarks the supposed invalid glancing at Mrs. Lovejoy maliciously and rather enjoying teasing a pretty woman after the taste of average masculinity.

At this the widow blushes and looks uncomfortable, and Lilly, eyeing her, knows that Doctor Fred has told her of the lie that he had written, and were it last night, she would hate—*hate*—HATE her; but now, this morning, noting the wondrous loveliness of her former rival she thinks: "No wonder Fred is spoons on that catchey Stella—George! what an ankle!" sneaking a peep at a delicious little boot that is making her heart beat very rapidly.

Then she continues aloud: "Of course I shall see Doctor Fred to-day. He is going to take me to the 'hop' this evening," and astonishes herself by being annoyed because she sees she has planted a dagger in the widow's heart, and wonders, "What the deuce can Stella see to like in Fred, anyway? I should think I would be more in her style."

A moment after the visitors rise to go.

As they shake hands, Doctor Cassadene is announced and enters to receive two fearful shocks to his manly vanity—which as usual in his sex is very great and exceedingly touchy.

Lilly shakes hands nonchalantly with the Doctor, and says : " How do, Fred ! " in a careless way that startles them all, for though she intends it to be simply the welcome of one man to another, it has given both Bessie and the widow a sudden intimation, judging from a feminine standpoint, that she is engaged to the Doctor, and intends in this way to announce her coming union to the handsome man who is standing before them. He responds to her salutation in an uneasy, embarrassed way, and is then introduced to Miss Constantia who receives him rather frigidly.

A moment after Bessie, having made her adieux, turns to the door, and would go on her way alone, but Lilly, actuated by some sudden emotion, says promptly : " Let me escort you," offering her arm with the grace of an avenue Adonis.

This Bessie takes very readily, giving her escort quite a shock as she remarks : " What an unusual treat ! Why, Lilly, you're as attentive as if you were a—a gentleman, this morning."

Mrs. Lovejoy is about to follow them. The Doctor gallantly says : " Let me put you in the carriage," and gets one of the shocks of his life.

For actuated by an unknown, yet potent feeling, the widow suddenly returns :

" Lilly has another arm at liberty—she will do for both me and Bess ! " and slips her pretty gloved hand under Miss Travers' arm, who looks back at Fred with mocking eyes, as she takes the two beauties out to their carriage.

They are at the gate, and Stella says laughingly: " I must have another one of your pretty kisses, Lilly! "

" And I, too! " cries Bessie, not to be outdone.

Whereupon the putative young lady kindly accommodates them both with an enthusiasm that astonishes them, and putting them blushing, laughing and very beautiful, into their carriage, would lift her hat if she had one on her head, after the manner of a Fifth Avenue swell, as they drive away.

Then she suddenly says to herself in an affrighted, reproving yet reflective manner: " Ah, naughty boy! " and gazing at her shadow on the sunlight of the walk murmurs, " I wonder what I'll christen you? " and looks complacently on herself, for verily the joys of young manhood are exceeding great! A moment after she gives out a low, affrighted " Wh-e-w! if Aunt Connie only knew she'd go out of her head! " then turns with merry laugh towards the house.

But at the threshold a fearful scowl comes over her mobile features. She hesitates and mutters : " I suppose Fred'll want to kiss me. My heaven, how sickening! " and a shudder runs over her. Then her face grows very determined and she cogitates: " If he does I'll fix him! " and with this threat to her own dear sweetheart of yesterday, she strides into the house whistling in easy abandon, " The girl I left behind me "!

A very few bars of her music brings Miss Connie

to her. That outraged spinster appearing on the portico whispers, " Whistling, Lilly ? " in a horrified tone, next remarks severely, " What's come to you this morning?—Your manners have been something awful for a young lady. Now go to your fiancé—I hope he has not heard you whistling—it would be quite a shock to him."

Taking her aunt's advice the late Miss Travers steps into the parlor where Doctor Frederick sits alone and sulking. Mrs. Lovejoy has wounded his pride ; besides, this young gentleman has somehow an intuition that his sweetheart knows of his defection on the night before, and that he has an uncomfortable interview before him.

Such ideas are soon driven from his mind. Lilly says in easy nonchalance : " Well, old boy, did you have a high old time last evening, with that pretty widow ? " and nods her head in the direction of the departed Stella.

" Yes, you see——" gasps Fred, astounded.

" Oh, her beauty is excuse enough. And how's the patient with the snake-bite ? Dead, I presume—most of your patients usually die."

" If you will let me explain, Lilly," mutters the Doctor.

" Oh, no need of that," says the putative young lady. " I know about how it is myself ! " and with these extraordinary words, she flops into a roomy chair, assuming such an easy and mannish attitude that her lover stares at her in astonished silence.

" What time are you going to take me to the ball —Eh ? Why don't you wake up, Freddie, and answer ! "

But Cassadene's love, like most men's, is increased by the lady's coldness. He says: "You speak to me that way. You refuse to hear my apologies —my excuses. We have been parted twelve long hours, and as yet not one kiss, my darling!" and approaches her with outstretched arms, to play the engaged and ardent lover, but finds her very coy.

She artfully eludes several strategic moves on his part, and then, he being on the point of victory, suddenly cries out in a desperate tone: "Not a kiss, Fred, until you have explained the snake-bite."

"My heaven!" he bursts out.—"How can I explain it, except that after writing you that note, just as I was mounting to gallop to my patient, a man rode up to the hotel and told me that there was no need of my going there. The man had *not* been bitten by a snake—it was simply the scratch of a thorn brush in the swamp that he had supposed the stroke of a water moccasin, and had nearly died from fear, not poison."

"Ah, that was the reason!" mutters Lilly, astounded at this audacious and ingenious lie, which had been carefully prepared by Doctor Fred in case of his perfidy being discovered. She is thinking, "I wonder if I'll ever learn to fib in that glorious manner," when she finds herself in his arms, and then kiss!—*kiss!*—K-I-S-S!—the agony has begun!

She groans inwardly, and struggling turns so savage and scowling a face over the Doctor's shoulder that could he see it despair would be upon him. She wants to clutch the brawny throat in front of her, and choke it with all her newly acquired muscle;

but the cigar-perfumed mustache is pressed again and again upon her lips that now shrink from it for the first time.

Then a sudden consciousness that she must play her part, in order to preserve her secret, coming to her, she tries to be the Lilly Travers of old, but does not do it very well, for a moment after he turns from her muttering : "Your kisses are cold—cold—cold!"

Then her very iciness adding to his flame, he cries out desperately, "Can you doubt the love of the man who would die for you? Your promised husband!" and goes into many other masculine rhapsodies and extravagances that would have seemed lovely to her but twelve hours before, but now make her laugh.

As she bursts into a sneering snicker, he becomes very angry and growls at her : "Not only coldness, but derision!" next goes on in a heart-broken voice, putting her into momentary panic as he mutters, "Your conduct is very unnatural."

"Unnatural? How?" gasps the girl. "You were indifferent to me last night. Why shouldn't I be indifferent to you to-day?"

"Some women might, but not the girl I worship —the girl I adore," he returns pathetically; and there are real tears in the great big flirt's eyes, for her indifference makes him desperate.

Then he frightens her terribly as he cries : "You are not the Lilly Travers of yesterday."

At this, fearing that perhaps he may suspect a miracle—she is delighted when Aunt Connie makes her appearance.

"Before you go, Doctor," says Miss Constantia,

" I want you to examine Lilly's throat and chest.
You notice how hoarse she is ? "

" Examine *me* ! " gasps her niece, all in a tremble.

" My heavens ! " exclaims Fred, suddenly ; for
he has been too agitated and excited up to this
moment to note anything but his sweetheart's indifference. " What a cold you have ! Allow me."

But she draws back from him with an affrighted
" No ! no ! "—and shudders with burning panic
blushes.

" As your physician, my dearest," remarks the
doctor tenderly.

" This is absurd delicacy in such a case," says her
aunt ; but to Lilly's relief, Doctor Fred remarks,
after looking at her attentively : " I do not think
her cold is at all serious." Then he adds rather
maliciously : " I am sure from the way she whistled
a few moments ago that her lungs are not affected,
and as she seems to be rather anxious to avoid my
attentions both as physician and lover this afternoon, I shall not force them upon her."

For this he gets such a heartfelt, grateful and
almost loving " Thank you " from his fiancée, that
joy flies into his eyes, and Miss Connie, having departed with a sniff of contempt at her niece's absurd
prudery, Doctor Fred falls to again rapturously
and forces the putative Miss Travers to undergo
some most tender and horrible caresses at his hands.
For she is desperately afraid of his physician's prac-
tised eye giving him some suspicion of the extraordinary change that has taken place in her, and tries
to play the sweetheart and the woman who has
parted from him but yesterday.

" Ah, now you are my own once more!" He has
seized her and is lavishing kisses upon her. "You
have missed me, haven't you, darling? A little
jealous, eh, but she couldn't be long angry with
her Freddie, could she?" Then he cries out, "My
precious one, you look pale and unlike yourself.
Come to the light." Upon this Lilly tries to droop
her eyelids in the old, submissive way, which is fortunate, as they veil two very savage looking optics
as he leads her to one of the open French windows
of the room.

"Now, look me in the eyes!"—he playfully
chucks her under the chin. "You have been griev-
ing for me—jealous and all that foolishness, my pet!
(kiss) Those lovely shadows below your delicious
eyes mean that—don't they, my sweetheart?"

" YOU BET THEY DON'T !!!" is the fierce rejoinder
spoken in so savage a whisper that he staggers back.

After a moment, however, attributing it still to
some remnants of the aforesaid jealousy he renews
the attack, and suddenly gives her a fearful shock, for
he says: "Darling, you must name our wedding day!"

" Not now! For God's sake, not now!" she
stutters.

" Well, then, my angel, to-morrow—you must tell
me when you will make me the happiest man in
Florida.—Don't forget—I will call for you at half-
past eight this evening." So, with a few more en-
dearments which yesterday she would have loved
but to-day she hates, Doctor Fred goes away in a
very happy and contented mind, remarking to himself *sotto voce :* "The widow may cut up rough, but
Lilly is mine anyway."

And she stands staring after him wondering to herself :

"How did I endure his suffocating and nauseating kisses? O-o-ugh! Name the wedding day? This is the deuce of a joke on Fred!—If he knew? Ha! ha! ha!—ho! ho! ho!—he! he! he!"

These are such masculine guffaws that Aunt Connie runs out upon the veranda where she is standing and asks her very savagely if she is crazy!

CHAPTER VIII.

THE HOP AT THE PONCE DE LEON.

"ANOTHER thing I will tell you," continues Miss Constantia, after this outburst is over,—"is that you do not go to the hop this evening."

"Not to the hop?" remarks Lilly piteously, thinking of how lovely Stella and Bessie will look arrayed for that entertainment.

"Not with that cold."

"I am going, cold or no cold. Besides, my voice is much better," and she attempts by raising her vocal pitch to give herself some of the tones of yesterday that made her voice so liquid, brilliant and beautiful.

"Well, anyway," remarks Miss Constantia, "you are not going to the ball in a low-neck dress; with that cold a decolleté gown would be death! I know your Parisian gowns—and I don't care if you have a pretty neck and shoulders."

This is a very pleasant suggestion to Lilly, who

has been in somewhat of a quandary as to what will be the best thing to wear on this occasion for the more effectual concealment of deficiencies.

"Very well, auntie," she says dutifully; "I think I'll wear my black lace robe, brightened up with flowers of some kind. It is quite high enough at the throat to cover the trouble. Now, a favor to me—you must go with me, you dear old auntie, and play chaperon this evening."

"In my day," remarks Miss Constantia severely, "a girl did not need a chaperon when she went with the man whom she was going to marry. I am down on these foreign notions; but if it will give you any pleasure for me to go with you, I shall be delighted. Perhaps Major Horton will be there also."

"Of course he will," cries Lilly. "He *must* be there with his daughter."

At this the old lady's eyes twinkle eagerly, for Miss Constantia Oglethorpe has a very tender spot in her time-worn heart for the dashing major of the passed-away Confederacy.

"Very well," says the niece shortly; "that is settled," and feels relieved, for she knows that her aunt's presence will be certain safety to her from any lover-like attentions that Fred may feel disposed to inflict upon her during the journey to and from the entertainment.

Half an hour after this Lilly goes for a drive, which she enjoys immensely, and coming home enthusiastically cries out: "I never thought there were so many beautiful women in the world before!" and goes into such rhapsodies over the ladies of St.

Augustine whom she has seen upon the streets, making such wild remarks about well-turned ankles, beautiful figures, lovely eyes, and drooping glances —that her aunt gazes at her astounded ; till at last, upon her excitedly suggesting that she has already gotten up one or two flirtations with beauties that passed her on the street, Miss Constantia raises up her voice in horror and shrieks: " What's the matter with you to-day ? Are you going crazy ? I never heard such talk from a girl before ! "—which frightens the late Miss Travers and makes her very demure until she goes up-stairs to dress for the coming hop.

In her room she has an awful spasm of bashfulness under the hands of the young lady hair-dresser who comes from one of the hotels to arrange her beautiful brown tresses, as well as several vigorous contests with Jane, who makes a number of attempts in her good-hearted, negro way to try to lace her young missus' corset and arrange her foot-gear.

But Lilly, to her horror, now discovers that during the day her feet have apparently been growing larger, and the dainty things that had fitted her so snugly but yesterday are all too small for her rapidly developing extremities. So on the pretext that her black slippers, the only ones she can wear with the dress selected for the evening, are shabby, she gets Jane out of the way, by sending her with a note to an Alcazar shoe-store. From where, fortunately having found it open, the maid returns with a pair of slippers that at least are comfortable, though they are not so pleasing to the eye as those that had formerly adorned her mistress's fairy feet.

The careful arrangement of her toilet takes so much time that she hears Fred's voice in the hall below before she descends, and gives a little grin as she mutters: "He won't find me changed in the matter of keeping him waiting. I am feminine at present in that respect anyway;" and so swoops down-stairs to do her best this evening to represent Miss Lilly Travers.

Miss Connie, having the major in her mind, is even slower than her niece with her toilet, and Lilly finds herself alone in the parlor. She glances out.

Doctor Fred is standing on the veranda enjoying his after-dinner cigar. He looks so handsome in his evening dress and light overcoat that the late Miss Travers suddenly thinks: "I wonder how I would appear in such a rig?" and then pauses abashed at the thought, for this is the first time that the idea of a masculine costume has entered her head.

A second later, the Doctor has tossed away his beloved weed and turned to the girl whose apparent indifference to him has made him all the more eager for her society. Coming slyly behind her, he gives her an ardent kiss and whispers, "How beautiful!"

"Then," she says, drawing away—"I wish to impress upon you the important fact, old fellow, that lace is the easiest thing in the world to rumple, so please keep at a respectful distance or I shall be a sight to behold."

"Very well," sighs the Doctor; "I will not destroy so lovely a toilet." Then he remarks: "I am gratified to see that you are beginning to regard my wishes, Lilly, about exposing to the chill weather

and—well, to other men's eyes—your bewitching
shoulders and arms. I do not mind other men's
sweethearts being dressed that way, but I want my
own dear love's dress high—even to the throat."

"If it pleases you," grumbles Lilly, "respect it,
—and don't rumple it."

"So I will,—going to the ball," says the Doctor ;
":but coming home "—he gives a longing sigh.

"I have provided for that," remarks Miss Travers
archly ; and she points to Miss Connie, now entering the door arrayed in her best black silk.—"Behold my chaperon !" at which her sweetheart becomes very sulky and she thinks she hears him
swear under his breath.

A few seconds after they are rolling away towards
the Ponce de Leon. As the carriage leaves the
shell-road to travel over the oasis of asphalt in the
centre of the town, the conversation, which has lan-
guished, becomes more rapid, and here Miss Lilly
brings rapture to Fred's heart.

She remarks sententiously : "You know the miserable dearth of men at all watering-place hops,—I
presume there will be fewer of these masculine deities here than farther north."

"Oh, don't fear," remarks her fiancé ; "you will
have plenty of partners to haul you about." Then
he continues : "I by no means approve of young
ladies dancing with every man they meet at such
public assemblies."

"Neither do I," says Lilly, and gives her sweetheart a sudden rapture, for she whispers : "Fred,
I have determined to give the ladies a treat this
evening."

" What do you mean ? "

" I'm going to dance only with girls. Will that please you ? "

" Please me, darling !" and he gives her hand in the convenient darkness a tender squeeze. " You will dance with no men this evening ? "

" With none," answers the girl determinedly; whereupon Miss Connie, awaking from a meditation on her ex-major of the Confederacy, remarks suddenly:

" Lilly, don't talk such nonsense. It is perfectly unnatural for girls to dance with each other, when good-looking, able-bodied fellows are about."

" Very well, aunt; to-night I am going to be unnatural," says her niece prophetically.

Then amid flashing lights, the hum of voices, the babble of fountains and cadence of the distant orchestra they roll into the covered driveway of the Ponce de Leon.

While Doctor Cassadene is carefully assisting Miss Connie out of the carriage, Lilly quietly opens the door and steps out on the other side, agilely dodging a team which is driving up after them, and thinking with delight, " I'm taking care of myself just like a man ! "

" You didn't wait for my assistance," remarks Fred, biting his mustache in annoyance as he sees her performance.

" No. I am trying to accustom myself to doing without it."

Unheeding her significant reply, a moment after he is by her side whispering: " You are very unkind, but I forgive you," and offering his arm, which the circumstances of the case compel her to accept, he escorts her and Miss Connie up to the second floor. Next remarking : "Mrs. Lovejoy has placed her suite of apartments at your disposition and that of some of her other lady friends, for a dressing room. I'll be waiting for you when you come out," he departs. Then before she even has a chance to hesitate, Lilly finds herself in this Holy of Holies of the fair sex, this temple where the finishing touches are placed upen feminine loveliness in supposed seclusion from the profaning eyes of man.

For one short moment she is abashed and would retreat and steps hurriedly back upon Miss Connie's foot ; whereupon that maiden, who is immediately behind her, remarks savagely : "Lilly ! My toes ! Can't you bear your Frederick's absence for one moment ? What are you running after him now for ? "

This attack brings her to herself, and remembering that eternal vigilance means safety from discovery, the late Miss Travers, assuming all the feminine airs, graces and coquetry that have been left to her from yesterday, though awfully self-conscious and somewhat awkward, strides into this conglomeration of subdued laughter, tumbled wraps on sofas and chairs, flowers, perfumes, flashing eyes, lovely lips; black, brown and golden heads; necks and bosoms of snow, gleaming arms, shining shoulders and radiant faces, in lovely abandon and charming disarray. A scene once familiar and devoid of charm to her, but now dazing, disconcerting and maddening in its allurements.

" Help me off with my wraps, Lilly, that's a good

7

girl," says Miss Connie; "what are you gazing about in that wild way for—one would think you'd never been at a ball before!" She forces herself to pay her aunt this attention, as it gives her a chance to collect her thoughts that have been driven wool-gathering, if not worse, by the enchanting scene about her.

Then, her aunt made presentable, she turns her attention to herself, and has just thrown off her cloak, when Mrs. Lovejoy's maid offers her assist-ance to remove her overshoes.

She waves the girl off almost rudely, remarking: "I can attend to myself, thank you;" and sitting down, adjusts her slippers in a bashful, diffident, but apparently awkward manner, and hears a muttered remark from some lady in the crowd: "I thought you said Lilly Travers had a small foot!"

This gives her a flutter; she thinks: "What a gawk I must look in this attire now! My heavens! —if they discover——"

This idea is so horrible that she turns pale and would fly from the room, did not a pair of soft, white, robust arms encircle her waist, and Stella's radiant face look over her shoulder, and Stella's blue eyes look into hers, and Stella's red lips come very near to hers, as the widow whispers: "Delighted you have come. I have been looking for you every-where, dear Lilly! You are going to dance?"

"Well, *rather!*" remarks the late Miss Travers, so enthusiastically and determinedly that for a mo-ment Mrs. Lovejoy is startled.

"You are devoted to dancing?" she murmurs, drooping her eyes.

" Yes—devoted enough to dance with a woman !"
answers Lilly craftily, " if you will let me. You
know how scarce men are here. To-night I am
going to devote myself to your—to our sex. Will
you dance with me ?"

" Y–e–s!" sighs the widow. Then she says suddenly, her eyes beaming brilliantly : " Such devotion
to our sex should be rewarded—you shall have *two*,"
and leaves Lilly delighted ; for though not now
jealous of Fred's attentions to Mrs. Lovejoy, she
has suddenly become worried at Mrs. Lovejoy's
fondness for the Doctor.

" I wonder if I could not cut Fred out—why
shouldn't I? I believe I could, if she only knew,"
thinks Lilly and utters a playful but malicious
laugh.

The next instant the widow is obliterated from
her heart. Miss Connie whispers, " Why don't you
help that poor child with her shoes ?" and with
throbbing pulse she gazes at Miss Bessie Horton,
who in charming disarray is seated upon a chair in
the corner of the room coquettishly struggling with
a satin slipper—and making too bewitching a picture for masculine eyes.

Unmindful of torn laces and feminine screams the
late Miss Travers forces her way through the crowd
of indignant beauty and is beside her love of loves.

As Lilly gains Miss Horton's side that young lady
conquers her foot-gear.

" I have been gazing at you for the last five minutes, and you haven't even noticed me, Lil," mutters Bessie, anger in her tones and pique in her
voice. Then she says inquiringly: " Just look—

Don't you think my slippers match my dress beautifully?" Casting her eyes down, the putative Miss Travers is enthralled and whispers, "You have the prettiest feet, Bess, in the world." And so they are, this evening, arrayed in the delicate hosiery and fairy slippers of a *toilette de bal.*

"I didn't ask about the feet, I asked about my slippers!" pouts Bess.

"You're altogether too lovely for anything!" cries the late Miss Travers overcome.

"I'm delighted you think I'm all right," answers Miss Horton easily, and a moment after asks: "Did Doctor Cassadene come with you?" perhaps a little too eagerly. "He is going to dance with me."

"Yes!" says Lilly snappily. Then she remarks contemplatively: "You must not give him any more dances."

"Why not—if he asks for them? He is very handsome, and men are very scarce"—this last with a little defiant *moue.*

"And for that reason," says Lilly, "I am going to take pity on you; I am going to dance with the girls this evening." Then assuming the attitude of a cavalier and the drawl of a dandy she lisps, "May I have, the—aw—honah of a aw—turn with you this evening, Miss Horton?" and pretending to stroke an imaginary mustache becomes suddenly red and then very pale, for she finds her upper lip has somehow grown very rough and exceeding fuzzy during the day.

"Certainly; take all you want," cries Bessie with such enthusiasm that Lilly forgets her alarm in the joy of Bessie's friendship.

A moment after her companion gives her a start by saying: "You have not told me yet what was in that casket you bought at Vedder's! Why, how red you are, Lilly! Here's my powder puff!"

But Miss Travers suddenly points across the room whispering, "That is the girl we saw in the balcony —you remember?—the one that was looking at Doctor Cassadene! Do you know her name?"

"Oh yes," babbles Bess, "I made a point of inquiring about her. She's Miss Rosa King of Charleston.—She met Dr. Fred last month and hates Mrs. Lovejoy.—Don't you think Stella is perfectly lovely?"

"She is very nice." This last diplomatically from Miss Travers.

"Mr. Wilkes introduced me to her yesterday, and she has been very kind and attentive to me all day," rattles on Bessie. "I think she is perfectly charming."

"Charming! She's adorable," answers Lilly with so much enthusiasm that Bessie returns reproachfully:

"Well, I don't like her as much as I do *you* anyway." An answer that makes Lilly's glances very ardent.

Under them her companion grows restless and suddenly remarks, "But we are missing all the dancing, Miss Connie is beckoning impatiently to us, and I suppose my father and Dr. Fred have been savagely pacing the corridor outside for the last ten minutes."

Thirty seconds after they are in the hallway of the giant hotel where Miss Lilly finds Bess's prediction is true—and the major and Dr. Fred both in very bad tempers.

So they all go down together through the great corridors into the rotunda, and so to the dining-room of this huge caravansary.

This has been turned into a ball-room for the evening, though only a portion of its parquet floor is used for dancing, the rest being occupied by spectators, for whom seats have been arranged. In one of these chairs Miss Connie is made comfortable, and Miss Travers, taking Bessie under her protecting wing, strolls about the ball-room, which is only fairly filled, the season at this Florida watering-place being still in its infancy.

Even now, however, there is quite an assemblage of women, though the dress suits of gentlemen are very few and wide apart, producing a dismal prospect of masculine companionship in the dance, to the numerous ladies who are strolling about in pretty evening costumes.

The music is just breaking into a waltz, and Cassadene overtaking Miss Bessie and her companion, remarks with the easy assurance of masculine proprietorship: " Miss Travers, my dance, I believe," and is astonished and disconcerted at her answer.

Lilly with a provoking smile returns: " You forget the promise I made you."

" The promise to dance with no other gentleman but me ?—of course I remember *that !* "

" I beg your pardon—the promise to dance with *no* gentleman this evening."

" Not even me ? "   The astonishment of this

Adonis would be ludicrous were his face not so pit-eous—for Fred always wants most what he cannot get.

"Certainly not. I am a man—I mean a—a woman of my word." And Lilly's voice and manner would be very dignified did she not get confused over the last part of her speech.

" Yes, she has promised to dance only with girls this evening, Doctor Cassadene," breaks in Bessie, "and I've got four of them." And before Fred can make reply, the two young ladies are in each other's arms whirling away to the soft strains of the " Estudiantina." Bessie whispering in her compan-ion's ear : " How beautifully you guide—just like a man ! Your arms seem so strong and firm and you never seem to hesitate like other girls when bumped about in a crowd."

A few moments after they stand by Miss Connie's side taking a little breathing spell, and Mrs. Lovejoy, turning from Mr. Remington, says suddenly : " Lilly, have you forgotten your promise—my turn next."

Unheeding Bessie's reproachful : " Why, our dance is not finished yet," Miss Travers whirls the widow in among the waltzers with as much grace and vigor as any of the dress-coats that are perform-ing beside her, and with such effect that Stella's eyes droop as her feet keep time to the music, and she whispers to her partner: " I could dance with you forever, if you were only a man. Your waltzing will make many a young lady happy this evening—Oh, you madcap ! " for Lilly has answered this eulogium by a sudden almost involuntary but fervid squeeze.

"Yes," whispers the putative Miss Travers, enthusiastically—for the music is in her soul and the perfume from the delicate bouquet in Mrs. Lovejoy's hands is in her nostrils and her arm is clasping her willowy waist,—"I intend to give the girls a treat this evening."

And so she does, making many a fair one, who has been lamenting the dearth of gentlemen, forget for a few short, blissful moments that she is not dancing with a claw-hammer coat and that a black broadcloth sleeve is not around her waist.

But she devotes most of her time to dear little Bessie, who, despite numerous applications from the other sex, gives Lilly about all the dances she wants. In one of the pauses of their exercise, Miss Travers mutters partly to herself, "And to think that I should ever enjoy dancing with a girl."

"Yes, it is funny!" cries Bessie, impulsively. "I like it also—give me another turn."

And the two fly about in each other's arms till the major, Bessie's father, remarks sarcastically : "You girls are mighty hard on the boys this evening."

With the widow, however, Lilly dances only twice ; for Mrs. Lovejoy has command of all the gentlemen she wishes and though she likes to dance with Lilly, she also likes the satisfaction of showing that she can have all the masculine devotion she desires.

As for the men, there are many of them about her during the evening, for Miss Travers has a reputation for both beauty and wealth ; sugar plums which always attract the masculine portion of humanity. But Lilly refuses them all in so off-hand and careless a style that Miss Connie whispers reprovingly to her several times during the evening, and young Mr. Wilkes, the Northern orange grower from Indian River, upon being introduced and his request for a turn refused, walks off savagely to the bar-room to forget his chagrin in the flowing bowl, and meeting some other gentlemen there, descants upon the Northern heiress's hauteur, remarking, "By Jove! fellows; I merely asked her to dance with me once, and she looked as if she would knock me down—hang me if she did'nt!"—a remark that is more truthful than Mr. Wilkes imagines as he makes it.

But the evening is not all triumph to the recently emancipated. Old Remington who is somewhat of a cynic and philosopher remarks to old Horton, "Isn't Lilly Travers changed? I saw her a year ago at one of the Patriarchs' in New York, and she was a perfect dream of beauty—and now by all the phosphates in Florida! she's a gawk—that what she is!"

"In truth, age does not improve any of us," returns the major sadly—"I knew her aunt when she was a girl of eighteen. She was the loveliest creature in St. Augustine. I and young Pinckney of Charleston fought a duel about her."

"And then——" suggests the Northerner.

"Then," says the Floridian, "she would have neither of us—and now——" he looks over at Miss Connie's prim and rather gaunt figure and spectacled eyes and gives a reflective sigh.

"Did you see that?" whispers Adams Winthrop Dunbar of Beacon Street, Boston.

"What?—my dear chappy!" lisps Prescott Cad Chowders, of Fifth Avenue, New York,

" That Travers girl—a waiter happened to bump against her, and she clinched her fist as if she would floor the darkey—she's strong-minded, I can tell you ! "

" Yaas—and strong-armed—my dear boy !—How she twists that widow about—steers her with as much power as Harvey de Witt Van Favors who leads all our Germans this year. Won't she give it to the fellah who marries her and her million ! "

Some of these floating remarks coming to Miss Constantia's ears make that ancient and prim spinster very savage with her niece.

This evening also there are certain things that do not suit the erratic Lilly—she cannot assume all the privileges of the sex, she cannot boast and brag to her fellows of her conquests—she can't stroke her mustache in a knowing manner when Stella's name is mentioned, she can't take darling little Bessie under her arm and elbow her way through envious swains and put her in her carriage with a soft squeeze of the hand and a killing glance in her eyes. —For the late Miss Travers is still only a reckless boy and has a young blood's eagerness to show off and triumph over and be envied by his fellows and his rivals.

So, as Miss Horton has departed escorted by another young gentleman to her carriage, upon whom Lilly looks with by no means angelic glances though very well pleased to see the old major is also at his daughter's side, and the hop being nearly over, these Ponce de Leon dances being generally early and hungry ones as the hotel provides no supper for its guests, Miss Travers strolls out into the beautiful court yard to sit among its flowers, listen to the babble of its fountain and hear the hum of the last expiring waltz of the orchestra.

This she does alone, for women wander about these Florida hotels in the free and easy manner peculiar to this Southern town that for three short months seems on a continuous picnic.

Solitude is pleasing to her, she wants to think over the excitement of this first evening of her boyhood, in which she has been so happy.—She thinks as she sits beneath a magnolia and shaded by its leaves—" To-night would have been perfect—if I'd had a swallow-tail.—That widow, OH!—And Bessie, AH!" these exclamations stand for sighs of ecstasy.

She would perhaps run on in this strain indefinitely, did not a faint sob from the other side of the little hedge that cuts her off from another path come wafted to her ears.

It is a woman's and as such appeals to the masculine heart. All the boy in Miss Travers is up to go to the assistance of beauty in distress, when a gentleman's voice comes to her ears from the same spot, and it is one that makes her hesitate and pause—the one that was like music to her but yesterday—Doctor Fred's !

It says very politely, " Rosa, I am astounded at this outburst.—How can I help myself!" and Lilly knows the lady he addresses is the one that looked in anguish on his attentions to Stella the day before.

" How can you help it?" the girl repeats, " How can you help it? You haven't even asked me to dance once to-night—when before Mrs. Lovejoy

came and that gawky Travers girl got here—you—
were so different.—Oh Fred, can't you remember?—
It's only two weeks ago—only——"

Miss Travers rises and walks off—smiling a little at
the thought that she is gawky now, and then muttering to herself in sneer at the sex she has deserted, "And yesterday I was one of those sighing, appealing, entreating creatures like her—I'm a
rather different article now.—From this time on
I do the heart-breaking."—And the recollection of
this scene hardens her against her erstwhile lover
and makes it easy for her to give him his *congé*—
which she determines to do this very night.

She strolls in, joins her aunt, and in a few minutes
they are ready for the drive home, Doctor Cassadene
coming up just about this moment with a somewhat
annoyed yet triumphant look on his handsome face
to receive a very free and easy " Hello, Fred, who
was the young lady in the moonlight?—We fellahs
are having a night of it—ain't we?"

This is answered by a frown from the gentleman
addressed and a subdued snort of horror from Miss
Connie as they go down to their carriage.

CHAPTER IX.

"MY MAN, JANE."

AND so they all drive home from the ball, the
aunt so savage at her niece's eccentricities that she
says very little, and Doctor Fred in very glum and

moody silence also, though the emancipated one does talking for the three.

She is in very high spirits, Bessie having promised to come and spend the next afternoon with her. This makes her very happy, and she rattles on, making some very peculiar remarks for a young lady.

" Fred, old boy, didn't we give the girls a treat to-night ? " she says enthusiastically.

" Lilly, you astound me," interjects Miss Connie severely ;—the gentleman addressed however listens in glum silence.

" Do you know—Frederick my chappie—I have only envied you two things this evening; otherwise, I flatter myself I had a *leetle* the best of you," continues the late Miss Travers airily.

" Indeed ? What were they?"—curiosity has opened the Doctor's mouth.

" Well, first, your enjoyment of your cigar on the veranda; and, second, the privilege you had of meandering towards the bar between dances. But I'll catch up to you—mighty shortly ! "

" Lilly, those are terrible words for a young woman," cries her aunt in horror, and is delighted to find the drive over and the carriage standing at the entrance to their house.

The two are assisted to alight by Doctor Fred, and Miss Connie, bidding him " Good-night " and thanking him for his escort, goes into the house.

Lilly would follow her, and is saying " Adieu," when Fred's hand clasps her arm determinedly—almost roughly. He whispers: " Before you go in, I want a word with you."

"Oh ! half a dozen—I'm not sleepy ! "

"Then come round the corner of the veranda ; we shall be out of the driver's sight and hearing."

"Certainly. Light your cigar? I see you are dying for a smoke ! If you have two in your case, I'll—I'll join you !—You—you don't offer it ?—Oh how stingy ! " remarks Lilly roguishly.

They have passed to the other side of the house now, and Fred turns upon her in severe displeasure.

"This last request of yours, Miss Travers," he says sternly, " is in line with your other performances this evening. Perhaps you wish by such unladylike conduct to alienate my affection."

"You have guessed it, Fred," she answers. "After this, I only wish to be to you as one good fellow is to another good fellow—friends—nothing more. I do not even "—here she smiles—" claim the privilege of sisterhood."

The reply she receives astonishes her.

"And do you think to destroy my love, by these pranks? Lilly—I—I love you all the more for your spirit—you can't deceive the eyes of love though you play your part very nicely ! " cries the Doctor in longing tones ; for now the girl who is passing away from him seems dearer to him than ever.

"Don't talk nonsense," says Lilly in a businesslike way. " It is impossible for me ever to become your wife."

"How long have you known this ? " gasps the man.

"Since yesterday evening."

"Ah, it is always yesterday evening." Then he whispers : " If it had not been for that unfortunate occurrence, for my stupidity—my neglect, if you

will—would you now have been my sweetheart—
my love—my Lilly of yesterday."

" I should," says the late Miss Travers.

" Then I'll retrieve myself.   I'll make you forgive
me.   In spite of yourself, I'll make you marry me
within the month ! "

With this audacious masculine threat, Doctor
Fred is about to stride from the veranda; but a
light though firm grasp is on his arm and a laughing
voice cries, "That is impossible, I love another—
she's a darling!"   And Lilly passes into the house
leaving him astounded and confounded.

After a time however he thinks the "*she* " is a slip
of the tongue, but goes off in a very bad humor to
the Ponce de Leon where he finds Mrs. Lovejoy
still seated on the veranda with some ladies and
gentlemen, and the widow's blue eyes have a very
soothing effect on this bird of passage.

This interview has taken hardly a minute, and
Lilly stepping into the house finds Constantia
awaiting her with words of reproof.

" You have broken with Doctor Fred ? " she says.

" Yes."

"And that was the way you took to do it? "

" Yes! "   Lilly is delighted at her aunt's taking
this view of her eccentricities.

" Then, you have made a fool of yourself," cries
the old lady.

" And why ? "

" Because you are not now the kind of a girl
men fall in love with."

" Why not ?   I have had plenty of devotees."

" Yes ; you *have* had them, but you have

changed. No man would love such a girl as you. It would not be natural. You are too bold. You are not retiring. You clenched your fist at a waiter this evening—I saw you; you needn't attempt to deny it, your glove is torn even now from your violence!" And looking down Lilly sees her aunt's remark is true.—During the evening her growing hands have made her gloves a torture to her, and now one has burst in a disreputable rent under the increasing strain.

"You would have knocked him down, had you dared," cries Miss Connie in continuation. "You are a tom-boy—that's what you are, and to think only yesterday you seemed so different—so womanly —so lovable! I—I am *dis-gus-ted!*" and a burst of tears closes this harangue.

Her niece's "Now, don't cut up rough, old lady!" "Just go easy, will you, a little while,"—and other masculine expressions of penitence produce new spasms in her aunt. She retires weeping to the solitude of her chamber.

A moment after Lilly runs up to her apartment, throws herself into a chair and mutters:

"I've had a pretty good time myself, but others don't seem to enjoy me as much, barring the widow and Bess.—This can't last long. I shall be discovered. My woman's nature is being kicked out of me by masculine impulses."

Then she glances at the glass and laughs at herself, remarking, "I shall soon have to shave! I hardly think I can ever persuade Aunt Connie and Jane that I'm a bearded woman!"

This sends her into a profound meditation as to

her future course—and thinking of Bess, she mutters, "I'll never go back to the trammels of young lady-hood—I love and can tell my love—unchained by the shackles of maiden modesty"—and so goes to pondering upon the best method of carrying out her plans. One thing strikes her at once. Jane will certainly discover her secret soon.—She turns this matter over in her mind and after a little bursts into a laugh and cries, " A gentleman should have a valet."

At this moment her meditations are broken in upon by a groaning and wailing and gnashing of teeth and she hears a subdued : " Oh, Gus ! yo' break my heart," coming from the dressing-room, that is occupied by Jane. The next instant she laughs : " I've struck it. I'll make her a *particeps criminis* in my offence of becoming a man !"—and with masculine promptness proceeds to act upon her idea.

She opens the door and finds her dusky abigail dressed and seated upon the bed in a state of darky frenzy.

" Didn't I tell you to not wait up for me ?" Lilly says sternly.

" Yes, miss ;—(*sob*)—" I knows dat ; "—(*sob*)—" but I couldn't go to sleep, I'se so wretched !" (*sob—sob—sob !*)

" Come in here and tell me what's the trouble with you," cries her mistress sharply, smothering a laugh, for she has made a shrewd guess as to what is the matter.

" It's dat Gus feller, dat's what it is. He's busted my heart !" answers Jane, and entering she gushes forth in rage, " He's been cuttin' up shines wid dat Antoinyet dat works in de ha'r-dresser shop in de

8

Alcazár ;—a low down Spanish nigger, dat's what
.she is. Some day I'll get desp'ret an' razor him—
I will ! "

"No you won't," says Lilly sharply. "And I
won't have such talk from you. You are jealous,
that's what's the matter with you."

"Jealous !—Well, isn't dat 'nuff ? "

"Jealous ! And I've got a remedy for it ! Do
you think you'd like to take something soothing to
the wounded female heart ? "

"If yo' could give me somethin' as would make
me close my eyeballs in sleep—and keep me from
goin' plump out of my head, I'd go down on my
knees to bless yo', Miss Lilly ! " sobs her maid.

"Then," remarks Lilly, unlocking her jewel case
and producing the vial with its three precious seeds,
"Open your mouth ! "

"Is dat med'cine ? "—suspiciously.

"Yes ; medicine for jealousy. Take it, and you
will be all right." And this fair intruder on the
domain of man selects one of the sacred African
pellets.

"Yo' sho' tain't pizen ? "

"Nonsense ! I took one last night myself. Wasn't
I jealous of Doctor Frederick then ? " answers the
mistress, and she places the seed in a glass and adds
a few drops of laudanum from her travelling medicine case, for she fears the vigor of Jane's lungs after
she experiences the effects of the weird pill.

"Y-e-s ; yo' was, jealous to death yo' was ! " mutters Jane with a guffaw.

"Very well ; have I been jealous of him since ?
Haven't I been light-hearted,—gay,—happy ? "

"Yes ; yo's been too almighty uppish, Miss Lilly."

"Very well ; open your mouth and be the same! Would you like it with a little whiskey?" and Miss Travers cunningly adds the spirit. "Open your mouth!"

And as Jane unable to withstand the temptation obeys, she skilfully flips the seed, whiskey and laudanum down the capacious opening, which gaps before her, nearly large enough to take in a cannonball. This closes upon the amber pellet and then suddenly flies open again to give out one long-drawn awful howl of astonishment and terror! It would give out a succession of these did not at this moment a pair of white and delicate but vise-like and desperate hands clutch her throat.

"What am de mattah wid me? What's got hold of my insides? It's pizen! It's pizen! dat's what it is, sho'!—I'se gone—I'se dead!" gasps the handmaiden in struggling gurgling whispers.

"Hang you!" whispers the late Miss Travers; "if you don't stop screaming, you'll alarm the house. Stop! or I'll throttle you!" and the white, desperate, vise-like hands give Jane's dusky throat another savage pinch.

"Laws! Yo's as strong as a man—yo' is—ough!" gasps the dusky abigail being propelled at this moment by the powerful arms of the putative Miss Travers into a chair.

"Yes ; wouldn't you like to be a man? Honest, now—tell me the truth."

"Ob co'se—I'd like to be a man, de bes' in de worl'! Did yo' ebber see a woman dat wouldn't be, ef she could—'cause I ain't."

"Nor I either, Jane," remarks her mistress concordantly. "It has been the universal desire of your down-trodden sex, from the time they can think."

"Yes, an' yo' down-trodden sex, too," returns the dusky abigail rather sleepily, for the laudanum is producing its effect.

But here, her mistress's words come to her in such a mysterious and awful manner that she wakes up with a horrified start and rolls her eye-balls, and her jaws shake and her teeth chatter, and she would howl but is too terrified to do more than gasp, for now Lilly remarks solemnly: "My down-trodden sex *yesterday*,—but, last night, Jane, an extraordinary change took place in me—I became a man."

Then she tells her, in as simple manner as she can, the wonderful story of old Hauser Oglethorpe and the extraordinary transformation that has been effected in her by one of the amber seeds.

"An' I took one ob 'em Obi-nuts too," cries Jane. "Oh, Lawdy! Lawdy! Yo' mean to tell me I'll be a man to-morrow?"

"Yes—or sooner."

"Tain't possible!—I know I'se goin' to die! Golly! my insides is bein' uprooted."

"You are not going to die,—so make up your mind to take it calmly. Supposing you had been born so—you would not have been frightened then, would you? Now, don't be astonished."

"Astonished? I'd be astonished now, I'd be howlin', but I'm too sleepy to do—much campmeetin' business—to-night."

"Yes, I have given you a narcotic.—Now, to-

morrow morning, when you awake, don't you let any
one see you until I have a talk with you;—remember that!"

"Yes'm; but I'se so sleepy, Miss Lilly.—Yo' let me
go to bed and I'll talk to yo' to-morrow mawnin';
—a man? Ef I was awake I'd be a-glorifyin' now—
a m-a-n!"

This last is a yawn from Jane who staggers sleepily into her room and punctuates the night with long-
drawn deep terrific darky snores; but unheeding
these, Lilly sits down to complete the plan she has
outlined in her mind.

She looks at herself contemplatively in the mirror
and says: "You're a nice boy. I wonder what I
shall name you. I must give you a pretty name,
because you are the one who is going to have all
Miss Lillian Travers' property. I'm going to make
you a rich young dandy, sir—but no dude and
no 'rounder'—remember that!"

After a little playful cogitation, she continues, giving a polite bow to her image in the glass, which returns it in true gentlemanly style: "You are going
to be Mr. Lawrence Talbot, that is to be your name,
sir;—Lawrence Talbot, né Lilly Travers.—What a
funny announcement that would be in the papers!"

Then she sits down and writes a check on the St.
Augustine bank which holds her Florida funds, for
a goodly portion of her balance there, and writes a
letter to that institution directing it to remit to her
New York bankers the balance of her account, signing "Lillian Travers," very prettily, though there is
a slight masculine boldness in the signature. Looking at it she remarks to herself playfully: "I wonder

if that is forgery. If so, I am going to do a good deal of it in the next few days."

Soon she jumps into bed and, turning various problems over in her mind, goes to sleep murmuring: "Dear little Bessie. I wonder if she'll think Larry Talbot is a nice young fellow. I'll give her a chance to judge of him before long." And so dreams come to her, and they are pleasant ones, for she laughs in her sleep—to be awakened from them the next morning by the sun shining brightly into her apartment, and, springing up, she looks at her watch and finds it nine o'clock and begins to think of Bessie.

Then she gives a sudden jump—for from the next room is coming in a deep, masculine tone, sung with emphasis and effect, and joyous enthusiasm :

> ' De Lawd am risen !
> Bress de Lawd !
> De Lawd am risen !"

"Ah! That's my man Jane!" says Miss Lilly Travers and tips a knowing little wink to Mr. Lawrence Talbot who returns it from the mirror.

The next instant the hosanna ends in a squeak of terror, the door from Jane's room flies open and that new recruit to masculine ranks dashes in, one shaking, trembling, flying mass of panic.

In another second she would be in the hall to arouse the household, but, like a flash of lightning Lilly pins her, and forces her into a chair.

"Let me get 'way from here—de Obi's workin' too much on me—de debble's conjered me.—I'se— I'se mose gwine!" gasps the dusky Jane struggling vainly.

"Keep still until your senses come back! Are you crazy—going on like this? Why did you say you'd like to be a man if you didn't mean it?"

"I did mean it, Miss—Massa Lilly; but I didn't know it was goin' to work so pow'ful—I was singing a jubilee for joy when I felt it—a big lump in my throat—it's goin' to bust an' let out de life blood.—Honey, I'se most gone now.—Look at de tumor," and Jane exhibits a well-developed and prominent Adam's apple to Lilly's relieved eyes.

"Pooh!" says the emancipated mistress. "That's only a proof of manhood. All men have one. I've one myself," and placing her hand to her white throat Lilly gives a start, for she has a very nice little one also.

"And did yo' hear my voice?" returns Jane more quietly—"I'se got a debble of a cold."

"So have I," says Lilly. "Didn't you notice my contralto yesterday? Now you listen to me: don't sing. If you do, Aunt Connie will think there is a man up here."

"An' so dere is, Miss—Massa Lilly—two ob 'em," retorts Jane, beginning to giggle, and recovering her spirits rapidly after the volatile manner of the negro. "We's bof in de same boat, praise de Lawd."

"Yes; and if we are to remain in the same boat, don't you speak of what has happened—not a word to any one. Jane, we might be arrested for walking about in women's clothes! Think of that!"

"Jailed! Den my lips has de lockjaw!" mutters the masculine maid-servant, and after a moment bursts into an uncontrollable guffaw, keeping this up till her mistress says angrily: "What amuses you so?"

"I'se jes' thinkin'—whaugh—whaugh—'bout dat Gus—how mad he's goin' to be—whaugh! whaugh! whaugh!" and Jane indulges in suppressed whoops till the tears roll down her face.

"Great goodness, you didn't think of telling him?"

"'Deed I did.—It would have made Gus feel so cheap.—Tryin' to be sweet to a man!"

"Gus is to know nothing about this business! Throw him over. Let him be as angry as he chooses, but hold your tongue to him!" whispers Lilly in alarm.

"But ef he comes roun' tryin' to kiss me, I'se sartin to slug him."

"Not at all—you must act like a modest, bashful young woman," says the late Miss Travers soothingly.

"Dat's purtty hard now, Massa Lilly—I means Miss Lilly. Lawd! I don't know what I mean! I'se so uppity, there'll be no keepin' me down."

"Very well; get rid of your surplus energy by helping me to dress," cries the mistress sharply; and Jane does so grinning and chuckling with darky delight over the efforts she has to make to get her master into his corsets and the groans and writhings that he emits under her strong and vigorous manipulations as she draws the lacing together. All this makes Miss Travers satisfied that the resolution she has made the night before is the only safe one: flight her only resource. She is now convinced that even if accident does not disclose the marvellous transformation of her life, her man Jane will do it for her in some unguarded moment.

This causes her to make a foolish threat. She says sternly : " Jane, do you like to be a man? "

" Yes'm : I'se feelin' fust rate 'bout it."

" Then, do as I bid you, or I'll give you one of those Obi seeds and change you back into a woman."

" Foh de Lawd's sake, doan' do it, miss — massa ! "

" I will, if you don't do exactly as I tell you : you are not to leave the house, on any account ; you must also stay as much as you can in my rooms until we leave St. Augustine."

" When 'll dat be ? " sullenly.

" To-morrow morning.—You may go to packing my trunks now.—Leave one open for me !"

" Well, Miss—Mr., I'll try to keep in ; but I be feelin' so fine an' uppity, I'd like to take a walk roun' town.—Doan' yo' think Malvina, Miss Constanshe's housemaid—is a kinder fine-lookin' gal, miss ? "

" Don't you dare think of girls,—until you have left St. Augustine. If you do, you'll be one yourself—I swear it," cries the author of Jane's mutation.

" Well, ma'am, I'll do as yo' orders," mutters the man Jane in a dogged and perhaps surly manner, as Lilly steps down to breakfast to try and play her part with Miss Connie who is waiting for her at the table.

CHAPTER X.

"HAVE I, LIKE FRANKENSTEIN, RAISED UP A MONSTER TO DESTROY ME?"

SHE enters the dining-room, kisses her aunt penitently and says: "Dear Connie, I hope you will forgive me for being so foolish and so unladylike last night; but my heart—my breaking heart—ran away with me. Fred has destroyed my—my happiness."

"My poor child!" and Connie's old arms go sympathizingly round her putative niece's waist. "What makes you think Doctor Cassadene has not treated you properly?"

"I—I know it. I've broken with him now, and can tell you." Then in a half sobbing way she relates to the sympathizing old lady the record of Fred's lying note and his treachery in taking Stella for the moonlight sail.

"Well," remarks Miss Constantia. "I have only known Mrs. Lovejoy one day, but I do not trust her. She is a very designing widow, Lilly."

"Oh, I have nothing more to fear from widows," says the girl of yesterday quite confidently. "I am going away from here. I am going North again. I —I came down to marry Fred, but now that is all over, and the sooner I go away the better. I—I can't stand it here." And she squeezes a counterfeit tear from her eye-lids, but recollecting that she is going to leave dear Bessie, makes it a real one.

"Yes—I expect it is the best thing you can do," returns her aunt contemplatively, for even in this short conversation Lilly has unwittingly let fall one or two masculine expressions. "When do you think of going?"

"To-morrow morning—'Florida Special.'—I must look after my tickets!"

Whereupon Lilly proceeds to make her arrangements as scheduled in her mind. She requests her aunt to return her horses and carriage that she has sent from the North and are now due in St. Augustine—drives to the First National Bank, cashes her check, and then to the railway ticket office in the Ponce de Leon, where she engages a state-room in the boudoir car that leaves for the North next morning. This is easily done, as the rush in February is all southward, the trains running out quite empty and returning very full to this Florida watering-place. Next a curious masculine idea having come into her head, she goes to a gun store and purchases a small revolver and has it loaded by the shopman who shows her how to work the mechanism of the arm.

This stowed away in her pocket, she drives back to her relative and falls to discussing with her aunt her return to New York, receiving some unintentional stabs from the dear old lady, who loves her as the apple of her eye and appears very loath to part from her, though in truth some of Lilly's performances of the preceding day have been very shocking and by no means pleasant to this good old representative of ancient etiquette.

But Lilly throws conscience to the winds. Her one thought is—Bessie will be coming *soon*!

So she steps into the front garden to be on hand to welcome her beautiful little sweetheart—for such she has got to calling Bessie in her mind. This she does impatiently some ten minutes before the girl is due; Miss Bess having quite a long drive into town from her father's orange groves and house, some three or four miles up the San Sebastian.

Astonishment and joy! the late Miss Travers finds Miss Horton is fully as eager as she is for the meeting, and Bessie's horses and negro coachman come into sight just as Lilly reaches her front gate to take an anxious, longing glance up the road for their appearance.

With a gentleman's ready politeness Lilly steps to the carriage, and saying to the coachman : " You needn't drive in ; I'll take care of Miss Bessie now," assists the sweet little lady to the ground and mutters into her ear : " You darling—ten minutes ahead of time!"

"Yes; my horses were very fresh and I told Nicodemus he needn't hold them—I like to drive fast, when I have pleasure ahead of me.—Ah ! going to play the gentleman again. How nice!"—for Lilly has offered her arm, masculine style. The little gloved hand goes confidingly into the nook made for it ; and they stroll up the walk to the house.

Arriving at the portico, Bessie gives a piteous pout and whimpers: " I don't like you this morning."

" Don't like me?" Miss Travers gives a horrified and reproachful stare.

" No ; you haven't kissed me."

" H-ah !—Wouldn't you like me just as well if I didn't?" asks Lilly contemplatively.

" No !"—imperiously. " Kiss me or I shall hate you !"

"Then, I suppose I must," mutters the late Miss Travers; "you are a wilful little despot,"—and she gives her tyrant a playful buss. But one playful buss brings on another, and before they go into the house Bessie cannot complain of Lilly's neglect.

Lunch is ready, and at this meal Miss Connie opens her eyes at her niece's gallant care of their guest. She remarks playfully: "I believe in hospitality, but, Lilly, Bessie will live if she doesn't eat strawberries and cream more than twice at a meal; and my cake is good, I know; but you will kill her if you force her to eat another mouthful."

"Yes," mutters Bess, with a sigh of repletion; "I think I'll do until supper-time"—then she continues anxiously, "Lilly hasn't eaten anything."

"No," cries Connie, "she has been doing nothing but watch you. She had a good appetite when she was here last, but now"—here the old lady gives a sigh, for she imagines that the broken engagement and Fred Cassadene's miserable behavior are the causes of her beloved niece's lack of appetite. Watching her opportunity she takes Lilly aside and says: "Don't grieve so much for him. Perhaps when you get away from here you will forget him and be happier."

"Happier? I shall not, I am sure," answers Lilly with a sigh, thinking of bidding Bessie adieu. "When I am away from her—I—I mean *here*—I shall be even more miserable."

"Then you had better stay!"

"Impossible!—I dare not."

"Dare not!" cries the aunt in rage and astonishment. "Do you love this miserable doctor so you fear your heart again? Lilly, you surprise me!" and with a snort of anger Miss Connie goes away, leaving Lilly to break the news of her intended depart-ure to the little blonde whose blue eyes have been merry and whose mouth has been laughing, but whose eyes now become sad and whose mouth goes into a pout of pain as she hears this terrible news.

She cries out: "You—you have only been here two days. What do you mean—going away? The season has not commenced yet;" and getting up from the table with a "gulp" in her throat suddenly walks into the garden.

"What's the matter with her?" ejaculates Connie, looking from the parlor. "You have set her to cry-ing;" for the suspicion of a sob floats in the door-way, which after the manner of most Florida houses in this beautiful spring climate is nearly always open.

"Oh, I'll fix her," says Lilly. "Just leave her to me," and runs to overtake the distressed damsel, rather delighted that her announcement has been so effective.

But Miss Horton has disappeared.

She looks for her through the orange vistas—in vain. She cries out "Bessie!"—no answer. She darts hither and thither in pursuit of this elusive chick—without success. Then she lifts up her voice and calls: "Bessie?—Dear Bessie?—Darling Bes-sie?"—until finally some of these adjectives appar-ently softening the secluded one, a broken-hearted voice comes to her through the grape vines that en-tirely screen a little arbor:

"I am here, but I don't want to see you—go away; leave me alone! One would think you loved

me by the things you call me—but acts are"—
(sob).

By this time Lilly has broken through the surrounding branches to find a bewitching but mournful
picture. Bess has thrown herself into a hammock
that has been swung in the little arbor for summer
uses and has given herself up to grief.

"Go away; I don't love you," she mutters.

"Oh, yes, you do," answers Lilly desperately.

"No, I don't"—(sob); "you're going away"—
(sob) "you don't love me"—(sob—sob—sob).

"Yes, I do," says Miss Travers with energy.
Then she cries out desperately: "Come, get up at
once. Your performances are driving me crazy,"—
as in truth they are, for Miss Bessie's easy abandon
of grief in the hammock is full of most potent and
distracting allurements to Lilly's masculine eyes.

"Come, sit up," she says; "sit up and talk sensi-
bly. You know I've got to go away from here to-
morrow. It is impossible for me to remain."

"Not one more day?"

"Not a day—not an hour—not a minute! My
stateroom is engaged. The 'Florida Special' has got
to take me away. Come. Make the most of this afternoon. Don't make our parting too hard, for I"—
here the emancipated one, having got her arms
about the tempting one, cries out: "I am unhappy,
also!" and her misery seems to soothe Bessie.

"Ah! you're sorry. That makes our parting
easier. If you are unhappy to leave me, I know
you will come back to me. Promise, and I will be
a good girl, even a glad girl, this afternoon," purrs
the blonde fairy.

"I—I swear it!" is uttered in tones of such determination that even Bessie believes, and suffers herself to be consoled; and still lying in the hammock, she turns a tear-stained but lovely face upon Miss Travers, and seizing some orange blossoms that are growing over the hammock, twists them into a wreath and crowns her lovely head, and tossing others about her, says:

"Do I look pretty?" And the orange blossoms getting into the late Miss Travers' brain, cause her masculine mind to think of what orange blossoms mean, and she looks upon the picture, and it is too lovely, too entrancing, too inviting for masculine eyes; for the girl's exquisite figure with its rounded, though maiden contours, is wonderfully outlined by her attitude, and two adorable ankles robed in gleaming silk and disclosing insertion are flashing in and out beneath the white muslin dress, as she swings in lazy motion.

The blood surges to the late Miss Travers' head. She gasps, "*Too* alluring! *Too* beautiful!" and unable to stand the fascination of the picture, destroys it; for she plucks Bessie out of the hammock bodily by force. Then she says: "Come. Let us take a drive about the town, and then——"

"And then, I suppose," pouts Bessie, "papa will take me home."

"Not immediately," remarks Miss Travers; "he shall stay to dinner, and then we will inveigle him into a game of cards,"—for she knows the major's weakness.

Thus the two walk about chatting while Constantia's carriage is being made ready for them; a few minutes of this and Miss Bessie, whose agile mind hops from subject to subject as a bird from twig to twig, suddenly says : " Oh! I forgot—Fancy! I forgot !"

"Forgot what ?"

"Forgot to ask you about the box you bought at Vedder's ? What was in it ?—something romantic, I am sure. You seem to have been a different girl since you got it," cries Miss Horton. Then gazing on the blushing emancipated one she continues, " I know there was something in it, because your face is so red."

" Pshaw !" jeers Lilly, attempting lightness ; " you saw the casket on our parlor table when you came in yesterday."

"Yes!"

"You saw it half an hour ago."

" Yes ; it was open."

" What did it contain ?"

" Nothing,"—disappointedly.

"That is what I found."

" Well, that is very curious," cries Miss Horton in suspicious unbelief ; " because I lifted that casket half an hour ago, and it was not nearly so heavy after it had been opened as it was before. Why, Lilly, what's the matter with you ?"—for Miss Travers has grown very pale.

A moment after, however, she forces herself to say, " There was nothing in it when I opened it. Bessie, you must believe me if you want to be my friend. Do you believe me ?"

" Certainly, I do ! Rather than quarrel with you I'd believe you if you told a lie."

9

"That is more blissful than complimentary," answers Lilly, with an attempted laugh.

"I expect Miss Connie must have opened it before you," says Bessie, "and got some great secret out of it—something so great she won't tell anybody else—I'll ask her."

This gives Lilly another shudder. She cries— "Not now; we haven't time—carriage is here."

With this she jumps the inquiring blonde into the equipage in such a vicious, vigorous and masculine manner that Bessie whispers, "You don't want me to ask Miss Connie, do you?"

"Stop talking nonsense," replies her companion. "Let us enjoy ourselves for this afternoon—the last I'll have with you for some time."

This silences Miss Horton, and when she opens her mouth again it is upon another subject.

So the two drive away to have a pleasant afternoon in the pretty streets of St. Augustine, and listen to the band at the Cordova, and see a swimming contest in the Alcazar bath, and come home, having spent a day that would be a happy one, were they not to part on the morrow.

The evening brings the major who has driven down for his daughter, but to the girls' entreaties Miss Connie adds her word and he finally is induced to remain an hour or two, though he says the night looks threatening.

After tea in the parlor they have cards, the putative Miss Travers making herself very attentive to the old gentleman, as if she were anxious to gain this respect and confidence.

Constantia, who has opened her eyes several times

at Lilly's deference to the rather dogmatic assertions
of the major, remarks aside to her: "What's come
into you?—you're as obsequious as if you were a
young gentleman with designs on Miss Bessie"—
and wonders what brings so much color into her
niece's cheeks.

But a chance shot of the major's wounds the
emancipated one most deeply.—There has been a
two-headed cow on exhibition on Bay Street, the
ex-Confederate has seen it and has not thought he
had got his quarter's worth, and tells his wrongs,
asserting that the two-headed critter hasn't brains
enough to run one animal; and thus being started
upon the subject he runs on in a most uncompli-
mentary way about dime-museum freaks, of whom
he has apparently seen a goodly quantity, remarking they are all frauds, and that living skeletons,
Siamese-twins, tattooed ladies, Circassian beauties
and bearded women should be all put under ground
as soon as born.

At this attack on bearded women Miss Travers'
face grows rosy and then pallid, and for her life she
can't keep her fingers from her fuzzy upper lip.
She feels she is being called a dime-museum freak
and wonders what the major would say to a woman-
man demanding his adored Bessie's hand in marriage, and sickens at the thought.

But the cards are now over and the major, rising
to go, perceives that his predicted storm has come
upon him—the rain which has been pattering unnoticed for an hour, is now pouring down in tor-
rents, and the wind is howling through the mag-
nolias, palm and orange trees.

"Great Goliah!" mutters the old gentleman, striding to the window. " What a night! The roads
will be fearful. Can you lend Bess a tarpaulin?"

But Miss Connie hurriedly exclaims : " Do you
suppose I'm going to let you and your daughter
pass out of my doors on such a night as this? I
have ordered your horses round to the stable and
they are taken care of and warm now."

These remarks are commonplace, but they bring
panic perspiration all over the putative Miss Travers' forehead; her heart beats wild and frightened,
her finger tips grow icy.

" Isn't this lovely, Lil?" Bess chimes in enthusiastically. " If I stay here all night I can go down
with you to the train in the morning and see the
very last of you."

But Lilly is not responsive and stands aloof nervously tapping on the window pane, and staring
out into the night to keep the agitation on her face
from notice. A moment after, the major having
yawned once or twice in a suggestive manner, Miss
Connie rings the bell and says to the answering
servant, " Malvina, show Major Horton to the blue
chamber. A fire is made up there ;—light it." And
having said " Good-night" the ex-Confederate is
ushered away to enjoy his solitary cigar and night-
cap and then turn in.

His departing steps have hardly died away when
Miss Connie, addressing her niece, says in tones
that seem like thunder claps, though not intended
as such, " Lilly, take Bess with you and go to
bed."

" I—I think she had better have the wing-room,"

answers Lilly nervously ; then seeing a wounded
look in Bessie's violet eyes, she continues : " Bess
would never be able to sleep in my room. My
maid's snoring is something awful, and Jane, you
know, occupies my dressing room."

" Oh, I don't mind snoring, Lilly," says Bess un-
concernedly. " Father snores, — you'll hear him
yourself to-night ! "

" Anyway, get along to bed, both of you," cries
Miss Connie. "Lilly, don't forget you have got to
get up early to-morrow morning to catch that train."
And the old lady having kissed them, goes away,
and Miss Bessie says—innocent words that make
the emancipated one very nervous :

" This *is* jolly ! " she cries. " Come along, quick—
dear ! It is going to be a cold night, and I love to
cuddle." At this a sudden gleam of fire comes into
the late Miss Travers' eyes and a fervid shiver seems
to fly through her body. " Besides, you can tell me
all about the mysterious contents of the black box
that you seem to wish to keep to yourself so much "
—whispers Bessie as they go up-stairs. " Why don't
you speak to me ? You seem to be thinking about
something."

" And so I am," mutters Lilly sharply—" thinking I am not going to keep you awake to-night by
snoring and kicking about as I always do in my sleep.
Which added to Jane's performances in the next
room, means for you a sleepless night."

" Oh ! what a whop—" cries Bessie in a rage, check-
ing herself, however, on the last word and going on
in a plaintive voice, " I stayed with you last spring
when you were here, and you were a lovely bed-

fellow. However," here she becomes pathetically sarcastic, " I will most willingly excuse you, though you know you are telling fibs by the wholesale. You wish to be alone, you selfish thing—that settles the question, Miss Travers!" This Miss Horton emphasizes by a formal courtesy.

This remark is made in the hall in front of Lilly's apartments, which consist of one big room, full of old-fashioned furniture, and beyond it a dressing closet which is generally occupied by Jane, but is now suspiciously silent. On the right hand of Miss Travers' apartment is the wing-room, a door connecting it with Lilly's chamber.

Striding into this wing-room, Miss Travers lights the lamp and says: " This is where you are to stay, Bess."

" So I cannot hear you snore ? "

" Certainly. So, go to bed! and now—good-night."

" If you don't kiss me good-night, I'll stay where I am." Bessie, not having followed her guide, is still in the late Miss Travers' chamber and seems loath to leave it.

" Very well—there ! "—the " *there* " is a short and savagely intense kiss. " I've kept my promise, now keep yours," mutters Lilly. " Disappear! I've got some packing to do before I go to bed."

With this after a playful struggle she pushes Bessie into the wing-room, and steps back into her own apartment, in spite of her little sweetheart's reproachful eyes at being thus deserted. Closing the door softly, Lilly sits down before a freshly made fire to meditate in its flickering light upon what course she shall pursue with the self-willed little beauty in the next room.

She is aroused from this reverie by a strange sound from the wing-chamber, and stepping cautiously to the door she listens. Bessie is sobbing in a heart-broken way upon the other side of it ; she whispers softly : " What's the matter ? "

" You—you know," comes from the other side. "I'm—I'm lonely here—in a strange room. How mean you are ! You've broken my heart."

This reproachful pathos overcomes the late Miss Travers. A sudden inspiration flying into her mind she opens the door, and stands dazed at the lovely vision, for Bessie has thrown off her gown and unbound her tresses and is beautiful as a dream, her blonde hair flowing over shining shoulders and white garments.

" Bessie, you know I've got some packing to do," gasps Lilly retreating but gazing.

" Yes. Let me help you ! "

" No—you'll only be in my way. It will take me an hour. Go to sleep and——"

" And when you've finished packing you will come to bed with me ?" savagely.

" Yes ! " desperately.

" Very well," says the girl tossing her hair about and making it gold in the lamplight. " It's a bargain, though I don't trust you. That ' Yes ' of yours was a kind of wail."

And Lilly turning from the lamplit beauty into the dim light of her own room mutters to herself : " For one night for my little sweetheart's sake I'll be once more a woman ! " and a chill of fear runs over her that manhood may never come again and the happiness of wooing her own sweet Bessie be lost to her forever.

But even as she thinks this there is a little patter of unshod feet upon the carpet, and a soft voice comes to her, "Lilly, I hate to trouble you but I'm—I'm laced so tight, I can't undo myself without my maid. Where's yours?"

"Jane!" This is a horrified gasp from Miss Travers.

"Of course Jane—she's in there!" and though Lilly hurriedly cries, "You—you mustn't awake her," Bessie has the door open and looking in says, "There is no chance of my waking her—Jane has gone out."

"Out!" and Lilly is at the door gazing on her man Jane's unoccupied bed and wondering what new embarrassment the untutored masculine maid-servant may bring upon her, gadding about the streets of St. Augustine.

"I suppose by your not wishing me to awake Jane, you intended to do me the kindness yourself. Lilly, please help me, I'm tied up so tight?" entreats Bessie.

So over corset strings with flushed cheeks, shining eyes, thumping heart and fingers made clumsy by haste the late Miss Travers toils, and Bessie smiling in her face sees admiration and laughs, "Don't you think I've a pretty figure?"

"You'd have a better one if you didn't lace it so tight," answers Lilly, with masculine devotion to hygiene.

"Why, what's come over you!" says Bess in

astonished pique.—" You used to be a wasp-waist
yourself, and now lecturing—you talk like an idiot
man ! Besides, I'm not laced tight—behold me !"
With this she gives a little shadow dance in front of
the fire that displays by its ruddy gleams such lithe
graces of pose and figure and glimpses of general fairy
beauty that the putative Miss Travers writhes under
its allurements and mutters hoarsely " Be still !"
But Bessie answers, " Say I haven't a pretty figure
now—mean one !" and would continue her "*pas de
fascination,*" did not her companion with tormented
eyes cry " Stop !" so imperiously that the *figurante*
gives a startled pause and asks, " What's the matter ?"
    " Nothing !"   answers   the   emancipated   one
shortly.—" But sit down on the sofa.—Be quiet—I
want to talk to you—I'm—I'm going away to-morrow."   This last sadly.
    " Do you suppose I've forgotten that !" murmurs
Bessie softly; then she says archly, " Say I've a
pretty figure and I'll sit down !"
    " Darling, you've the loveliest in the world," cries
Lilly, tenderness and admiration fighting with each
other in her voice.
    " Well, having convinced you I'll sit down !"
With a purr of content Bessie cuddles herself in a
white beauty-ball upon the sofa, while Miss Travers
who somehow appears afraid of being too near this
torturing loveliness sits in a chair and watches the
firelight play about her charmer's golden hair and
throw soft shadows about her fair young head.
    A second after Lilly says suddenly, " Bess, you
would like a lover ?"
    " Pooh !" says Miss Beauty " I've had lots !"

"Lots!" Miss Travers gasps—"you're—you're only eighteen!"

"Certainly lots—I began at five. Don't you think I'm a catchy girl?" returns Bessie.—"What a funny thing you are—you were angry a second ago, now you're laughing!" and Miss Blue-eyes looks amazed.

"You're a cute little puss who should have a—a husband!" mutters the transformed one.

"Yes, a husband might do!" sighs Bessie contemplatively.— "Boy lovers are such unsatisfactory creatures.—But a husband.—Now if you had a brother, Lil!"

"Wouldn't a cousin do?" cries out Miss Travers in joyous tone.

"Y-e-s—perhaps——"

"Perhaps what?"

"Perhaps if he looked like you!"

"He does look like me."

"Ah, he exists!—a real cousin." And Bessie flies on excitedly: "Tell me all about him—like you— he must be awfully handsome—what's his name?— How old is he?—Pshaw! you're making up a fairy story—I never heard you had a cousin before——"

"But I have," says Lilly confidently. "He's a— a young Englishman, a distant cousin.—You know I've some English relatives on my father's side."

"Yes—what's his name?"

"Lawrence Talbot." The words come slowly from Miss Travers' lips as if she must be very careful to make no mistake.

"That's a nice name," babbles Bessie. "Tell me all about him!"

And in the firelight with a tremble in her voice as if she were pleading her own cause, not another's, the late Miss Travers tells the present Juliet the sad story of the absent Romeo. " He has but few relatives and is very well off—I am sure he will make a good husband," she concludes.

" Oh, but he may not want me ! "

" He *will* want you ! " says Lilly impressively. " He *shall* marry you ! "

" What a matchmaker you are ! " answers Bessie lightly and then she laughs. " Send your Lawrence Talbot along and I'll inspect him."

" Yes, he's coming from England—he'll be in Florida within a month. I'll give him a letter of introduction," cries Miss Travers enthusiastically.

" All right—but I sha'n't love him half as well as I do you ! " says Bessie.

" And why not ? "

" Oh, he won't boss me about as you do, Lil— you're such a lovely tyrant ! "

" Then I'll earn my title—" returns Lillian lightly. " Go to bed : get your beauty sleep and let me pack ! "

" I won't ! " says the obedient one defiantly.

" To bed ! or I revoke my promise ! "

" Oh, what a boss you are, Lil. But there ! " and two soft white arms close about the putative Miss Travers and fresh sweet lips press upon her trembling ones and give her courage to make her sacrifice, as Bessie trips away to bed.

The instant she is alone, with a sigh of resignation, but determined mien and eye, Lilly is at her jewel case in which she has locked up the sacred seeds.

The key is in the lock—Astonishment! The vial, seeds and record are all gone—Despair!

For a moment, she tremblingly thinks she may have carelessly left the key in the lock; she may, in some temporary fit of caution and forgetfulness have secreted the vial and its precious contents in some other hiding spot.

She flashes up her lamp and makes hurried—anxious—trembling search—tumbling over her unpacked things with careless speed and reckless noise.

Upon this Bessie's voice comes from the next room in protest. " What are you prowling about for, so Lil ? " she growls.—" Why don't you come to bed ?—I'm—I'm cold."

This sends a shiver through Miss Travers. She is at her search again. A sudden thought! Jane may have packed the seeds in one of her trunks. Into her locked-up boxes she plunges. Their carefully arranged contents fly out. In a jiffy robes are tossed one way, bonnets the other.—She is bending down anxiously into a saratoga when Bess springs from the next room in lacey night robe and paralyzed horror and whispers " Burglars!"

" Burglars, nonsense!"

" A burglar; I hear his steps on the roof of the veranda—Listen—Oh mercy!"

For at this moment mixed with the sound of raindrops a heavy tread is heard outside the window.

" I'm going to scream!"

" Stop!" mutters Lilly desperately—" You'll alarm the house! Not a word!"—and perhaps anxious to play the hero before such a lovely heroine, and perchance making a shrewd guess as to the

truth, the late Miss Travers produces her newly
purchased weapon—and springing to the window
she throws it open and claps the pistol to the intruder's head—whispering, " Speak, or I shoot ! "

" Don't—for de Lawd's sake ! Don't ! I'se
Jane ! " gasps a voice outside.

" Jane ! " echoes Lilly.

And Bessie gasps in admiration, " How brave you
are !—You're like a man ! "

" Nonsense," mutters Miss Travers. Then she
cries, " Come in, you hussy ! " and her handmaiden
in dripping dress and muddy boots totters in and
horrifics her.

She says, " I'se got clean away."

" Got away—from whom, Jane ? "

" De constable ! "

" Why, what have you been doing ? " This is in
Bessie's voice and puts Lilly into instant action.
In a second she has dragged the white-robed one
into the wing-chamber, crying, " With that window
open—you'll catch your death of cold—Get into
bed ! " And before the astounded Bessie can lift up
her voice in expostulation Miss Travers has dashed
back into her own room and locked the door between
and is standing in judgment over the errant Jane.

" Now," she says in an awful voice, " where have
you been ? "

" Jus' round a leetle, Miss—Mister Lilly ! "

" Round a little ?—What have you been doing ? "

" Gurl huntin' ! " says Jane stolidly ; then she
grins towards the room into which Bessie has just
disappeared and mutters, " Yo's been doin' something in dat way——"

She gets no further. The last word is squeezed back into her throat by Lilly's clutch. " Keep your tongue quiet or I'll—fix you ! " she whispers. " Now answer my questions as quickly as you can. You say the officers are after you—what have you done ? "

" Well, I kinder wandered round to the servants' quarters of de Ponce, and Gus Duncan he seed me and wanted to make up, and I kinder led him on till he tried to kiss me and den——"

" And then ? "—says Lilly anxiously.

" Then I let him have it good. Dere was quite a crowd round and it did me proud to see how 'sprised dey was at a woman laying out de second man in de Ponce de Leon dinin'-room, de one what shows de folks to der chairs."

" Did you injure him ? " queries Lilly uneasily.

" No marm—I means sir—I only jumped on Gus a few times.—He's gone to de hospital. He said he'd get a warrant for me ! "

" A warrant ! " mutters Lilly in a despairing voice ; then she cries suddenly, " Jane, where are those seeds ? "

" Dem seeds ?—Am dey gone ? " asks the abigail —" Oh Lawdy ! Lawdy ! More trouble ! " and she would raise her voice in lamentation.

" None of that for me—you—you ! " Lilly stammers in rage. " Now just tell me exactly where you put them."

" I didn't put 'em nowhere ! "

" Jane, if you're afraid I'll make you take one and become a woman again, I swear to you I will not— only I must have the seeds ! " pleads Lilly, who is very anxious now.

" I don't done nothin' wid de seeds. Please let

me alone. I'se so cold and wet and scared I can't
think of nothin' else—What'll dey do wid me when
dey cotch me?   Golly! what'll de jidge say when he
finds I'se a man!—Oh, camp-meetin'!" and Jane
gives a guffaw which is answered by a gasp from
Lilly, to whom these words strike terror.

With Jane arrested the secret is sure to come out.
She says hurriedly—"Go into your room and change
your damp things. You'll be put in the chain-gang or
sent to the convict-camp if they catch you."

"De convict-camp!" gasps Jane, her face dusky
with horror, for she has heard of the monstrous
cruelties of these hells of justice.

"Yes—your one chance is for me to get you out
of St. Augustine this morning"—answers Lilly,
glancing at the clock which points to two. "Get
clean things on and help me pack my trunks."

And Jane departing—the late Miss Travers gives
a shiver of misery. An angry voice comes from
behind Bessie's door, and her sweetheart is rattling
the handle of the lock savagely and calling her
names, and she thinks, "Jane arrested—My secret
discovered—My God! the major—! what will he
do?"—and shudders with fright and mutters—
"My Heaven, am I like Frankenstein? Have I
raised up in Jane a monster that will destroy me?"

CHAPTER XI.

"GOOD-BY, BESSIE!"

BUT the thought of the major's future rage is
driven out by his daughter's present one—Miss

Bessie's tones show she is in an awful temper. She now cries, " If you don't unlock this door in one second I shall scream—'*Murder !*' " this is a faint yell.

Anything but publicity. Miss Travers throws open the portal, and wounded affection and insulted pride stand in front of her. Miss Bess is in an awful state.

" How—how dare you lock me in?" she stammers in fury. " My—my own father wouldn't dare to lock me in! One would think you—you were Miss Prince—" The lady last mentioned is her former schoolmistress and about the only being who represents discipline to this young beauty, who has been petted and humored by her doting father ever since her dying mother placed a blue-eyed baby in his arms.

" Well," says 'Lilly, who has heard of this school tyrant before, " suppose you imagine me Miss Prince for to-night, and go to bed;" here Miss Travers tries a ghastly smile.

" I—I could never imagine you Miss Prince," mutters Bessie savagely.

" And why not ? "

" Because I was afraid of her, and—you don't frighten me a little bit ! "

" Please go to bed—if you don't I won't kiss you in the morning," murmurs Lilly, attempting a bribe.

" You won't ! you *needn't*—you SHA'N'T kiss me in the morning.—You shall never kiss me again," cries Bessie. " You lock me in—you go prowling about so I can't sleep—you won't come to bed—you're the meanest thing on earth—I—I wouldn't treat—you—so!" and rage turns to tears that touch Miss Travers to the heart.

Her voice grows very tender and her eyes grow very sad and she gasps out, "You—you wouldn't reproach me—if—if you knew!"

"Knew what?" Bessie's blue eyes open with interest.

"That Jane's going to be arrested in the morning."

"Arrested! For what?" Bessie's blue eyes blaze with curiosity.

"For thrashing his—her sweetheart Gus Duncan, the second man in the Ponce de Leon dining-room, because he wanted to kiss her."

"What—that highfalutin darky who waves you to a seat—Jane whipped *him!* Oh, my! How—how lovely!" and Bessie, who sees this grand dark mass of conceit and hauteur coming to grief, in her vivacious imagination, becomes very merry.

"Oh, you laugh! It's funny to travel without one's maid—and—and look at my trunks—How shall I ever pack them?"—Here Miss Travers gives a despairing sigh as she surveys her ravaged boxes.

"Why, what ever made you toss your things out in that way?"

"I thought I—I had lost some diamonds," mutters the emancipated one, who has learnt to fib during her two days' manhood.

"And you've found them?"

"Yes."

"Very well, I'll help you pack!"

"Not in that costume—you'll catch cold. Jane's —Jane's coming!" cries Lilly in an uneasy tone.

10

" All right, I'll dress—I love packing and I see some divine toilets ! " says Bessie, casting her eyes over the display of millinery on the floor—and with this departs to her own room.

A few minutes after as Jane and Miss Travers are working over the unpacked trunks—Miss Horton makes her reappearance in her dress of the evening before, and cuddling up in a warm place on the sofa, looks on and criticises and babbles and finally goes to sleep, to awake with the morning sun shining upon her and making a halo about her golden head.

Lilly is sitting by her side gazing upon the girl's loveliness. In her eyes is some subtle something that appeals to dear little Bessie's heart. She murmurs—" I—I love you, Lil, though you treat me badly. You're the first girl who ever tried to boss me that I didn't hate. You—you are going away ! Kiss me."

She is accommodated vigorously but sadly. Miss Travers' boxes ar: all corded and strapped. And that young lady, looking at her watch, says, " Why, it's breakfast time," and in a few minutes they are both ready to go down-stairs.

As they get to the door, the expressmen arrive to carry away Lilly's baggage, and that putative young lady says severely, " Jane, go down with my boxes to the train."

Whereupon Bessie whispers excitedly, " She'll be arrested."

" No—I think not. Your father has already prevented that, I hope. He is an early riser, and hearing him walking about I asked his assistance,"—replies Miss Travers.

"Then Jane's all right!" laughs Bess, who has a great opinion of her father's general potency.

This idea is borne out by the major's entering the breakfast room just as the ladies sit down and remarking: "Miss Lilly, that hundred dollar bill of yours soothed the wounded Gustavus' feelings.—He will not swear out a warrant, though he swears that he'll never marry Jane."

This news so relieves Miss Travers that Bessie thinks her spirits are too good for the occasion and remarks reproachfully : "Why, you are happy and yet are going away!" Which brings tears to Miss Connie's eyes and to Lilly's also, for she knows that her aunt will never again see the niece she has loved so well ;—and as she parts from the dear old lady, she embraces her and seems loath to tear herself away from her arms, for it is to her like—the parting of death.

But trains wait for no man nor woman—and Lilly and Bessie find themselves in the carriage ready to drive to the depot; Miss Connie and the major remaining behind—they thinking the girls will have some confidences to make during the drive.

"Come back soon, Lilly," says Constantia, trying to smile.

"Bess, what are your eyes so red for?" asks the major, raising his hat.

"I should think they would be red—" replies his darling, "I stayed up all night!"

"Good Scott—What for?"

"Helping Lilly pack!"

At this the major gives the late Miss Travers a

very savage and reprimanding glance as they drive
away. But the journey to the depot is a short
ten minutes—and Lilly has lots to say and hardly
knows how to say it, and gets to talking of Lawrence Talbot so much that Bessie says petulantly—
"Put him away till next time. Tell me when
you are coming back—and I—I've something for
you—"

"For me?"

"Yes. Tell me how you like 'a silent Bessie'?"
and slipping from round her white neck a little
gold chain she shows to Lilly's eager eyes a miniature of her own face with smiling violet eyes and
golden hair and says: "I give it you—'A silent
Bessie'!"

"You darling!" and Lilly kisses first the picture
and then the original—and would do so much more
but they are at the station.

Here they find Jane in her mistress's stateroom
with a frightened, dodgy look on her face—and taking her to one side Miss Travers whispers: "I've
saved you from the convict gang—this time—but if
you don't do exactly what I say I'll revive the
warrant against you and in you go!—Do you understand, my man!"

"Yes!"—answers Jane, apparently impressed.

"Now leave us alone!" orders Lilly, and she and
Bess have a tender but peculiar five minutes.

"Next time you go North I'll ask father to let me
go with you—I would this time but you've fled so
suddenly!" says Bessie—then she mutters: "You'll
come back, Lil, sure in a month!" and her companion grows very sad as she thinks that Bessie must

mourn for Lilly Travers—for they will never meet again.

She says, attempting lightness : " I'll send Lawrence Talbot down to replace me—Bessie, you will love him for my sake—Good-by ! " for the conductor has called " All aboard ! "

" Tell me you'll come back soon ! " and two blue eyes grow desperate.

" I'll—I'll try."

" That won't do—You'll run off to Europe or something awful if you don't promise—Promise ! "

" All aboard for the last time ! " The bell of the locomotive is clanging its warning.

" You must go now, Bess." Lilly has got her to the platform of the car. Their lips meet in a rage of kisses and Bessie is on the wooden walk of the station trying to keep up with the moving car and crying, " Promise you'll come back soon ! "

" If possible ! "

" Promise. Don't go away and not promise. The train's moving so fast ! "

" I'll send Lawrence Talbot to——"

But here Bessie stops running, fire flashes from her eyes, she stamps her little feet and clenches her dear little hands and gives Miss Travers a shock, for she screams out, " I hate Lawrence Talbot. There ! You hear me ! I HATE LAWRENCE TALBOT ! "

And so the train parts Lilly Travers forever from Bessie Horton as the locomotive turns its face from Florida, the land of sunshine, and dashes on its fiery path for far-away New York and February snow and ice.

Miss Travers waves a last adieu and then steps

into her stateroom and meditates : " Wonder if I've
overdone Lawrence Talbot ; " then thinking of the
sacred seeds that have disappeared, the only path to
departed womanhood, she mutters, " You're on the
Lawrence Talbot side of the fence, and that's the side
that leads to the minister—I rather imagine the reason
that Bessie Horton thinks so much of Lilly Travers
is because Lilly Travers has become Lawrence Talbot."

————

CHAPTER XII.

THE MONSTER BECOMES DANGEROUS.

THE next day, as dusk is falling upon New York,
the Pennsylvania Railroad ferry boat brings what
is called Lillian Travers, and what is named Jane
Rouser, into that great city. The two are very tired,
for a thirty-three hours railway journey, even on that
most luxurious of trains—" the Florida Special "—
is wearisome, and Miss Travers has had a great many
precautions to take during this trip, that are not
necessary to ordinary travellers. Besides these she
has been compelled to keep a very wary, watchful
and suspicious eye upon her man Jane, who, though
confined as closely as it is possible, to the stateroom,
has made several furtive but dangerous attempts to
enter into a flirtation with the pretty quadroon
stewardess attached to this sybaritic train, to look
after the special wants of women.

These, with two or three other erratic performances of her putative maid, such as his answering
promptly " Yes, sir " and " No, sir " at various inop-

portune times, have put Lillian into a nervous frame of mind.

She knows she has made an unwise move, in trans-forming her faithful maid-servant Jane, into her un-ruly man "Friday." That though Jane intends to be faithful to her interests, and keep the secret, still, instead of a prim lady's maid, she is now a head-strong, wild and harum-scarum darky boy, with that peculiar addition called down South "nigger-brains," at this time peculiarly dangerous to her from its idiotic logic and extraordinary syllogisms.

During the last few hours of the trip, she has got to thinking Jane once more "her monster" and likening herself to Frankenstein in his unfortunate experiment. She therefore welcomes the sight of 633 Fifth Avenue, her old family mansion, which is at present in charge of the cook, a darky woman of wondrous potency with canvas-back ducks, and woful avoirdupois. This lady of color has been left in charge of the house, Miss Travers wisely thinking the cook the nucleus of all domestic bliss.

This servitor, having been notified by telegraph, admits Miss Lilly and her maid.

"I am only going to remain for a few days, Dinah," remarks Lilly, "so I shall not add to my establishment. An omelet, steak, and some of your coffee and rolls, are all that I shall want here. More elaborate meals I shall get at a restaurant," for she knows the fewer servants in the house, the greater safety to her secret.

Then Miss Travers goes up-stairs, and after get-ting a shock from many of the pretty feminine arti-cles in her dainty boudoir, that remind her of the

refined femininity that she had—but has no more; of
the womanhood that was—but is not, turns, and
says to Jane with masculine severity : " A few words
before you go to bed, my man.   First of all, you
are still to be a woman."

" That ain't possible, Mr.—Miss Lilly."

" You are still to *appear* a woman to the outside
world."

" What—no promenade down Sixth Abenue wid
de boys, no showin' de gals what a han'some youn'
man I is ? " mutters Jane ruefully, he having appar-
antly laid out for himself what might be called " a
high old spree " upon his first visit to New York as
a gentleman.

" Not until I tell you to ; probably not till we
leave New York."

At this disappointing statement, Jane turns away
in disgust, his master adding : " You had better go
to bed now ; you are tired out.   So am I, and I
have lots to do in the morning.   And don't you
call me Mr. Lilly again, as you value your situation."

" No, sir—yes, miss," answers Jane hurriedly and
disappears.

The next morning, Miss Travers, who has apparently made up her mind what to do, sets about it
with energy and rapidity.

She drives to Tiffany's and selects a ring that she
knows will make Bessie's heart glad.   This being sent
home to her later in the day, she forwards to Miss
Horton with a little note saying, " Dear Bess, I send
you this in return for ' the silent Bessie.'   You will
see it has engraved on it ' To B. H. from L. T.'—By
the by, L. T. stands for Lawrence Talbot as well

as Lilly Travers.—Why not consider it an engagement ring from him?"

Meantime she has called upon her lawyer, and incidentally looking over her securities, found a good portion is in convertible bonds. This is satisfactory to her. She asks that gentleman a few questions, and then departs in search of further information. This she picks up deftly, in the course of the next day or two, from various friends of hers—brokers, real estate speculators, etc., by feminine questions, aided by a masculine fixed purpose.

Some of her queries, however, are of a very astonishing nature to be put by a Fifth Avenue belle, and one of her friends, a stock broker, incidentally remarks at his club, that he thinks "Lilly Travers is going into business. By Jove! the way she asked me about convertible securities, unindorsed stock, and non-registered governments, made me think she'd got Wall Street in her eye. Perhaps she's a coming Hetty Green, and'll make me her broker. I wonder how long it would take her to get away with the million and a half that's been left to her by the old gentleman."

And, in fact, Miss Travers seems to be bent upon getting away with her fortune. She instructs her real estate brokers to sell all her realty in New York. They open their eyes at her orders, but do her bidding, Miss Travers being her own mistress, and any conveyances she may make perfectly valid and good.

This is very shortly done, for New York realty well located, is a very convertible asset, and though she loses a slight percentage upon its actual value, still being willing to make a sacrifice for speed in transfer, she gets it in a surprisingly short space of time, the lawyers making the examinations of title, being spurred on by a liberal *douceur,* accompanied by the statement that Miss Travers wishes to hurry the business as much as possible, on account of her intended departure from New York. These transfers are made and the money paid into Miss Travers' account.

Meantime she has converted all registered securities into cash, and has abstracted the stones contained in the family jewels from their old settings, for she wishes to obliterate everything that can tend, by any means whatsoever, to the suspicion that Lilly Travers has been generous to Lawrence Talbot.

She looks in the glass each morning, into the smiling, bold, and rapidly becoming masculine face of the young gentleman who nods back at her, and says : " I'm going to treat you very well, my young man, for Bessie's sake. You shall be very rich— almost as rich as Lillian Travers was. I can't give you real estate ; that would force you to be identified, and you are unknown to every one but me. I can't make a will in your favor, for it might be disputed by envious relatives, who would say I was insane to leave to you—even handsome fellow that you are—my property, from my kindred. Consequently, I've got to give you unregistered government bonds, my boy, and you can re-invest them carefully for yourself and Bessie."

And then the handsome young gentleman smiles back at her, and says : " Thank you, Miss Travers. You're uncommon good to an unknown fellow like me. I'll try and make myself comfortable upon your liberal donation." And the two laugh and shake hands together, and have a very pleasant time, one with the other.

Until suddenly, some new idea coming into the young lady's mind, she shakes her fist at the gentleman, scowls at him, and says threateningly : " If you don't treat Bessie well, look out for me ! Lawrence Talbot, Lilly Travers is going to be your mother-in-law ! " and so turns away laughing, to do a great piece of work for the young gentleman this day.

She goes to the Central Safe Deposit Company, and there engages one of the larger boxes, such as are fitted with combination locks, paying the year's rent in advance.

She enters her name on the books of the institution as requested and says :

" I wish to make this deposit box open to myself and one other, Mr. Lawrence M. Talbot. I shall be away from New York, but Mr. Talbot will bring a letter of introduction from me to you ; he will also give you the pass-word : ' My turn next ! ' This is his signature ; " and she hands them a card, upon which she has already written in as masculine hand 'as she can command : " Lawrence M. Talbot."

She goes over these methods of introduction and recognition, that Lawrence Talbot will have, with the Safe Company's officers, so that there can be no mistake, telling them Mr. Talbot will also receive from her the combination of the lock to the box she has engaged, which will be an additional proof of his identity. This shall be all the identification they can require from Mr. Talbot, as she will be out of town, and he has no friends, she thinks, in America.

All this being very definitely and accurately settled, through various brokers she converts her whole fortune, with the exception of a few thousand dollars, into unregistered U. S. Government bonds, and this being done, in the course of a few days, she deposits them in the box in the Central Safe Deposit Company, which is open to Mr. Lawrence Talbot, as well as to herself.

All this has been accomplished with as much speed as the transaction of the business will permit, for she is spurred on by the following letter, that is addressed " Miss Lillian Travers " and post-marked " St. Augustine, Florida," and is in Bessie's pretty and feminine handwriting.   It reads:

ST. AUGUSTINE, *February* 9th, 1891.

DEAR LILLY :

Your lovely, lovely present is here, and I have been thinking about you all night ; not of my present, but of your letter.   Somehow I've cried over it.   Its words were cheery but its tone gave me the shivers !   It seemed almost to say ' Adieu !' to me.   It didn't say it, but it seemed to say it.   But then, you know, I am a creature of impulse—and perhaps it didn't say anything of the kind, except to my excited longing for your quick return.   Besides I have thought over it all night, and have just got the clue, and I think you're the meanest creature in the world not to tell me about it before.   I have just been reading a Jacksonville paper which says in its horrid society news that the beautiful and accomplished New York heiress, Miss Lillian Travers, has gone to New York to order her trousseau, for her approaching marriage with Doctor Frederick Cassadene, the distinguished and popular physician at the Ponce de Leon Hotel.

If this is so (and I don't believe it) write me at once.   Any way I know the report will make that beautiful Mrs. Lovejoy very angry.   She is so very—but oh, I must be careful, especially if you're engaged to him.   I'll turn to another subject—myself.   Perhaps you'd

like to hear a little bit about Bessie. Bessie is getting along very
well. She has a very nice time. She has lots of beaux—one of
them in particular, is very nice—so you needn't send Mr.
Lawrence Talbot down here at all. But please come yourself, right off—as
soon as possible, immediately—for I shall not be happy until I hear
your voice again. Papa was very angry at your keeping me up all
night, packing your trunks ; he has forgiven you by this time, at my
intercession, and sends you his love. I know Miss Connie does the
same also, and so do I—lots of it—from

Your loving

BESSIE.

P. S.—How do you like " the silent Bessie " ? Is she behaving herself well ? I send you the enclosed notice.

The newspaper clipping reads :

It is reported on the best authority, that Miss Lillian Travers,
the lovely and fascinating New York heiress, who has spent several
of her springs among Florida orange groves, is shortly to become a
real Floridian, by marrying Doctor Frederick Cassadene, the very
accomplished and popular physician of the Ponce de Leon.

Our reporter mentioned this rumor to the Doctor, who smiled, and
looked as men always do, when they expect to become benedicts,
though he refused to commit himself. In support however, of our
statement, Miss Travers has gone to New York, suddenly, with the
intention it is understood, of ordering such a trousseau as only a New
York heiress can order. We presume some of these beautiful toi-
lettes will be seen in the parlors of the Ponce de Leon before the
season closes, as we understand that the wedding is to take place
before the end of March.

Over this notice Lilly bursts into laughter; but
Bessie's remarks about beaux, and that Mr. Lawrence Talbot's appearance will not be necessary, give
her a fit of the blues, and the late Miss Travers
knows that masculine jealousy is as potent a factor
of misery and anxiety as feminine jealousy. .

She is also incited to further speed by two or

three ominous occurrences that have taken place, from time to time, which indicate that if she does not change from the feminine to the masculine mode of life, of her own volition, Providence will change it for her.

A moustache, day by day, to her dread, but also to her pride, becomes beautifully developed. Not daring to trust to a barber's skill, she has been compelled to try her own, and her first shave has been a gory operation, and is not considered a success.

Besides this, on cashing a check the paying teller, who knows her very well by sight looks up and says: "Ah! personal application!"

"What does that matter?" she asks.

"Well, if you had not brought it in person, Miss Travers, I should not have paid it."

"Is not my account good?"

"Perfectly—*very* good!" with a great emphasis on the very. "But to tell you the truth, this signature does not seem to be exactly that of a woman."

"Indeed?" she says, struggling to restrain the agitation that, despite herself, flies into her face. "What is it then?"

"Why, it looks like the signature of a man."

"Ah! delighted to hear that!" she returns, forcing a smile. "I'm trying to make myself a business woman, and a masculine handwriting will perhaps assist me!"

But all these portentous incidents are as nothing, to the dread and horror brought upon her by her man Jane.

She has driven home one evening, after a hard day's work in making her various business arrange-

ments, when as she steps out of her coupé, about
nine o'clock in the evening, the night watchman,
chancing to pass by, salutes her.

He says respectfully : " Miss Travers, can I say a
word to you ? "

" Certainly ! " she replies. Something in his tone
giving her alarm, and fortunately putting her on her
guard.

He asks : " Have you a negro man in your employ ? "

A sudden instinct prompts her to gasp " Yes !—
my maid—" then getting confused she corrects
herself and murmurs : " I mean, my valet—my foot-
man. Why did you ask ? "

" Well, Miss Travers," says the watchman, " quite
often, early in the morning—a negro man lets himself into your house. I supposed he was some
sweetheart of one of your servants, but still I
thought it was best to ask. Now that I know he is
in your employ, it is all right."

" I'm very much obliged to you," remarks Lilly.
" Please take this for your care of my interests ; " and
pressing a liberal tip into the watchman's hand, she
goes up the stairs, enters the house, and mutters to
herself these feminine words : " Damn him ! It's
that infernal Jane, I know. I'll fix him to-night ! "

That evening she kills time by a novel and thinking of Bessie. At eleven o'clock, she investigates
Jane's room. That putative maid-servant is not in.
Then she sits down in her abigail's apartment and
waits—and waits—and then waits.

As the clock strikes two, she gets what she is
waiting for—a sensation, and would scream, were

she a woman, but being a man, she stands, gazes and gasps, for with a flippant air, and a smile of triumph on his face, and two or three chuckles on his lips, a typical Sixth Avenue darky dude enters the apartment.

With flashing eyes Lilly cries: "What are you here for? Out of my house this instant! Are you a sweetheart of Jane's?"

"Whaugh! whaugh!—I'se Jane hersel'!" cries the dude and bursts into a guffaw. " 'Clare to goodness—oh Lawdy! yo' didn't know me, Mr. Lilly."

"I know you now! So you've been masquerading about in men's clothes, night after night, to destroy my secret, my happiness, my life!" Lilly mutters, a fearful intensity in her tones, and the ferocity of despair in her manner.

"Got to wear dis kind o' clothes, Mr. Lilly. 'Gin de law to wear any oder!"

"Never you mind what the law is. My law is that you are still my maid-servant, till I permit you to assume the sex I gave you."

"Yo' can't turn me back into a woman agin, any way, Mr. Lilly," remarks Jane, with a grin.

"No, but I will send you to the Florida convict-camp. I'll get Gus to revive his warrant against you."

"Guess dat wouldn't go," remarks Jane, with a grin. "Gus'll swear a woman whipped him—I'll prove I'se a man. Golly, I'se got yo' dar. I'se been gettin' pints on de abenue."

"My Heaven! Have you told any one?" gasps Miss Travers, turning very pale.

" No—no—but I'se been gettin' pints without tellin', and I'se diskivered that I'se worth a thousan' dollars a week, to a dime museum, as de greatest freak on earth ! "

" Very well ! " cries Lilly desperately. " Go to your dime museum, and tell them your story, and they'll put you in an insane asylum—that's where ' the greatest freak on earth ' will land. Who would believe you ? "

" Believe me ! They'se got to believe me ! " mutters Jane excitedly. " I'll prove it by DE SEEDS ! " He makes an attempt to choke the last word in his throat, but is too late !

With the power born of desperation, the late Miss Travers is upon him. She has thrown him down. Her hands are at his throat. She chokes him till he is gray in the face. Then she mutters slowly : " Give me those seeds, or I will kill you ! Tell me where they are ! "

" 'Deed, Miss Lilly—— "

" Never mind about your ' deeds '—tell me where the seeds are ! " and she emphasizes her command by producing her pistol.

" Dey is hid in one of my ol' stockin's in de bottom of my trunk !—Please—please let me git some wind ! "

" Very well—get them ! " and Jane, who is apparently subdued, sullenly fishes them out from this odd receptacle, and Lilly once more has the little vial with its two magic seeds in her possession that sparkle in amber beauty. She looks on them gloatingly—lovingly.—They seem to give her new power.

11

" Why did you take these?" she asks.

" 'Cause yo' said if I didn't behave myself yo'd turn me back into a woman agin, and I wasn't goin' to habe one of dose things forced down my throat, and I won't habe it now. ✳I'll go away from yo' fust," cries Jane savagely.

" Promise to obey me and I will promise to let you remain as you are, though I don't think you are an improvement upon my obedient and faithful maid-servant, Jane. Any way you won't have to remain as my maid much longer. We leave New York soon, and in a few days you shall be no more my maid Jane Rouser, but my man, Jack Robbins!"

" An' yo', Miss Lilly, what'll yo' be?" mutters Jane.

" I shall be Mr. Lawrence Talbot!"

This name evidently impresses Jane. He mutters: " 'Pears to me, as you habe done such mighty high work for yo'self, yo' could do a little better fo' me, Mis' Lilly?"

" No. Jack Robbins is good enough for you," remarks the master, sternly.

Then, after a few more admonitions and directions, she goes away and carefully securing the glass vial with its potent seeds in a little bag she hangs about her neck by a thin golden chain she gets ready for bed. While doing this a mocking smile is on her lips, she sneers, " I wonder how much a dime museum would give for me?" then shudders: " My monster, Jane, will destroy me. Like Frankenstein, I have raised him up to be my ruin!"

And this idea running in her head, she goes to

sleep, and has a fearful nightmare ; and sees three-sheet posters like the following, in gigantic type and lurid characters covering all the city walls and billboards.

DIME MUSEUM.

THE FREAK OF ALL AGES!

THE WOMAN MAN!

LAWRENCE TALBOT née LILLIAN TRAVERS.

Only One More Seed Left.　BID HIGH!

$3,000,000 Offered

A female member of the Rothschild family bought the previous one and has just been voted into the

PARISIAN JOCKEY CLUB.

The richest widow in New York is in negotiation for the LAST Seed.

Also a

QUEEN who wants to be a KING before she dies.

| **3** PERFORMANCES A DAY | In conjunction with **The Missing Link** and **The Living Skeleton.** |

CHAPTER XIII.

DOCTOR FRED WOULD LIKE A KISS.

ALL these considerations urge desperate haste. Lilly forces the last few remaining preparations for her departure, finding time, however, to initiate her maid Jane into acting her man Jack. Every morning, they rehearse.

Miss Lilly calls in authoritative gruff voice: " My shaving water, Jack ! "

" Yes, Mr. Lawrence," replies Jane.

Or: " Put cigars and whiskey on the table, Robbins."

" Yes, Mr. Lawrence ; " and Jane doing as she is bid, places cigars, cigarettes and fiery spirits on the table, which Lilly, by way of educating herself to her new manhood, forces herself to indulge in, though she hates the taste of whiskey, and the cigars make her very sick.

One of these *petites comedies* is taking place when she is startled by the cook bringing up to her an epistle in a masculine hand which she easily recognizes as that of her erstwhile fiancé. It is a hastily written, impulsive letter, of the discarded suitor style; full of wild outcries of wounded love, complaints and reproaches. For, after the manner of his kind, Doctor Freddie has got to longing and mourning and suffering for lack of the love he has destroyed, and Lilly Travers now seems to him the only woman who can ever make his life happy. This he tells her in his letter, the conclusion of which is so dictatorial that it is scarcely polite. It

says: "If you do not return to Florida very soon,
I shall go to New York after you. You remember
my boast, Lilly—within four weeks you shall be the
bride of   Yours till death,   FRED."

The first part of this epistle produces a smile;
the latter part causes consideration, even concern.
Doctor Cassadene hanging round the skirts of Miss
Lilly Travers will embarrass her preparations to
become Mr. Lawrence Talbot!

This is another motive for speedy departure
from New York, which place has been getting
gradually distasteful to her. She longs to enter
society as one of the sex into which she has grad-
uated, and cannot do it.

She has got to muttering to herself savagely: "I
am tired of being a hermit."

As she drives down Fifth Avenue, she has fallen
into the habit of looking at the club buildings of
this most clubby street and thinking she would like
to sit in their windows, like other male bipeds, and
enjoy the feminine beauty that passes in parade in
front of them, while sybaritic man gazes on, enjoying cigars, cocktails and other frivolities peculiar to
the sterner sex, that she is getting gradually to like
with the love of the manhood that has come to her.

Driving past the Manhattan, the New York, or
the Union, she mutters: "I'll be put up there some
day; I'll sit in that window and that chair myself."

She has a tremendous hankering after the delights of Delmonicos' café, sacred to gentlemen.
She has even wild ideas of donning some of Mr.
Lawrence Talbot's new clothes and "doing" Kos-
ter & Bial's, or taking a merry little spree on the

Bowery, and would do her will, did she not dread that such adventures might lead to the revelation of her secret.

Actuated by these motives and impelled by a great longing to see Miss Bessie Horton, Lillian Travers makes her final preparations to depart forever from life as a woman and enter upon the glorious manhood that is before her, for which she longs as a child does for a new toy.

She surreptitiously expresses to Orlando in Southern Florida two large trunks addressed "Lawrence Talbot, Esq.,—to be retained till called for," and looks gloatingly at the name as the boxes are carted away.

Her fortune, now almost entirely in non-registered bonds, is in the vaults of the Central Deposit Company, ready to open to Lawrence Talbot's greedy hand, the moment he appears. She makes a last visit to that institution, and deposits everything of value that belongs to Lilly Travers, save one little article that she cannot find it in her heart to give up; for "The Silent Bessie" has been a great comfort to her in the absence of the chattering one. She looks upon the beautiful face of the miniature that smiles at her from its surrounding circlet of pearls, and mutters to herself: "My little sweetheart, I'll take you with me. It will be a risk; but for your sake I'd risk everything but being a woman again!" and so pockets it.

The next morning, booked as Miss Lillian Travers of New York, with three thousand dollars in large bills in her pocket-book, she takes passage on the Florida Special, accompanied by her maid Jane, and, arriving at Jacksonville, stops at that thriving town. For, after a great struggle with herself, she has made up her mind another parting with Miss Connie would be too dangerous as well as too painful to her.

She mutters to herself: "Lillian Travers has passed out of my loved ones' lives. Let us see if Lawrence Talbot cannot make up her loss to them."

She lingers in Jacksonville one day, fighting with the various emotions that are in her and seeming to hesitate at leaving every friend she has on earth and casting herself alone upon the world with her new manhood for her only support.

Then she desperately takes train for Ocala, having determined that she will make the trip down the Ocklawaha River, for a very curious idea has gradually formed itself in the last few weeks in Miss Travers' mind in regard to that cypress-shadowed, alligator-haunted region, which she is now about to execute.

She journeys leisurely by way of Palatka, and at Hawthorne changes to the Florida Central and Peninsular Railroad and passes down the eastern side of Orange Lake to Citra; remaining at this place over night and inspecting, next morning, the beautiful orange groves that here grow in the wild luxuriance of a forest, dotted with other trees to make them look the work of nature, not of man as they are, for the sweet oranges of the East have been budded upon the wild and bitter native trees of Florida, and the groves still have the irregularity and beauty of the wild-wood.

She has an object in this apparent leisurely travel.
She wishes to appear simply as being on a pleasure
tour, so that when ill-adventure comes to Miss
Travers the world will think it is accident, not de-
sign.   But this plan brings with it delay and delays
are dangerous.

Leaving Citra, she finds herself at Ocala the same
day, accompanied by the faithful Jane, who has
grown very much excited during this trip and who
frequently asks her with an agitated guffaw, " When
is it comin'? What time does de change take
place? When is we goin' to use de new clo'es?"
and other remarks that make her mistress nervous
and excited also.   Here she puts up at the well-
known hotel which has been christened after this
town.

A sleepless night—the last she will pass in
woman's night gear—and she is up early the next
morning to take the train for Silver Spring. On
this trip she brings with her only a small trunk
which Jane easily carries, for the Ocklawaha boats
have but limited accommodation for baggage in their
staterooms, which are little bigger than saratogas
themselves.

A few minutes of railroad and she looks on the
fairy beauty of the great Silver Spring, once thought
the fountain-of-eternal-youth, to find which Ponce de
Leon journeyed till he died—these wondrous living
waters that spring a full-grown river from the earth.

This dazzling stream that in its tossing ofttimes
magnifies the things that lie on its sandy bottom
and the fish that swim within its crystal ; these
weird half-tone shadows from the cypress on its

banks; these living waters that are liquid-ether as
they bubble from the grottos that give out the
purple tints; all seem of another and unreal, though
perchance a happier state, to this being, who, still
calling herself Lilly Travers, is living a life no other
being ever lived before.

But she has short time to gaze astonished,—the
train has scarcely run upon the little wharf before
the steamer blows its whistle, and freight and lug-
gage and passengers being hurried on board, the
pygmy *Okahumpka*, her stern wheel revolving, is
gliding out from her landing, past " The Ladies'
Parlor" and " The Gentlemen's Smoking-room "—
fountains of weird, cloud-like water, but of earthy
name—and darting down this marvellous river,
whose silver stream within a few miles will be swallowed in the slimy, blackish oozes of the swamp-
born Ocklawaha.

Water ethereal supports the tiny steamer, and
Lilly Travers, looking over its side, for a moment
grows dizzy and staggers back—thinking she is an
aeronaut; for the boat seems like a balloon with
air above her and air beneath her. A moment after
she calms her nerves, and standing on the upper
deck gazes at the panorama through which she
passes—long vistas of cypress trees, rising from
this glassy water mirror like giant storks' legs to
their canopy of green and moss above.

Impressed by her strange position she thinks:
" Like Ponce de Leon, who came to find youth, I
have come here to find manhood. He failed and
died. Shall I be disappointed also ?"—and looking
at the clear, living stream upon which she is float-

ing and which in an hour will become dark and
turbid, wonders .if this is allegorical of her coming
change.

Her meditation is broken in upon by a most
unexpected *contretemps.* A masculine voice comes
to her ears with a recognition that makes her start.
It says : "How did you enjoy your New York trip,
Lilly? Did my letter have any weight in causing
your return?"

Turning round with a gasp of astonishment
and dismay, she sees the stalwart figure of Fred
Cassadene, who is looking upon her with triumphant and longing eyes. A moment after there is
some disappointment in his glance; for curiously
enough, the Miss Travers he is gazing upon seems
to have deteriorated since he saw her last, and appears not so graceful and not so beautiful as the
girl who had given him back her troth, scarce a
month before, in St. Augustine.

He chews his mustache rather disconcertedly, as
he mutters to himself, "By Jove! how she has
changed!" Then masculine vanity comes to him
and he thinks: "Joy will bring back beauty to her.
I'll make her happy."

Miss Travers gives a startled "You here!" and
then forces herself into the commonplaces of social
recognition. A moment after the Doctor whispers
in her ear, "You have suffered too!" and is surprised
and shocked, for the delicate Miss Travers replies
savagely "Rats!" an expression she has learnt from
Jane and cultivated for masculine use.

On this, the disconcerted Frederick drawing back
from her, she goes into meditation herself, and won-

ders : " What cursed ill-luck has sent this love-sick sop here to make my task more difficult? "

Though she does not know it; her day's delay in Jacksonville, her additional lingering twenty-four hours in Citra,—have brought this misadventure upon her.

Cassadene, glancing over the papers, has noted in the society columns that Miss Lillian Travers, one of the great catches of New York and the reported fiancée of the dashing doctor of the Ponce de Leon, is now in Jacksonville, accompanied by her maid; that she in the next day or two is bound for Ocala with the object of making the celebrated Ocklawaha trip, for which she has already engaged a stateroom. This has put a sudden idea into the Doctor's mind. He will meet the boat at Silver Spring also, and Miss Travers, being on board, will perforce be compelled to accept his presence, which she will not be able to dodge, these steamboats being very small. In the twenty hours' run through romantic cypress swamps and in the shadows of the great trees and at night by the light of the burning pine knots, he will again press his suit, and having been made vain by his fortune among the fair sex, he has no doubt he will once more be successful.

This is the reason that Doctor Fred, chewing his mustache savagely, is now gazing upon Miss Travers, whose conduct again surprises him.

The boat has already plunged into the cypress swamps. The crystal waters of the Silver Run have been swallowed by the dark stream of the larger river which cuts them off, sharp as a knife blade. The steamer is now some miles down the Ocklawaha.

Swinging round one of the narrow turns, the boat runs within a few feet of a cypress tree, one of the long branches of which is covered with crawling, slimy, venomous snakes,—the dreaded water-moccasins of Florida.

Several ladies on the upper deck shudder and cringe away from these reptiles, that seem almost near enough to be dangerous. But Miss Travers, unlike her sisters, gazes upon the slimy things without apparent outward discomfort, and seems to enjoy the vigor with which one of the negro deckhands whacks them off the branch with a pole into the water. The Lilly Travers of a month ago would have shuddered and turned from this sight, though the young lady who is now gazing upon it seems rather interested in the darkey's assault upon the reptiles that open their cotton-mouths at him and show their fangs as they wriggle about in vain endeavors to dodge the blows from his far-reaching pole.

The Doctor's vanity again deceives him. He thinks : " Lilly attempts to be masculine and used that frightful exclamation to so disgust me that I will not renew my suit ; for the dear girl knows that if I once make serious love to her, she will be a goner." Then meditating : " I will give her a little rope. I will leave her alone for an hour or two. She will be sighing for me by that time,"—he devotes his attention to other things and consoles himself with a cigar. While enjoying his Havana he keeps one eye upon Miss Travers, who, he shortly discovers, is gazing at him in a longing way, which elates him greatly.

He strolls up to her and murmurs in his sweetest voice : " Ah, Lilly ! the old feeling is coming into your heart. Your eyes have again a longing look in them."

"Yes—for a cigar," mutters Miss Travers snappishly ; and again disconcerted he retreats from her.

And this is true ; for it is a hankering after his cigar, not him, which has attracted the late Miss Travers' eager eyes. She is gradually acquiring, among her mannish accomplishments, a love for the weed, and thinks a cigar would be uncommonly pleasant, dare she but use one. This makes her angry and she says to herself : " To-night, whether he is on the boat or not !—To-morrow I will have the privileges and rights of a man ! "

Her unfeminine disregard, as Doctor Fred terms it, of his feelings, has made that gentleman sulky and surly, and, greatly to her relief, he does not bother Miss Travers for some hours.

After a time, at a little landing Lilly sees an orange grove and stepping on shore gathers aided by the lady of the plantation a branch covered with juicy fruit and coming on board again goes to eating and tossing the peels over the side as the steamer pushes along under palmetto and cypress that shadow her decks and make leafy arches overhead.

So Lilly putting Fred out of her mind gets to looking upon and enjoying the panorama that unfolds itself as the boat threads its way through this foliage-lined stream, making turns innumerable, and sometimes appearing to drive straight for the cypress belt to plunge within its swamps, then suddenly poled off by the sable deck-hands turning from it and bending, as it were, back on its course, after the style of the letter S.

Next she notes the skill of the negro pilot as he swings the craft on its course, and gets to looking for alligators, a few of which she sees. Most of them are not very large, though extremely wary, for until a few years ago, sportsmen brought their rifles and shooting-irons on deck and the boat's passage was marked by a fusillade on the inhabitants of the swamp, so now the surviving alligators skulk away from the path of the steamer and into the swamps which lie for miles and miles on either side of the river, a mass of submerged cypress, dense undergrowth and jungle, impenetrable to man and still the haunt of the hunted " gator."

Thus the day wears on, Miss Travers making but one appearance in the dining-room of the little craft, for anxiety has taken away her appetite. And now after passing two giant cypresses that graze the boat on either side, early night falls upon the river, for the great trees grow so thick together that the declining sun cannot penetrate their leafy screen.

After a little the noises of the swamp begin to be heard in the stillness of the night ; and knots of fat pine are lighted on the pilot-house to throw a glow over the river by which the boat can feel its way round the bends and sometimes in the trees torches blaze in the hands of kindly darkeys to help the pilots of the boat.

At the little landings negroes come down with blazing pine knots to light the deck-hands as they take on cargo.

This romantic scene impresses Miss Travers and

gives her a gloomy fit. She grows timid and shudders at the thought of losing her name, identity and
kindred: and once her hand goes to the little vial
that is still hanging closely held in its buckskin bag
about her neck, and for one short moment she
thinks: " Why not take one of the mystic seeds that
have brought disquiet to me and return to the life I
have led—the womanhood I have left behind me?"

But even as she thinks this, the voice of Doctor
Freddie, who is trying to make himself very agreeable to a pretty. young lady from Cincinnati, comes
to her and she pauses and mutters : " My Heaven!
—and love *him* again?" Then suddenly dear little
Bessie's face rises before her and she is strong to do
the work she has planned for herself this night.

The decks of the boat gradually become deserted,
for it is getting late, and most of the passengers
have squeezed into their staterooms, a rather difficult job for fat people. A few, perhaps unprovided
with sleeping accommodations which are limited
upon these boats; or perchance, anxious to still look
at the great moss-laden trees, as they move past
them or hear the plantation melodies of the darkey
crew—remain. Often as the boat makes sudden
turns the cypress branches scrape its sides. Now
and then a warning cry is heard as some great limb
sweeps the deck giving danger as well as romance
to this night.

Looking at her watch, Miss Travers asks a careless question of a negro deck-hand : " What will be
our next landing?"

" McBride's," he says ; " den yo' come to Gray's
Cut—and keep yo' eye out, miss, for de way we

twists 'bout, right dar. Den we come up to Enoch & Collins', an' den Needle's Eye, an' after a little while we's at Orange Spring Lan'in'."

As his words come to Lilly's ear, her heart gives a bound; for, ever since she has made some apparently careless inquiries at Citra, Orange Spring Landing is the place she has selected where the earth will know Miss Travers no more.

Even as she thinks this, Doctor Fred is at her side. This gentleman has apparently got over his huffiness of the morning. Her very rebuffs have made him more eager for her favor. In the darkness he cannot see the change that has come to this woman when he still loves in his own desultory fashion, perhaps as well as he can love anybody— except himself. He pictures in his imagination the girl he was once engaged to, and Lilly Travers in the darkness of this night is as femininely beautiful as the Lilly Travers of a month ago. He commences to plead with her. He tells her how he loves her, and, receiving no answer, his vanity whispers to him, "You will succeed this time!"

"Dear Lilly," he continues, "you love me still. You have stayed on deck so as to hear from me once more the tones you used to love—the words you used to drink in from my lips." Then the two being alone and in the shadow, Doctor Fred follows a maxim he has laid down for himself: "Strike while the iron is hot." He suddenly gives the putative Miss Travers a tender yet enthusiastic embrace, and whispering "I love you," would again feast upon the lips whose sweetness he remembers.

But this young delicate lady, to his surprise, tears

herself from him suddenly, with a force that astonishes the stalwart Frederick, and whispers in tones of deadly rage, " Hang you, sir, if you dare to touch me again, I'll knock you overboard to the alligators ! "

Then a sudden change seems to come over the girl, and she says to her astonished, dismayed and disgusted suitor : " Forgive me.—Good-night, Doctor Freddie. We shall be better friends when we meet next."

⸰ This idea seems to amuse her, for she passes from his side and goes off to her stateroom, laughing an uneasy, mocking laugh, and this is the last that Doctor Frederick Cassadene ever hears from the lips of Lilly Travers.

Half an hour afterward, the boat pulls up at Orange Creek Landing. There is quite a lot of freight to put aboard, the deck hands are busy, 'the captain and pilot occupied, and Fred Cassadene is carelessly smoking a cigar near the gang-plank, looking at the labors of the night and ruminating over his ill-success with the New York heiress,— when, a young man in gray travelling suit, with a fishing-rod in his hand and attended by a darkey servant carrying a gun case and small satchel, passes quickly over the gang-plank. The pine knot in the hand of a negro standing on the landing for a moment lights up the face of the young man, though partially concealed by a slouched hat, and Cassadene gives a momentary start ; then mutters : " It's funny I can't get Lilly Travers' eyes out of my head. Everyone I look at seems to have her optics! " Then, he queries wonderingly : " That young sportsman must have kept himself pretty well boxed up in his stateroom this trip; funny I haven't seen him, before."

But the whistle of the boat sounds, the great stern wheel revolves and the *Okahumpka* is on her way again, while Lawrence Talbot and his valet, Jack Robbins, are tramping along the Orange Creek road towards Orange Springs; but they do not stop at that little place, turning off instead to the north and making along the road that leads to the railway, some ten miles distant in that direction; for Mr. Talbot seems to have a desperate desire not to be seen in the neighborhood of the Ocklawaha River. And so they make the longest march young Mr. Talbot has ever made, for he is a delicate young gentleman as yet and has not met with the fatigues incident to manhood, nor many of its responsibilities which are shortly to come upon him; and his man-servant, who wears his clothes in an awkward, ungainly, unaccustomed way, during one of the many stops—for they make many—says with a guffaw: "Golly, Mr. Lawrence! wouldn't we be skeert ef we was gals?"

"Yes," remarks Talbot, lighting a cigar to soothe the weariness of the way; "a month ago, Jack, we would have died of fright, out here alone, with the owls hooting like that!" Then he says suddenly, "What did you do with our clothes?"

"Tossed 'em all overboard!"

"That's the proper place for 'em!" remarks the gentleman cheerily. "How any human being can wear the disgusting unhealthy corsets and street-sweeping gowns women will insist upon flaunting about in is more than I can see! But we have a pretty good step to go before we reach Clark's Mill,—so trot along, my man!"

Then the two trudge sturdily on, and in the early morning find themselves in pine woods, here and there made bright by little lakes; but they still press on, until, foot-sore and weary, this young gentleman and his man-servant reach the railroad, where they take the first train for Southern Florida, arriving at Orlando. Here Mr. Lawrence Talbot finds his trunks ahead of him, and proceeds to make himself comfortable and apparently having plenty of money—hires a guide and explores the Kissimmee region in pursuit of game, without much luck, however; the "Cracker" who attends him remarking on their return, one day in a bar-room in Kissimmee, that young Mr. Talbot is the worst "shooter" for a human being he ever. "seed"; that he has only succeeded, so far, in shooting the air.

All this time, the neophyte is hurriedly cultivating a handsome mustache and a well tanned skin, and learning to become a shot and to handle his masculine muscles for all they are worth and is thoroughly indifferent apparently to what is going on in the country to the north of him; though he sometimes wonders what the world says at Lilly Travers' being out of it.

Curiously enough Miss Travers has not been missed as yet. The *Okahumpka* arrives at Palatka before sunrise, Doctor Fred bolts off to sleep and the Putnam House in a huff and a hurry, and when daylight comes upon the town the passengers have all left the steamboat, Miss Travers and her maid being supposed to be among them.

And though Bessie's face has begun to be anxious among St. Augustine orange groves and she sometimes mutters, "Why don't she write?" and Miss Connie ofttimes says, " Lilly must have gone straight to Havana, that's the fad trip this year,—she'll be back soon," very little has been thought of Miss Travers' disappearance.—What's one little girl in this great world of ours—even if she be a beauty and an heiress—save to those who love her?

BOOK III.

THE WONDERFUL ADVENTURES OF MR. LAWRENCE TALBOT.

CHAPTER XIV.

WILD OATS.

SHORTLY after this—the Palatka train brings in one evening to St. Augustine a dark-skinned, sun-burnt young man who says to his servant, "Jack, tell the hackman the Cordova. Wilson always makes everybody comfortable!"

In this gorgeous hostelry, Mr. Lawrence Talbot soon finds himself very cosily housed, occupying two of the small but pretty tower rooms that look out on the Alameda, diagonally opposite the Ponce de Leon. He is fortunate in securing these apartments, but the season is drawing towards its close and already travellers are commencing to turn their faces in search of a new spring that will soon be found in Virginia and North Carolina watering-places.

It is altogether too late by the time Mr. Talbot receives his trunks, for him to achieve a toilet and make any visits this evening, though he is desperately anxious to see a pair of blue eyes that exist some three miles out of town in the orange groves on the St. Sebastian. So he spends his evening meditating upon his future course, and drawing his inspirations from the strains of the band in the " sun parlor " and the whiffs of a cigar, which he has learned by this time to smoke very nicely.

He apparently has no friends in the hotel, though once or twice he looks at people as if he expected recognition but does not get it. His appearance and general style however attract the gaze of several beauties who wonder who that natty young fellow is and think he would probably be nice to know and perchance to flirt with.

Noting this handsome, dark-eyed, slight-figured young gentleman's lack of companions and acquaintances, the host of the Cordova with his characteristic *bonhomie* and put-everybody-at-home manner steps up to his lonely guest and enters into conversation with him, striving to make him forget his lack of acquaintances by genial anecdotes of Florida and St. Augustine, with which, curiously enough, his hearer seems to be extraordinarily well acquainted for a person who has never visited the place before.

In the course of conversation, young Talbot, noticing ladies passing out in gala array, asks incidentally where they are going.

"To the hop at the Ponce de Leon," says Mr. Wilson. Then he remarks suddenly: " Wouldn't you like to see it ? I think I can get you a ticket if you would."

"Would I like to see it ? " echoes the gentleman

addressed. Then he answers himself eagerly, "Immensely!" a longing light coming into his eyes and his countenance growing vivacious, for sudden thought suggests—" Perhaps Bessie will be there," —as he bounds up-stairs to encounter that joy of budding manhood, his first dress suit.

Calling in his servant, he says: " Jack, get out my swallow-tail; I am going to christen it to-night," and soon finds himself arrayed in a well-fitting evening costume that suits his lithe, though slight, figure perfectly, having come from the hands of a first-rate New York tailor. Looking at the glass, Mr. Lawrence Talbot remarks: " I think this will do the girls this evening; " and then mutters in sudden joy: " My first hop as a full-fledged man!"

A moment after he steps down-stairs, to find his invitation waiting for him at the office. Then shielded from the evening mist by a light overcoat he crosses the Alameda, and entering the gardened court-yard of the Ponce de Leon and passing its sulphur-scented fountain, he strolls into that great hostelry to see Bessie and not be over-pleased with what his sweetheart is doing.

Having put away his hat and overcoat, he enters the dining-room, where the dance is going on, and joins the spectators.

It is the usual watering-place hop, that Lawrence gazes on—the dancing ladies many, the dancing men few.

As Lawrence's eyes rove over the assemblage seeking his little sweetheart's pretty figure, his inquisitorial glances bring odd feelings with them. Mr. Talbot sees acquaintances and intimate friends of Lilly Travers, and would like to recognize and speak to them, but dare not. Then he notices some gentlemen who once bowed down at the shrine of the late New York heiress's beauty, and mutters " Wouldn't they jump, if they but knew!" Incidentally, among these he sees the stalwart form of Doctor Fred, who is just entering the ball-room with the radiant Mrs. Stella Lovejoy on his arm. This lady appears even more beautiful than before to Mr. Talbot, who divorced from the society of women for the last two or three weeks, now hungers for it with all a boy's enthusiasm.

But even as he drinks in the widow's beauty, a voice beside him makes him start and blush with joy. It is from blue-eyed Miss Bessie, and says to the gentleman upon whose arm she is leaning: " Mr. Wilkes, your description of your orange grove on Indian River gives me a yearning for oranges ! "

"Ah, thank you," remarks that gentleman excitedly. "Then," he says with insinuation, " you must also like orange blossoms?"

"If the right man came with them !" answers the young lady, and the blue eyes droop coquettishly.

Lawrence Talbot looks at this little scene, and rage comes into his heart ; he thinks savagely : " How dares Bessie talk of orange blossoms to any man but me?—What a little flirt she is—for of course she don't care a copper for that idiotic Wilkes."

With this fires of masculine jealousy come into his brain and make his eyes glare upon the offending orange grower. Mr. Wilkes however is so wrapped up in pretty Miss Horton that he does not notice these glances from the dark-eyed slender gentleman standing close to him.

Then of a sudden, Lawrence Talbot, forgetting the present, would treat Bessie Horton as Lilly Travers did in the past, and is about to embrace Miss Bessie impulsively and kiss her, and call her his little darling and bring confusion upon the young lady and attack and horsewhipping upon himself from her fiery father—but recollection stays him just in time; he mutters to himself: "Great Heaven! What an insult she would think it! I dare not even speak to her. I must run back to the hotel and get my letter of introduction. A ball-room isn't exactly the place to present it, but anything rather than bite my nails with rage and permit that drawling idiot to monopolize her this evening."

But as he turns on his errand, he fortunately sees the only man he knows in all this world led up by her father and very kindly recognized by Miss Bessie. This is a gentleman who has been examining some phosphate lands belonging to Major Horton in Southern Florida. Lawrence and he have been thrown together in Kissimmee. A week in that not over exciting place, has set them to playing billiards and over the green-cloth they have become quite friendly and chummish. The moment this gentleman has left Miss Horton, Talbot speaks to him, and, trying to keep excitement out of his voice, though it will tremble a little, he remarks : " That is quite a pretty young lady you were speaking to, Mr. Malcolm. What is her name?"

" Pretty ? Well, rather," says Malcolm, who is a man past middle age. "She is Miss Bessie Horton, one of the belles of this place. Would you like to be presented to her? Dancing men are scarce about here, and you look as though you might make yourself useful, Talbot!"

"Miss Horton?" remarks Lawrence, as if trying to recollect something. Then he says suddenly : "Oh yes—Miss Bessie Horton; I remember. I believe I have a letter of introduction to her in my trunk at the hotel. I should be delighted if your kindness would permit me to anticipate it this evening."

"All right, my boy; I'll speak to her," answers Malcolm, who is rather proud of his acquaintance with this eligible young gentleman, whose clothes and general get-up are unmistakably those of a New York swell.

A moment after, the debutant in manhood sees him speaking to Miss Bessie and her blue eyes getting very big with sudden interest, as she hears that Mr. Lawrence Talbot would like an introduction ; then his head buzzes; he is standing looking into his sweetheart's eyes and listening to her soft Southern voice and thinking her even sweeter, prettier and more piquantly charming than the dear little Bessie of old.

" Mr. Lawrence Talbot?" she remarks, looking him over. Then she says impulsively, " Has Lilly Travers ever spoken to you of me ? "

" Very often," replies the young gentleman eagerly. " I have a letter of introduction to you from her. I intend to present it to-morrow!"

"You mean you intended?" corrects Miss Bessie.

"No, I still intend.—Please don't cut me out of a visit to-morrow!"

She doesn't answer this; some curious idea seems to have come into the girl's head, her eyes look excited and astonished. She says: "How like your cousin! Your eyes have the same flashes; your voice—if I may use a slangy expression, the same twist in it." Then she goes on suddenly, a shade of anxiety in her tone, "When did you get your letter of introduction from Lilly?"

"In New York, four weeks ago."

"And no letter from her for a month!" mutters Bessie with a pained and anxious voice. "Then she puts this startling question, "Do you know where Lilly is now?"

"I—I—I believe she is somewhere about here," is Mr. Talbot's rather confused though truthful answer to this question. "I know where she would like to be," he goes on with a meaning smile.

"Where?"

"Where I am now. From what she said to me, I know she loved—I mean loves you very much."

"So, you have often discussed me," murmurs Bessie looking interested.

"Very often; where could we find a pleasanter subject?"—says Lawrence gallantly, his eyes emphasizing this passage, and a quizzical look coming over his mobile features as he continues, "I presume, in return, Miss Travers has often spoken to you of me, eh?"

But Miss Bessie turns away her head, without answer though a bright blush on the cheek that remains in view makes Lawrence think it hardly fair to continue in this strain, and he whispers, " Did you say you would like to dance?"

"I didn't say so," laughs Bess, "though I would, very much."

So the two move together in very much the same fashion that Lilly Travers a few weeks before danced with Bessie Horton.—so much so that in a pause of the waltz, Bess remarks, looking in her companion's face with some admiration and perhaps a little wonder : " Your step is just the same as Lilly's.   If I did not know you were her cousin, I might think you were her big brother."

" The brother you said you would like to marry one night ? " is on the tip of Lawrence's tongue ; but prudence checks him ; though these remarks of Miss Horton give him a confidence with this young lady that later on this evening brings him to grief.

At present the two chat very gayly and happily together, Miss Bessie playfully remarking that Lilly has told her that her cousin shall make up for her absence, and he must keep Miss Travers' word good.   Then she inquires : " How long will you stay in St. Augustine ? "

" So long as it is pleasant for me," returns the young gentleman ; then continues pointedly : " You see, the matter is in your own hands."

At which the young lady, thinking this gentleman rather bold on short acquaintance, replies : " Then I will begin my office and introduce you to my friends."

Which she does, presenting him to Mrs. Stella

Lovejoy, who looks with kindly eyes upon Mr. Talbot, and thinks he might make a new recruit in her ranks of adorers and a pleasant foil to Doctor Fred, and a card with which to draw out that gentleman's trumps in the game in which the widow and he are playing. An idea which shortly afterwards produces some curious complications in Mr. Lawrence Talbot's life.

Miss Bessie in her warm-hearted, impulsive, Southern way does the introduction business by the wholesale, and Mr. Talbot soon finds himself once more acquainted with many of Miss Travers' old friends, having great difficulty in preventing himself from treating the ladies with the familiarity that Lilly was wont to do.

These peculiar actions of her escort coming under Miss Bessie's sharp eyes, she gives a little laugh and whispers: "I am afraid you are a very bold young gentleman."

"Indeed? Why?"

"Oh, because—because you look so familiarly affectionate at many of the ladies on introduction."

A moment after she says: "You must know my father," and presents him to the old major, who, learning that the young man has been in Southern Florida, grows effusive about his phosphate properties in that region, telling him that he is forming a company that will deliver an "A, No. 1," eighty per cent. fertilizer right on the Liverpool docks, for five dollars a ton, and remarks: "What do you think of that?"

To which Lawrence, in bad judgment, replies: "I can't exactly tell—I am not a business man."

"Ha—ah! Then we'll teach you! America is a business country. Perhaps you will make your fortune here!" remarks the major patronizingly.

But Lawrence does not care for his future father-in-law to imagine that his future son-in-law's fortune is yet to be made. He says airily: "Oh, my ancestors did that for me long ago!"

And so turning to Mrs. Lovejoy's attractive side he leaves the future father-in-law impressed by the to-be son-in-law's wealth. For the major remarks to Miss Bessie the first chance he gets in a playful father's aside: "Has she caught a young and rich beau, papa's wise little girl?" playfully pinching Miss Bessie's pretty ear.

At which the girl says: "Pshaw! I have only known Mr. Talbot ten minutes. What makes you say such horrid things? Do you like to make me blush?"

But this conversation is interrupted by the attentive Mr. Wilkes, who again makes his appearance with some more remarks about oranges and orange blossoms and takes the young lady to dance.

Looking upon this, as he is conversing with the radiant Stella, jealousy again gets into Mr. Talbot's heart, and a moment after, the opportunity coming to him, he takes Miss Bessie upon his arm and proposes a little promenade in the big corridors of the hotel. The girl assents so readily to his proposition that this rash young gentleman becoming very bold, thinks to take up his running where Miss Lilly Travers left off—a mistake which brings its own punishment with it.

After a few commonplaces, he twists the subject

round to the aggravating Wilkes, remarking in the assurance of his new-born manhood : " You don't get very much advice, Miss Bessie, I should imagine ? "

" No ? " mutters the girl. Then she suddenly says, her eyes gleaming a little : " Do you think I *need* it ? "—and growing red at the implied criticism, remarks : " You have had such a long time to study me !"—this last with an air of sarcasm.

" Personally," says Mr. Lawrence airily, " I have not had much time, but I have received a good deal of information about you from Miss Lilly Travers."

" Ah ! Perhaps you would like to stand in Lilly's shoes," returns Bessie, haughtily.

" Wouldn't I ! " This is said with so much meaning that Miss Horton looks at her escort a moment in dismay, and then remarks, with additional color in her cheeks : " And what advice do you suppose Miss Travers would give me ? "

Just here Lawrence Talbot makes one of the mistakes of his young life. He says : " Miss Travers I imagine would suggest that a young lady of your beauty and fascinations should be able to find a more brilliant escort than a man who talks about nothing but oranges and orange blossoms "—the orange blossoms with rather a savage accent.

" Oh ! " cries Bessie, opening her eyes in indignation ; " you mean Mr. Wilkes."

" Miss Travers would mean Mr. Wilkes."

" Then Miss Travers had better speak for herself," cries Bess, who has been gradually working herself up into a Southern passion. " Let me give

you a little information also, Mr. Talbot: Do you
know what were the last words I ever uttered to
Miss Travers?"

"You—you needn't tell me," mutters Lawrence,
getting very red in the face and so much confused—
that Miss Bessie suddenly cries, "She *has* told you
already—Oh my! How mean of her!" and her
lips quiver with mortification. Next she ejaculates
—"Ah! here's Mr. Wilkes himself. I believe he has
the next dance." And turning from the abashed
young gentleman before her, her indignant but
troubled eyes become soft and alluring as she fixes
them upon the orange-grower, and taking that gentleman's arm, trips away in hot indignation.

Then savage, wild, torturing masculine jealousy in
its full-grown form enters Mr. Lawrence Talbot's
soul, and with a muttered anathema on Wilkes and
women, he strides off among several male acquaintances he has just made, to console himself with
champagne, thinking, "Why not—I might as well
sow my wild oats now as never!"

A glass or two of wine, and he chances to encounter Mrs. Stella Lovejoy. Made enthusiastic
by the grape he opens a violent attack upon that
lady's heart, to the rage of Doctor Frederick, who
looks very glumly on at this young gentleman's performance; till after a while tiring of this, Lawrence
goes gloomily home to the Cordova and tumbles
into bed.

But now he is no poor wounded Lilly Travers to
toss and writhe and utter tearful moans of wounded
love, and in the pride of new-born manhood he mutters: "Bess is an awful little flirt, but I'll fix her

good. I'll play the Lovejoy widow against her—
Watch me!" and so goes to sleep.

He awakes next morning, notwithstanding his
boast, in rather a doleful and disgruntled state of
mind, which does not cause him to respond very
effusively to the merry guffaws of his man Jack as
he lays out his clothes for the morning and remarks
in the happy-go-lucky style of his race: "Golly!
Massa Lawrence; won't we lay out de whole
worl'!"

CHAPTER XV.

FLOATING GARMENTS FROM THE OCKLAWAHA.

A MOMENT after, while dressing, chancing to look
through the casements of the Moorish windows of
his room in the Cordova, he sees Stella Lovejoy
taking her morning drive, for Mr. Talbot's slumbers
have been long and the day is somewhat advanced.
The sight of this beautiful woman brings with it
activity. He dresses, whistling vivaciously, and
going down to the dining-room, enjoys his breakfast
hurriedly. For the idea of last night has returned
to him, and he thinks he will make Miss Bess very
jealous, forgetting, with a vanity peculiar to adoles-
cence, that he must first make Miss Horton love
him, before he can make her jealous, and up to the
present time that young lady has not shown any de-
cided preference for him, though he has for her.

In pursuance of his plan, he keeps a bright eye
out for the widow's equipage, and fortunately catching sight of it in ample time, steps briskly over to
the Ponce de Leon and is ready to most politely doff

his hat and offer his arm, as the beauty descends from
her victoria. Escorting her into the gardens, he
speedily has a couple of seats (for he has been liberal, last night, with the servants of the Ponce de
Leon, and they remember him), and the two sitting
down amid flowers and sunshine listen to the band
playing in the *loggia*. In their conversation, Mrs.
Lovejoy soon discovers that this young gentleman
is a distant cousin of Miss Travers. This lady, she
at present considers her rival with the medical
Adonis, and becomes anxious for Mr. Lawrence's
intimacy, thinking she may obtain from him information of the Doctor's position with that New York
belle, that may be of use to her.

A few minutes after remarking with an entrancing smile : " The band has stopped work ! " She
suggests, " Why not come up to my parlor, Mr.
Talbot ? It is cooler there, and in a few minutes it
will be time for lunch, and you can be my guest."

So in a very few moments Lawrence finds himself seated with the beautiful Stella on the very
balcony which Miss Travers saw occupied by Doctor
Cassadene and this dainty charmer when the first
pangs of wounded love came to Lilly's heart to
make her on that eventful night turn away from
weak womanhood to obtain, perchance, weaker manhood.

On account of Mr. Talbot, Mrs. Lovejoy and Doctor Fred have had a lovers' quarrel the evening
before, and as Lawrence and she say sweet nothings
to each other on the balcony, this gentleman's card
being brought up to her, the widow returns "Not at
home ! "

This makes Mr. Talbot very proud and conceited, he thinking that his charms have literally floored the handsome doctor in the very first round. He strokes his not entirely completed mustache contemplatively and meditates: " I believe I could capture Stella myself—for keeps, if I but wanted her;"and thoughtlessly proceeds to put some nails in Doctor Freddie's amorous coffin in the easy way that one gentleman rival does to another.

" I believe you know my cousin Lilly, Mrs. Lovejoy," he remarks casually.

"Yes—slightly," replies Stella, forgetful of the kisses she has placed on Miss Travers' lips in the very room into which they are looking—the one that had been occupied as a dressing-room on the occasion of the hop a few weeks before. Then she says anxiously: " The papers have given us rumors that Doctor Cassadene is engaged to your cousin. Do you know whether there is anything in it?"

" Don't know whether there is anything in it *now*," answers Lawrence nonchalantly; " but at one time I am very sure the doctor was rather far gone on *la belle* Travers."

" At one time? What time?"

" Oh, not so long ago."

"You are sure?"

" Yes, ra-th-er certain," the words are drawled out by the young neophyte in manhood. " Just ask him about the Ocklawaha boat three weeks ago. Do!—I want to hear what he says about it?" and Lawrence laughs. " Ask him if he didn't pester Lil with his attentions until she actually threatened to knock him overboard."

"A very curious threat for a young lady to make," mutters Stella with pale lips, yet blazing eyes.

"Yes, my cousin was—I mean, is a very extraordinary girl."

"And she has made you very much her confidant," remarks Mrs. Lovejoy, eager to get more information, yet dreading what she may hear. Then she says suddenly, "Oh! perhaps she was also interested in you."

"I never tell tales," remarks Lawrence in the easy vanity of his new-found manhood; "but why ask me of other women? At present, I remember only——"

"Who?"—says the widow impulsively; for she knows that at present she is in a very becoming position in her lazy chair with a most alluring glimpse of arm and a very slight but catchy peep of ankle in view. Upon this Mr. Talbot,—who from the knowledge bequeathed him of her sex by the late Miss Travers, understands very well how to woo and win women,—rises from his seat, walks deliberately over to the fascinating, knock-every-thing-else-out-of-your-head picture before him, and is about to whisper, "YOU."

But at this moment, the fair Stella gives a sudden start, and cries: "No, don't answer that question"—though her eyes droop under the ardent glances of young Mr. Wild Oats.

"If not now, very soon," he murmurs. Then he says laughingly, "Why didn't you let me answer you?"

"Because I saw a naughty boy's eyes were full

of nonsense!" answers Stella rising and tapping him with playful fan. " Now we must have lunch. Will you escort me to the dining-room?" As she says this Lawrence Talbot sees a sight that makes him start. From the selfsame balcony upon which Lilly Travers suffered but six weeks before Doctor Freddie stands and glares at him with jealous anguish; and mocking laughter comes to Talbot's lips.

"You seem very merry!" remarks Mrs. Lovejoy.

" Have I not cause to be ! " cries Lawrence signifi-cantly, and feeling very proud at having the prettiest woman in the hotel to sit opposite him he takes her to lunch to make other men jealous, especially Doctor Frederick. This gentleman shortly enters the dining-room, slight and insult in his soul and hate and rage in his heart for this young popinjay who steps so easily between the medical Adonis and the woman he regarded as already conquered.

As for Lawrence, unheeding the lowering glances which the unfortunate Cassadene gives him from a neighboring table, he vivaciously and carelessly chats over his meal with the pretty widow, thought-less of how his words about Miss Travers' trip upon the Ocklawaha may yet be brought back to him by a man who hates him; careless, though he dearly loves Bessie, yet will, after the manner of his sex, scent forbidden fruit, the perfume of which is sweet unto his nostrils.

Lunch being finished, he proffers his escort to Mrs. Lovejoy for a drive to the base-ball grounds, near the railway station, where two professional clubs from great Northern cities are getting into early spring training. Here they meet a number of other people from the Ponce de Leon, and Lawrence makes new acquaintances and, generally, has a very pleasant time; for somehow or other, the report has got about that he is a very rich young gentleman, and the eyes of the fair are generally kind to the petted ones of fortune.

So going home from a pleasant afternoon, after a very lingering hand-shake, bestowed upon Stella at parting, and making some future engagements with the widow who has very kind and languishing eyes for the "naughty boy" as she has got to calling him, he passes Doctor Frederick Cassadene. To his polite nod this gentleman replies in a surly, bull-dog sort of way, and as Lawrence passes on suddenly mutters to himself, "Where have I seen that 'popinjay before? It was some out-of-the-way place!" and goes to thinking of the matter with all the energy of jealous hate.

As for Talbot he steps elated to the Cordova, to find a little note waiting for him, and curiously enough recognizes the handwriting, though Lawrence Talbot has never seen it before. A little whistling: "Didn't I tell you?" and opening it, he finds inside the envelope the following:

"Miss Horton presents her compliments to Mr. Talbot, and asks him if he can spare the time this evening to call upon Miss Constantia Oglethorpe at Sunny Grove, as that lady is anxious to learn the last news that he has of Miss Lilly Travers, as she is greatly concerned at her niece's prolonged absence, and failure to communicate with her.

"Miss Horton will herself be, in company with her father, at Sunny Grove, where Mr. Talbot can present his letter of introduction to her, which she is sorry to see he failed to bring her, as he promised last evening."

Upon reading this, Lawrence's eyes become

bright with triumph. He ejaculates : " I have her ! She can struggle—but I have her !" and hurrying through his dinner makes a wondrously elaborate toilet for the benefit of old Miss Constantia Oglethorpe.

Thus, attired and embellished, this young sprig of fashion about eight o'clock in the evening strolls up the well-known walk that leads to his aunt's house— to receive a pang from conscience. He has not thought much, in the excitement of his adventures, of the sorrow that Lilly Travers' disappearance will bring upon those who loved her best. But now this is to be brought home to him.

Forcing himself to remember who he is and to forget what he has been, Mr. Talbot succeeds in preventing himself from walking in unannounced and giving Miss Connie the affectionate salutation that Lilly was wont to bestow upon her dear old relative.

He rings the bell and is shown into the parlor by the brown Malvina, who tells him that Miss Oglethorpe will be down in a minute, and leaves him sitting in the very room in which six weeks before his marvellous change had been foreshadowed by old Hauser's narrative. There it is—the little ebony casket—open as Lilly left it. He gazes at it in a benumbed, dazed sort of way, for the memories it brings to him would appall an older man.

This reverie is suddenly broken in upon by Miss Bessie's voice in the hall. That young lady who has just come in with her father, is saying : "Very well, papa ; if you have business in town this evening, you may leave me here and come back for me ;—only, don't let your phosphate negotiations keep your little Bessie out too late."

A moment after the front door is closed by the major's retreating hand and the veranda echoes with his departing footsteps, while Miss Bessie turns to the servant and remarks : " Malvina, tell Miss Connie I am in the parlor ; " and walking in, is surprised to find Mr. Lawrence Talbot, who has risen with expectant pleasure on his face.

" Ah ! you have come. How good of you ! " says the young lady, who has apparently made up her mind to forget her anger of the night before. She smiles sweetly upon him and continues : " I hope you have left your advice behind, but brought your letter of introduction. You might have driven out to have delivered it to-day as promised ;—but I hear there are very beautiful widows at the Ponce de Leon "—which shows that somehow she has learnt of how Lawrence has passed his day ; this town of St. Augustine being rather small and gossip travelling very rapidly about it.

" Do you think your reception of me last evening warranted my bringing you this letter to-day ? " remarks Lawrence, passing over the document in question.

" My reception of *you* was all you could ask," laughs Bessie ; " but my reception of your advice " —here she pouts a little,—" my reception of *all* advice is generally unsatisfactory to those who give it. You will shortly discover that, Mr. Lawrence."

Then, opening the epistle from Miss Travers, Bessie has no more eyes for anything else. This pleases Lawrence who sapiently thinks, " Is not love for Lilly—love for me!"

But here Miss Connie comes in to welcome him very cordially, and say : "I am delighted to see you, Lawrence—you will pardon an old woman calling you that, because I understand from Bessie you are a cousin of Lilly's, though she never mentioned your name to me."

" A distant one," murmurs the young gentleman looking with very kindly eyes upon his aunt and fighting down a sudden impulse to seize the dear lady in his arms and give her one of Lilly Travers' old-time kisses.

" And yet," goes on Miss Connie musingly, " as I look in your face, I know you must be some relative of Lilly's. Why! you are as much like her as man can be like woman."

A minute after Lawrence making some unconscious movement, she mutters : " Lilly's very gesture! and—and—I have not heard from her for three weeks," and tears come into the dear old lady's eyes and produce pangs of conscience in the prodigal, for whose return the fatted calf would be killed did his relative but recognize him.

Then Constantia goes on eagerly to question Lawrence about what he knows of her niece's latest movements, and some of her queries are more pertinent than she imagines and give the young reprobate pangs while answering them ; for they run like this: Does Lawrence know when Lilly will return to St. Augustine? Did her niece appear well when he last saw her? That Lilly seemed to have something on her mind when she went away, and Miss Connie hopes that is all over. Then she whispers: "As her cousin perhaps you are already her confidant. Did she say anything to you when you last met her about Doctor Cassadene?"

"Oh! on that point," remarks Lawrence easily, happy to be able to remove Connie's fears, "I can assure you she cares no more for Doctor Fred than I do,—which is very little."

"But where do you think she is now?" queries Constantia anxiously.

"She came to Florida some three weeks ago. She should not be—very far—from here," murmurs the transformed one, struggling with a blush.

"Well, I have always said she went to Cuba. That is the latest travelling fad," remarks Miss Connie. "Though Bessie says she would have surely visited us had she come within a hundred miles of St. Augustine!"

"But I know she was here," cries Talbot impulsively. "I am almost certain she took the Ocklawaha trip about that time."

"Indeed?" returns Miss Connie. "I shall write to the officers of that line of steamers in Palatka to-night;"—which she does this very evening, to receive an answer some time after which produces more effect on the young gentleman who is talking to her than he at present imagines.

But at this moment they are startled by Bessie Horton. That young lady having finished a second perusal of the letter of introduction, suddenly hands it to Miss Oglethorpe crying: "Connie, read it yourself. Every letter that girl has written to me since she left for New York has had a meaning between

the lines. Tell me—does not this say 'Adieu' to
me? It does not put it in so many words, but I feel
'good-by' as I read it. What has become of Lilly?"

"Well," says Constantia, looking over the letter,
"I do not see anything in it but a plain note intro-
ducing a young gentleman"—here she looks at Lawrence and laughs—"whom Lilly recommends very
highly and seems to want to put before you as a
very desirable beau and perhaps as a——"

"You needn't continue," interrupts Bessie with
sudden blush. "You read between the lines very
differently to what I do!"

Then they fall into a general conversation which
lasts but a short half-hour, being broken in upon
by the return of the major, who has not found
the phosphate speculators that he expected to meet.
And Miss Connie, devoting herself to the ex-Confederate, leaves Lawrence free to make himself agreeable to the major's daughter. So the two wander
out on the veranda together, into the light of a new
moon—a different one to that which shone upon
Lilly Travers and Bessie Horton one night in the
same spot, not two months ago.

Then anxious to put off the look of anxiety that
is upon his sweetheart's face (as this rapid young
gentleman has got again to calling Miss Bessie in his
mind) he remarks: "Don't you think you are a little
morbid in your views about Lilly?"

"If you love her as I do, you would be as anxious
for her as I am," says Bessie. Then she continues
suddenly: "And I suppose you love her very much,"
and a moment after smiles uneasily and inquires:
"How much?"

"About as much as I do myself," answers Lawrence, the earnestness of truth in his voice.   This
reply gains him Miss Bessie's good graces.

She says hurriedly: "Ah, you love her *almost* as
much as I do!" and after this the conversation is
very pleasant, and some of the old look with which
she regarded Lilly Travers in the two days before
that young lady departed from St. Augustine,
seems to come into the girl's eyes.   After a little
she gets to telling Lawrence anecdotes about herself and Lilly and about the night the two girls
had spent together in the rooms up-stairs, where
Lilly dinged into her ears all evening—the name
of a young man—as she made her pack her
trunks.

"Yes, I know," answers Lawrence, recollection
making his eyes bright and his heart beat fast.

Whereupon the young lady looks at him in astonishment for a moment, and then says: "Lilly
Travers must think a great deal of you.   She told
you everything—even that last unfortunate remark
I made about you.   But we won't think about that;
we'll forget it!"   Then she cries imperiously, "You
must try to make me forget it!"

"I will," says Lawrence gallantly, and he keeps
his promise so well that their *tête-à-tête* is only
broken by the major calling out in paternal chaff:
"Come in, Bess; it's eleven o'clock. I must take
you home from your beau."

"Oh, don't mind what papa says!" whispers Bessie with a blush.   "He thinks every young man that
talks to me adores me, and sometimes makes fearful
mistakes."

To this, Lawrence answers with intention : " He seems more discerning than his daughter."

" Oh, if you are going to talk to me in that way," says Bessie, " it *is* time for me to go ; " and she passes into the parlor, pausing at the open window, to toss over her pretty shoulder a glance that shows she is not very angry at the gentleman she is leaving.

Driving home that evening, she remarks to her father : " I wonder if the young men were as nice when you were a boy, papa ? "

" Much finer," replies the major decidedly. " In my day the bucks and blades would fight for a woman as well as love one." Here the veteran chuckles to himself and continues : " Young Talbot seems to have made a very favorable impression on my little Bessie ; " and gives her ear such a playful pinch that little Bessie gives a playful little squeal.

As for the young gentleman spoken of, he bids Miss Connie an extraordinarily tender farewell for one who has known her an hour or two, for he says to his aunt : " Do you know what I am going to do ? "

" No," remarks that lady, somewhat astonished at the affection in his glance.

" I am going to give you a kiss, and I am going to adopt you as my aunt—for Lilly's sake," and does so though Miss Connie is astounded.

She has a very tender heart, and something in this young man's demeanor seems to have got very close to it, and she mutters, returning his salute : " You have so many little tom-boy ways that remind me of Lilly, my dear, that I adopt you as my nephew."

So he goes away, murmuring to himself: " The nephew will try to make up the loss of the niece," and gets home to the Cordova in a very happy state.

Here he is greeted effusively by his man Jack. That sable worthy says : " Yo' did yo'self proud to-day Mr. Lil—I mean Lawrence. Yo' skooped in de widder from de doc, I seed yo'. I'm doin' a leetle myself; I'se caught Gus's new gal—Antoinette of de Alcazar—Gus'ld like to razor me, he would.—And by de way, Massa Lawrence, I'se been making queries about heah, and twenty dollars a month may be good wages for a maid but fifty's 'bout de figure for a gen'man's body-servant. I rather cal'late my wages has been riz by act of Pro'dence, Massa Lawrence."

" Yes—I rather think they have ! " assents Talbot. —Then he says suddenly, " But keep the act of Providence to yourself for heaven's sake ! " and so goes to bed.

The next day Lawrence finds his way to the orange groves on the San Sebastian, and passes a very pleasant afternoon with Miss Horton. Where he must have done some good for himself, as the girl's eyes look very tenderly after him as he drives away.

So the days run on, Lawrence struggling to gain her heart and forgetting everything but Bessie's smiles.

But devoting himself too closely to his work he wounds some others. First young Mr. Wilkes whom he succeeds in ousting from his sweetheart's mind, orange groves and all : and second Mrs. Lovejoy, who is not accustomed to being neglected by gentlemen and takes his defection in very bad part, though she is kindness itself whenever she chances to meet Mr. Talbot. Thus time goes on till one spring day brings first the great joy of life to Lawrence Talbot, and afterwards—concern, anxiety and perhaps terror.

It is an afternoon when his happiness comes to him. Miss Bessie and he have by an accident that takes place quite frequently, happened to drop in upon Miss Constantia about the same time, and that lady having said to them with a meaning smile, " You young people go and amuse yourselves," the two have wandered off through the grounds to the shores of Matanzas Inlet, and are there amusing themselves in the childish sport of teasing the unfortunate little fiddler crabs of this region, which infest in myriads the vicinity of the inlet.

Bessie is making a very pretty and exciting picture, as, with dress gathered up in one hand and Mr. Talbot's dude cane in the other, she prevents the retreat of these hideous little creatures to their holes of refuge in the neighboring sand. Mr. Talbot in the easy manner of his sex is enjoying her vivacious exclamations rather languidly, enveloped in the smoke of a cigar in which Miss Bessie has given him permission to indulge.

The girl in the excitement of the chase has ungloved her hands and is at present maliciously filling up the hole of an unfortunate " fiddler " towards which its owner is travelling with the speed of despair ; when suddenly she gives a little startled " Oh !—Oh goodness ! " and grows pale, and Lawrence coming to her says : " What's the matter ? "

" Oh, my goodness ! "

" What's the matter—*darling ?* "

" Oh, gracious! I've lost the ring Lilly gave me down that horrid fiddler's hole."

" Never mind," says Mr. Talbot grandiloquently, " I'll get you another."

" Get me the *same !* " implores Bessie, " Lilly would never forgive me, if I lost it. She will be coming some day, to cry ' Bess, where is that ring?' " and tears of appeal come into the blue eyes. Then Miss Horton suddenly ejaculates : " Look out ! they'll bite you." For Lawrence has pulled up his coat sleeve and is digging with his hand into the den of the fiddlers.

" Pooh ! " remarks that young gentleman ; " they are more afraid of me than I am of them ; " and after a little excavating with his cane in the sand and groping around in the hole with his finger, he finally brings out two fiddlers and the ring ; the fiddlers very much the worse for wear and the ring as good as new, as he laughingly remarks.

" Oh, thank you," says Bessie in an excited way. " How brave you are, to put your hand among those awful things."

" I am delighted to be able to restore the ring," says Lawrence, taking her hand. " How did you come to lose it ? "

" Well, Lilly didn't seem to have the right measure. Her second finger was the same size as my big finger, and I suppose she selected it by her own, and made some mistake."

Of this statement Lawrence has no doubt, for he remembers that Lilly Travers' hand had grown very rapidly just before sending the present, and easily

sees how it could be much too large for the little
fingers he still holds very tight.

He says : " I am sorry the ring is too large," then
goes on very seriously, " Let me fit this finger,"
selecting the engagement one, " with a ring that I
hope will be exactly the right size ? " and his face
grows pale, while hers becomes very red.

" I—I couldn't take a present from you," mutters
Bessie, who loves beautiful things, though her self-
respect prompts her to refuse this one, " unless I
asked Papa."

" Very well," says Talbot brightly ; " we'll ask
Papa together : " his arm going around a lithe graceful
waist that thrills under his clasp, as Bessie droops
her head and murmurs : " Ask Papa !—*what ?* "

" Ask Papa, WHAT ? " echoes Lawrence indignantly
(for he mistakes maiden bashfulness for maiden
idiocy)—" ask Papa for his daughter of course !
Tell Papa that I am dying to marry the sweetest—
dearest—doviest—darling—girl—in the world ! "

Each of these assertions, Mr. Lawrence who has
inherited from the late Miss Travers a very deft
knowledge of her sex, emphasizes quite tenderly
and very beautifully and carries his suit on in such
a vigorous manner that when he brings the young
lady, under his charge, back to Miss Oglethorpe's
house, he says : " Aunt Connie, don't look at
Bessie ; she's very much embarrassed, she has just
become engaged. This is her first engagement,
and she is not accustomed to it." Then he goes
up to the girl and whispers, almost tremblingly :
" *Is* it the first engagement, Bessie ? "

And Bessie answers humbly : " *No !* "

14

"You have been engaged before," gasps Lawrence, growing pale.

"Yes!"

"My God!"

"When I was ten; that is the only time," mutters Miss Horton. "Little Willie Johnson said I was to marry him, but he didn't give me any ring." Then Bessie commences to laugh, and says: "What makes you so jealous, you foolish fellow;" and continues eagerly: "Have *you* ever been engaged?"

"Never to a woman!" stammers Lawrence.

"Well, then, you may commence with me," says Bessie archly.

So the two turn again to Miss Connie, who has been enjoying a distant view of this scene, and Lawrence remarks: "I will leave her in your hands. Her father will come for her soon. I believe there are rings in jewellers' stores in St. Augustine, but none worthy of her. Bessie, would you like to wait until I can go to New York for it?"

"No; give me a moss agate, but don't go away!" answers Bess anxiously.

Then they walk down to the gate together, where Lawrence entraps his sweetheart by asking: "When will you go to church with me?"

"Next Sunday, with pleasure."

"Done!" cries the boy.

"Oh! not to get married!" screams Bessie. "I—I don't mean that." And looking at him with maiden dignity she says: "Certainly not until you receive my father's consent, Mr. Talbot. Besides—Lawrence, I am going to wait until Lilly can be my bridesmaid."

This brings dismay upon him and he cries eagerly:

"Wait till then! Miss Travers may be—in Europe ; may be dead."—Then he mutters "Oh, no ; I don't mean that. I don't mean that," for tears have come into Bessie's eyes at his thoughtless suggestion.

To this the young lady after smuggling away the dewdrops from her eyelids whispers, as if struck by a sudden idea : " Lilly told you everything. What made you such great friends ?" and a little blush of jealousy comes on her cheek.

But not to remain, for Lawrence says solemnly: " YOU ! She always told me you were the girl I must marry."

" Why, that is what she insinuated to me very frequently. That makes the reason greater that we should wait until she can be my bridesmaid."

These words make Lawrence ponder as he goes to his hotel, after a parting that puts him into the seventh heaven.

He meditates on this clog to his happiness over his dinner and then suddenly thinks he'll go and ask Major Horton for his daughter—that will give him another interview with Miss Bessie who must be at home by this time. Thus resolved he drives rapidly up the San Sebastian road immediately after dinner, to receive another sensation.

He is greeted by the major on the door-step of his house : who says, in a very solemn voice, " Lawrence, come this way."

" Bessie has told you ? " gasps the youth growing frightened.

" That you want to marry her? Certainly—my daughter has no secrets from her father ! "—remarks the ex-Confederate confidently. Then he goes on

"Show me that you are able to take care of her, and as you are a relative of Miss Travers I shall be happy to consider your proposal.

"Very well," assents Lawrence. "A letter from my bankers will convince you that I am worth considerably over a million dollars!"

"Wheugh!" This is a surprised but joyous whistle from the future father-in-law.

"I know," the young man mutters impulsively, "that a million dollars is little enough for such a young lady as Miss Bessie."

"Yes; she'll agree with you on that," remarks the major dryly. "But, still, you must do the best you can on a million. It's very hard, but you must fight your battle on the line of a million," and the vendor of phosphate lands chuckles to himself quite cheerily.

"Very well," cries Lawrence enthusiastically; "I'll tell her."

But to his astonishment, the old gentleman stops him, saying: "Not now!" in solemn voice. "Do not speak of your wedding now. At present she is too heart-broken."

"Too heart-broken?"

"Yes—over the news," adds the major. "You haven't heard? Miss Connie has just received information——"

"Of what?" gasps Lawrence, some undefined anxiety coming to him.

"Of Lilly Travers."

And before he can reply to this, Bessie has come out of the house and is sobbing in his arms, "Lawrence, Lilly is dead!"

" Dead? Impossible," he cries. " I know she is alive."

" No, you are mistaken; Lilly is dead. The Ocklawaha steamboat people have just sent Miss Connie a dress picked up in the river and she has recognized it as one of Lilly's. You remember— you said she had taken the Ocklawaha trip. She must have been swept off unnoticed by some branch from an overhanging tree, in the darkness."

" You say they found the dress," asks Lawrence meditatively. Then he says eagerly and confidently : " Did they find the body in it ? "

" Oh ! " cries Bessie, with open eyes ; " I never thought of that."

And the major adds approvingly : " Young man, when Bessie has spent your million for you, you had better go into the detective business."

" I will," returns Lawrence. " But first I will prove to you that Lilly Travers is alive."

" Do that," says Bessie, joy drying up her tears and making her eyes flash, " and I'll——"

" Marry me ? " interrupts Lawrence with even greater enthusiasm.

" Yes ! " answers the girl.

" Without Lilly as bridesmaid ? "

" Without anything save a minister and a ring and—a father ! "

" Very well," cries Lawrence in happy voice ; " I take you at your word.—But don't cry ".—for the girl is sobbing on his shoulder. " Don't. Lilly Travers is alive !—I'll prove it ! " for into this young gentleman's head has suddenly come what to his inexperience seems an idea worthy of a Solomon.

CHAPTER XVI.

DOCTOR FREDDIE PLAYS THE VIRTUOUS DETECTIVE.

IMPRESSED with the brilliancy of the novel scheme that has sprung into his brain, Mr. Lawrence continues his conversation with his fiancée; her father having wisely left them to themselves; and obtains from his sweetheart the following additional information: that not only Lilly's gown has been discovered in the Ocklawaha, but also the dress of her maid Jane.

" That adds to the mystery," remarks Miss Bessie.

" Not at all; it elucidates it. The chances are altogether against Miss Travers and her maid having both been swept off the upper deck of the boat by the same cypress branch at the same moment. I presume the gown would hardly be considered valuable," he remarks. " It was rather old, wasn't it?"

" Oh," replies Bessie, " about the poorest one I imagine Lilly had."

" Very well; she probably thought the Ocklawaha River was a good old-clothes basket and tossed it overboard before she left the boat. However," he continues, " I am positive no accident has happened to Miss Travers, and will very shortly obtain a communication from her to that effect."

" It seems to me you can do everything," murmurs Bessie in first-love admiration.

" I can do this—as soon as I can obtain Lilly's address from her lawyers or bankers;—which I will do

the day after to-morrow in New York," returns Mr.
Talbot stoutly.

"rit, New York? You are going to leave me?"
cries the girl making a sorry face.

"Yes!"

"Oh!" There is a choking in Bessie's little
throat.

"But in five days I will return," answers Lawrence
reassuringly. "During my absence I must make
the necessary financial arrangements for our marriage, so that I will be free to take you for a long
trip to Europe. You would like to spend the summer there, darling?" he adds inquiringly.

"Wouldn't I?" replies Bessie, her eyes blazing at
the thought of making the great trans-Atlantic ferry
trip ; "that is, if Papa will let me go."

"I will persuade him," says Lawrence confidently.

Then after a tender parting—for Miss Bessie, having promised to marry him, now makes no further
concealment of her devotion for this rapid wooer—
he departs suggesting that the young lady soothe
Miss Connie's fears as soon as possible, for Lawrence
cannot bear the thought of looking on his dear
aunt's grief, that he could assuage in an instant but
at awful sacrifice. At the Cordova, not finding his
man Jack at his rooms, he goes to packing on his
own account. He is interrupted, in his occupation,
by the entrance of his worthy, who comes in in a
state of tremendous excitement.

"Golly!" he says, his eyes and teeth both gleaming very white—"Mr. Lawrence, does yo' kno'
dar's a repo't 'roun' town dat we's bof dead?"

"We're both dead?" echoes Lawrence in sudden interest.

"Yessah; dey has it 'round at de Ponce dat lly Travers an' Jane Rouser has bof been drownded in de Ocklawaha.   Gus, de secon' man at de Ponce de Leon, tole me all 'bout my death.   He was cryin' ovah me—my 'lobed mem'ry' he said—whaugh! whaugh! whaugh!"   And the valet goes into a hideous guffaw at the tenderness displayed by his old adorer.

"My Heaven! you didn't say anything to Gus?" cries Lawrence suspiciously.

"No, sah; I was laughin' so I couldn't speak, sah; an' Gus he call me an unsympathetic scal'wag, sah!"

"Very well," says his master; "keep a quiet tongue between your white teeth and finish packing our trunks.   We leave here to-morrow."

Relinquishing this duty to his man, Mr. Talbot strides out of the hotel, and lighting a cigar sits in the plaza and listens to the fountain and meditates upon his future course.   He thinks what a wonderfully brilliant mind he has for one so young; for this sudden idea has come to him: he will go to New York and first make everything certain with regard to his fortune by removing all the securities deposited by Lilly Travers in the safe deposit company's box she had engaged.   This he considers, and very rightly, may save trouble, as rumors of Miss Travers' death coming to her relatives, some investigation might be made of her estate, which would perhaps disclose the locality of her strong box and place serious obstacles, both legal and otherwise, to his obtaining possession of the bonds that are to furnish support to himself and his charming bride. Immediately after this, from New York he will mail a letter, written in his very best imitation of the late Miss Travers' feminine style and hand, to Miss Constantia Oglethorpe, informing that lady that her niece is well and happy and of her intended immediate departure for Europe.

This he fondly expects will eliminate any idea from his aunt's mind of her beloved niece being out of the world and pave the way to his nuptials with his charming sweetheart, which he determines shall take place before the end of the Florida season, if possible.

The details of these transactions having been settled to his own satisfaction, he goes back to his room in the Cordova, to find his trunks already locked and strapped, and to think that his man Jack is turning out a better valet than he had at first supposed to be possible.

So the next morning, after liquidating his bill, he drives to the " Florida Special " in company with his man, to receive a most charming and delightful surprise from his little fiancée, for that young lady, in company with her father, is waiting for him at the depot. His parting from her makes him curiously happy, as she, in the sorrow of losing him for a little while, promises that the next time this train runs out for the North with Lawrence Talbot, he shall take her with him as his very own—his bride.

The sun shines brightly as the train moves out of the station, and Mr. Talbot is exceedingly content, and thinks the world before him is now very easy, and does not know at this careless and happy

moment that both he and his man Jack are wearing
the two identical suits of clothes in which they departed from the boat on the Ocklawaha River, some
three weeks before, and that Dr. Freddie Cassadene,
having incidentally come to bid adieu to a lady
patient to whom he wishes to show particular attention, has put his eye upon these two same suits of
clothes and has suddenly said to himself: "Jove!
I know where I first saw Lawrence Talbot.—He and
his man left the boat at Orange Spring Landing that
night on the Ocklawaha—the night Lilly Travers
disappeared—the night she perhaps was drowned!"
For the rumor of Miss Travers' fate has travelled
pretty quickly about the town and has reached Doctor Fred's ears.

So this medical gentleman goes to turning this
matter of Lawrence Talbot leaving the boat the
night his cousin Lilly Travers disappeared, and some
curious diagnosis of the case of the missing heiress
coming into his mind, he writes a letter to the
Ocklawaha boat company, the answer to which
leads him in the course of time to an extraordinary
conclusion.

Thoughtless of any links he may be weaving to
connect himself with his earlier self, Lawrence Talbot arrives in New York, taking up his residence at
a hotel, and the next day, giving the pass-word, "My
turn next," and signing his name in the books of
the Central Safe Deposit Company, turns the combination in the lock of the private box left open to
him by the bounteous hand of Lilly Travers and
proceeds to make himself the possessor of the wealth
that young lady had deposited.

This in the course of the day he transfers to another box engaged in his own name in another safe deposit company; and these securities being deposited for his own special use and benefit, he remarks to himself: " If Lilly Travers comes to life now, she will be a very poor girl ; in building up my own fortune I have wrecked hers."

A small portion of these bonds, however, he sells and opens an account in a well-known bank, leaving with them a thumping big balance for future emergencies and the wedding trip that is now growing gradually nearer and more certain.

Then he turns his attention to Miss Lilly Travers' affairs, and indites a letter in that young lady's handwriting to Miss Connie in St. Augustine, Lilly stating that she has heard from Mr. Talbot the anxiety felt for her by her relative, and writes to reassure her. That her maid Jane has confessed to her that she tossed the garments over from the Ocklawaha boat that night in her careless negro way to avoid the trouble of carrying the worn-out things along. Miss Lilly further states that she is going to Europe for an extended tour and may perhaps even visit Egypt and India and return via Japan and San Francisco ; consequently, her aunt is to put all anxiety out of her head regarding her.

This letter Mr. Talbot himself posts in New York, and then an emotional idea coming into his head— that poor Bessie will feel slighted if Lilly does not write to her—he chuckles to himself at the thought, and sends a very gushing girl's letter, also in Miss Travers' handwriting and bearing Lilly's signature, to his sweetheart, giving a very good recommendation to himself and congratulating Bessie upon the fine fellow she is going to get as a husband; stating that Miss Travers cannot be present at the wedding, on account of her immediate departure for Europe, but that she sends through Lawrence a present that will show her love for " dearest Bessie " and " dear Lawrence," whom she hopes to meet in Europe very shortly.

Looking over this, Mr. Talbot thinks he has perpetrated a very sweet, practical joke upon his fiancée, and sealing it hands it to his man John to post; for inspired with the delights that New York offers to a wandering bachelor, he is anxious to go to dinner with one or two gilded youths erstwhile adorers of Lilly Travers whose re-acquaintance he has made by letters of introduction to which he has also attached Lilly Travers' signature, this youthful penman seeming like most other forgers to glory in his art.

In company with these young gentlemen he has a very astonishing and enjoyable and perhaps wild evening, for he sees New York by gas-light for the first time from the standpoint of a man of wealth and fashion and it appears to him a very beautiful though a wondrously wicked city: and leaves his companions vastly delighted that he has never married one of them.

The next morning finds him on a south-bound train, with a very handsome present he has bought at Tiffany's to give in the name of Lilly to his sweetheart, and an engagement ring that he fondly thinks will make Bessie open her dear blue eyes.

So on the evening of the fifth day from his de-

parture, Mr. Lawrence Talbot, accompanied by his
man John Robbins, arrives once more in St. Augustine, to encounter more exciting adventures than
ever dreamed of in his philosophy; to learn that a
man's life may be more free and easy than a woman's,
but that it has dangers and anxieties such as seldom
come to the other sex to make it bald.

These troubles do not come upon him immediately. The first few days of his return are very
rosy ones. Miss Connie has received her letter, and
relieved of all anxiety about the fate of her beloved
niece, thinks only of furthering the happiness of the
young gentleman who journeyed all the way to New
York, to bring back peace to her mind.

Seconded by this lady, in the course of a few days,
Lawrence, though slightly opposed by the major,
who thinks it would not be complimentary to Bessie,
to let her go *very* easily, succeeds in getting his
sweetheart to mention the day upon which she will
make him her husband, without the assistance of the
absent Lilly, as bridesmaid. Upon which Mr. Talbot gives her the present he has brought with him,
purporting to have been sent by Miss Travers, and
is very much astonished, and perhaps somewhat dismayed, to find that the artful letter he had forged
to Miss Bessie has not yet arrived from New York.

"You are sure you didn't get it?" he asks anxiously.

"Certainly!" answers the girl. "You are positive
she sent it?"

"Yes—she told me she did—in fact, I saw her
write it," mutters this young man, who has got to
chuckling at his own prevarications.

But at the same time, the non-arrival of Miss Bessie's letter gives him an indefinable fear, and remembering he had intrusted its posting to his dusky valet, he very shortly interviews that sable gentleman on the subject.

"Robbins!" he says, assuming his most dignified and severe air. "I gave you a letter in New York to post. What did you do with it?"

"Posted it, sah!"

"No, you didn't!" cries Lawrence angrily.

"'Deed I did, sah. I remember de box on Sixth Abenue. Dey was havin' a dog fight at de time, in de neighb'hood—" but here Jack suddenly knows that he is lying, and remembers that in the excitement of the dog fight he had forgotten to post the letter, though he keeps on asserting: "'Clare to goodness, I did, sah! I posted dat letter, sah!" and makes this assertion so often that Lawrence thinks it must be some error in the mail service that has produced this *contretemps*.

This is apparently borne out by the fact that next day Miss Bessie, coming down the walk to meet him, in all the beauties of white muslin, brilliant ribbon-sash, and pretty slippers, waves a letter jubilantly and cries: "Lawrence, you were right! Here's Lilly's letter written in her own dear hand. She didn't forget me quite as much as I had imagined!"

To this her lover returns conceitedly: "Didn't I tell you!" and is quite contented over the matter.

He would perhaps be somewhat less easy were he cognizant that his man Jack, with the best intentions in the world, has found the unposted envelope in his coat pocket, and desirous of rectifying his error, has walked down to the Cordova letter box, and not being well up in the postal service of the hotel, has asked Doctor Cassadene, who is lounging near, the proper way of disposing of the epistle. That gentleman, glancing at the envelope, has recognized the well-known writing of his lost fiancée, as he reads the address, and after showing Jack the letter box in which to deposit it, has asked excitedly, " So, Miss Travers is in town—after all ! "

" No, sah ! " gasps Jack.

" Why, she must be here ! That letter is from her."

" No, sah ! I got de letter in New York. Mr. Talbot gave me dat letter in New York, to post. I forgot to put it in, sah."

" Well then, Miss Travers is in New York."

" Certainly, sah ! Miss Lilly Travers in New York. —Saw her maid Jane der, sah—de Hotel Buckin'ham, sah. Mr. Talbot told me Miss Travers is gone to Europe." And having settled this matter in his easy darkey way, Jack Robbins, nee Jane Rouser, departs up-stairs, chuckling to himself triumphantly : " Reckon I had dat damn Doctor ! "

He does not say anything about this, however, to his master, thinking perhaps that it is just as well not to confess he had forgotten to post the letter in New York.

And to this thing being added other information that Doctor Frederick now receives from the Ocklawaha boat company ; this gentleman's eyes open very wide, as he says to himself : " Can it be ? The infernal scoundrel ! " A moment after he mutters, " Pshaw ! Impossible ! What motive ! " But still goes on thinking and putting two and two together and finally writes to the Buckingham Hotel, New York, and also to the firm who had been Miss Travers' lawyers.

And an incident that occurs shortly thereafter, adds newer, stronger, and more deadly hate to the stock of malice and malignity that Doctor Fred has on hand for Mr. Lawrence Talbot. This comes about, as usual, through a woman.

Mrs. Stella Lovejoy is not accustomed to being deserted by gentlemen, and resents defection in the ranks of her adorers as a personal slight. And though Mr. Talbot has made no deep impression upon her heart, and she loves the Doctor much better than her "naughty boy" as she calls Lawrence, partly in sarcasm, partly in affection, still the rumor that now floats about St. Augustine, that Bessie Horton has captured this handsome and rich young springald, makes her clench her beautiful hands, and swear she will get him back again, and make him love her, just to have the pleasure of saying "No" to him, and do another of her "great refusal acts" —a scene in which by force of habit she is past mistress.

She has always been pleasant to Mr. Talbot, even in the moments of her chagrin at what she considers his slights, and making it her business she contrives to meet Lawrence on the Alameda one afternoon when he is trying to pass a longish day, his sweetheart and her father being in Jacksonville, Miss Bessie being engaged in gathering up sufficient of a trousseau to take her to Europe; Lawrence having proudly told her he would do the rest in Paris.

At this encounter Mrs. Lovejoy suggests that the

young gentleman shall call upon her that evening, as she expects a few friends for a euchre party, and idleness prompting this careless young man, who has not yet learned enough of beauty to fly from it, he accepts with alacrity her invitation.

So that evening about nine o'clock, sending up his card, he is shown into the parlor of the widow's extensive suite of apartments, where the servant asks him to wait, stating that Mrs. Lovejoy will be with him in a few minutes.

The euchre party apparently have not yet arrived, and Lawrence idles his time away inspecting curios and knicknacks about the room.

While doing so, he hears the servant announce to Doctor Cassadene, who apparently has called in person, that Mrs. Lovejoy is not at home, and with the vanity of very young men smiles and mutters, " I down Freddie every trip. He's not even invited to the euchre party."

The door has hardly closed upon the Doctor's retreat, before Stella proves to him that she is very much at home, by coming in laughingly, and saying, " My party has disappointed me. You are the only one!" Then she adds: "I am glad of it!" with her tenderest smile.

" And I, too!" returns Lawrence, for he is looking upon a beautiful woman, who has made herself even more radiant and dazzling than is her wont, for his undoing, though in the innocence of his heart, Mr. Talbot does not know it. "Your servant said you were not at home, a minute ago," he continues.

" Yes, not at home to anybody but you. I thought as the euchre party had disappointed me,

15

we would have a pleasant evening together," and the widow's eyes grow drooping and tender, and those of Mr. Talbot grow flashing, bold, and daring, for in her costume this evening, Stella Lovejoy has a beauty that is almost not of this earth, but whether of Heaven or of Hades, young Mr. Talbot is too much fascinated to decide. All he knows is that she is marvelously lovely, as she nonchalantly motions him to a chair, and sinks down amid the cushions of a sofa, to make her very prettiest picture, which she does, for this lady is mistress of the art of fascination.

She is in some white, shimmering, glistening robe —part ball dress— part *negligée.* The invention of some Parisian man milliner villain to give women domination over his sex. Her eyes, blue as turquoise, have the varying flashes of opal. Her polished shoulders and bare white arms gleam in the mellow lamplight, and the floating lace about her dress makes it fairy-like, though the rounded outlines it drapes are those of a statue.

" Now, my boy," she says playfully, assuming the rôle of a woman old enough to flirt with this young gentleman, without damage to the hearts of either, " over a cup of tea we can pass a pleasant evening, one of the last I shall spend in Florida ; " and a slight sigh seems to float from her lips, which is echoed by her guest, who seems sad at the thought of her departure.

A moment after she murmurs : " So you must try and make my recollection of it pleasant."

" As you will do to me also," suggests Lawrence meaningly.

As he emphasizes this with his eyes, she rings a bell, and tea being shortly brought in, is poured out by her, in the free and easy manner of an accomplished hostess, and gulped down in a nervous excited way by the youthful Mr. Talbot, who sits with uneasy eyes gazing at the alluring loveliness which has been thrown before him, to make him forget everything in this world, save the beauty of Stella Lovejoy, so that the lady may have the pleasure of hearing him speak some wild words of love, and tell him what a naughty boy he is, just to soothe her vanity —just to show him that all men are as wax before her.

And this dashing, reckless young gentleman, who has had no such experience before in his short existence as a man, seems about to play the rôle expected of him.

His eyes look tenderly upon the gleaming picture before him and grow wilder and wilder and flash more and more fervidly as his Circe plies him with the blandishments her experience has taught her effective with youthful worshippers of her charms. Her eyes seem misty with tenderness, she shows him bashful blushes that enchant him and make him lose his adolescent head.

Each pose she gives him of her lovely self seems more beautiful than the one she moved from—she tantalizes him with her varying graces. Once she seems angry with him and pouts and turns her back upon him, but it is to show the dainty dimples in her shoulders—she laughs because her teeth are pearls, she waves her hands because her arms would make the lost ones of the Medicean Venus, she playfully shows him the step of the last new society fad polka, but it is only that her little feet and adorable ankles in their silk and satin adornments may complete this boy's conquest. And all the time by subtle arts of look and tone and gesture, she says to him " I love you !" though not in words—and he is as tinder ready to blaze up—when she applies the spark.

"Lawrence, play the gallant again !" she cries, " and put my tea-cup away."

He does so—their hands meet—their hands clasp —the tea-cup falls and is broken upon the hearth-stone.

Lawrence's eyes seek hers that droop before his impetuous glances; he hoarsely mutters : " Stella— my God! how beautiful you are ! I—" and in another moment would show his temptress, by some wild cry of passion, that Lawrence Talbot has forgotten the tenderest, dearest little sweetheart upon this earth.

As for the widow, her eyes are triumphant. She feels she has this fluttering, adolescent heart in her grasp. But at this moment, dallying with her power she destroys it.

She whispers coquettishly : " Why, what would Miss Bessie say to this ? " and expects him to answer, " What do I care what she says ! " or other wild words that will give her triumph over the innocent girl whose heart she would sacrifice to her vanity. But with Bessie's name, the charm is broken, the string of passion is snapped.

Mr. Talbot turns deathly pale to his very lips and gasps these astounding words—" She would say I

was an infernal scoundrel—as I am." Then he says
agitatedly: "I—I believe I must go now. I have
had my tea—awfully obliged to you for a pleasant
evening!"

And the girl entering at this moment, to take
away the tea things, he murmurs: "Good-by, Mrs.
Lovejoy. I hope I will see you at my wedding. I
know Bessie would like you to be there," and getting
into the hall, puts his hat on, and leaves Stella
gazing at him too astounded to speak.

As he passes from her apartments into the great
corridor of the hotel, he sees glaring at him Doctor
Frederick Cassadene, whose card has been slighted,
and who has been told but an hour before that Mrs.
Lovejoy was not at home—while she was tête-à-tête
with this favored springald.

"That man will never forgive me!" thinks Lawrence to himself; then shudders: "My Heaven! In
another second I would have lied to her. I would
have told her I loved her. My God! If Bessie
knew this it would break her heart!" So going
to the Cordova, he comes into his room, looks in
the glass, and shakes his fist at the agitated young
gentleman who gazes at him, and says: "Do you
know who's speaking to you, my masher? It's your
mother-in-law Lilly Travers. No more of this, Lawrence Talbot! I see what you'll make unless I put
my hand upon you! You'll be a 'rounder'! A
good for nothing! A 'thoroughbred'! who will
break Bessie's heart—confound you! If you don't
behave yourself I'll give you one of old Hauser's
Obi-seeds and make you into a good little girl again,"
and feels from very force of habit to see if the vial is

hung round his neck in its usual place where it dangles against the " silent Bessie."

Then he becomes meditative, and mutters, " If you can keep your head in the presence of such beauty as you've had thrown at you to-night, I think I may trust you anywhere, my boy!"   Next he laughs to himself : " George !   Wasn't Doctor Fred angry !   I do so love to down 'him!" and thinks no more of the occurrence, because he is very sleepy and tired, and Bessie will be here again the next morning, and he's going to be up early to meet her at the train.

Perhaps he wouldn't sleep so soundly did he know that Dr. Fred, with anguish in soul and battle in his eye, has determined to call him out and shed this favored young gallant's blood upon the field of honor.   For Frederick Cassadene, M.D., who has been doing detective duty for the last few days—but as yet has not proved his theory of Miss Lilly Travers' disappearance, has just said to himself in the privacy of his office these astounding words : " D—n that infernal young pill—if I don't hang him by the law I'll shoot him outside of it !"

CHAPTER XVII.

A DUEL AMONG THE ORANGE TREES.

THESE peculiar remarks have been brought about in the following extraordinary manner.   Cassadene has been investigating Lawrence Talbot's record, ever since he has heard the rumor that Miss Travers may have been drowned in the Ocklawaha, and recognized his rival, and his valet Jack Robbins, as the two men who left the *Okahumpka* that same night at Orange Spring Landing.

Filled with the idea that there was something mysterious in the whole affair, more especially as, after casual inquiry, he has discovered that the supposed missing heiress was a cousin of young Talbot's, he has written to the Ocklawaha Boat Company, and received from them a reply that makes him wrinkle his brow very thoughtfully, for it states that no person by the name of Lawrence Talbot travelled on the *Okahumpka* from Silver Spring on that trip. In fact, that no person by the name of Lawrence Talbot has ever registered upon any of their boats.

Doctor Fred utters a prolonged whistle on receiving this information, and mutters to himself: "The fellow travelled incognito—surreptitiously. Besides, he sneaked off the boat at an inconvenient place on the river, apparently not daring to remain on the steamer till she reached Palatka. Therefore this young man's presence on the boat was for some purpose that he dared not disclose to others—perhaps with some criminal intent. His presence on the steamer may have had something to do with the mysterious disappearance of his cousin on that trip. Though what motive could the young popinjay have had?"

He has said this to himself several times. But upon the knowledge being made public in St. Augustine, that Miss Constantia had received a letter from her niece in New York, Cassadene has put from his mind this suspicion as being impracticable for his purposes of revenge.

Though, seeing the letter addressed in his old sweetheart's handwriting, in the hands of Mr. Tal-bot's servant, it has again revived in his mind, and he has written to New York to the Buckingham Hotel, where Jack had stated Miss Lilly Travers had stopped, for information of that young lady's movements. Furthermore he has also written a let-ter to her New York lawyers, asking for information as to the date of Miss Travers' departure for Europe, knowing that they will answer him, as these gentle-men, he is confident, are aware of Miss Travers' en-gagement to him, and probably she has not taken the trouble to tell them of the affair being broken off.

The answers to these letters have not yet arrived, and at present he is in doubt as to what course he shall take on this point with the young gentleman whom he hates so cordially. But in investigating Lawrence Talbot's record, he has also learned of the young man's visit to Southern Florida, and inciden-tally heard of the remark of his guide, that Lawrence Talbot was the worst " shooter " he had ever seen, and had never hit anything in a three weeks' sport-ing tour, save the air.

This fact coming strongly into his mind on the evening of the last terrible laceration of his vanity and pride as a capturer of women, and more par-ticularly the beautiful widow of the Ponce de Leon, it suddenly occurs to him that he can cover himself with glory and honor, at comparatively little risk to himself, by wiping his irritating rival out of his track by means of the good old-fashioned duello—the cus-tom of which has not yet entirely passed away from Florida. An affair of this kind he fondly thinks will make him quite a hero, and will probably reinstate him thoroughly in the affections of the rich Mrs. Lovejoy, upon whose hand and whose fortune he has determined to make a desperate onset, ever since he suffered the shame of a second refusal from the New York heiress, upon the Ocklawaha boat.

Filled with this idea, the next morning Doctor Freddie proceeds to put his bloodthirsty plan in operation, and as usual in such matters, is very cheerfully aided and abetted by the father of all duels—his Satanic Majesty!

Mr. Talbot, aroused to bolt a hasty breakfast and make a hurried toilet, by his faithful servitor, John, goes to the depot, filled with the hope of again meeting his sweetheart, but finds himself disappointed.

Her father, stepping off the train, greets him very kindly, however, and says: " My boy, you will have to wait till to-morrow. Bessie couldn't get through her shopping as quickly as she expected." Then the ex-Confederate gives a sigh, for he knows his daughter has contrived to spend the value of a good many acres of phosphate land the preceding day in Jacksonville, and he imagines that she will make even a more aggressive attack on his check-book when she has a full swing at the dry goods stores, uncontrolled by his presence and advice.

The absence of his fiancée is not pleasing to Mr. Talbot, who has got desperately anxious for a sight of Bessie's blue eyes, and he mutters several anathemas under his breath, as he and the major drive back to the centre of the town, where that gentleman leaves his future son-in-law, and goes off on business of his own,

So, Lawrence, in rather a huffy temper, wanders into the Ponce de Leon billiard room, thinking he will kill time over the green cloth, and having been quite a feminine expert as Miss Lilly Travers, goes to knocking the balls about in a vicious and reckless, nervous way, waiting for some acquaintance to come in and indulge him in a game. This individual soon makes his appearance, in the person of Mr. Wilkes, the Florida orange grower, who doesn't love Mr. Talbot particularly well himself, but is very willing to win a few dollars from the young man, who, though he played well for a woman, is by no means an expert for a man.

After a little, it chances that Doctor Freddie Cassadene saunters in, his mind full of the purpose that had entered it the night before. So sitting down by the table, with this idea in view, he proceeds to make ill-natured, ill-mannered, and gibing remarks about young Talbot's performances with the cue, laughing at his shots in a boisterous and sneering manner.

To these, after a time, this young gentleman, not being in the best of tempers, replies quite warmly, and with equally well intended witticisms, and finally remarks to the doctor: "Why don't you go upstairs? I don't see what you can enjoy down here. This is the gentleman's department, and the lady's is more in your line." Then he sneers, "Have they all deserted you? Is the big Adonis lonely? Can't he find a single sweetheart on the piazza?"

Which remark makes the Doctor chew his mustache very savagely, for it reminds him of the discomfiture this young puppy, as he dubs him, has

brought upon him, and he thinks Lawrence's insinu-
ations are as so many allusions to that young gentleman's triumph with the flirtatious Stella.

"Look here!" he says grimly, "you'd better keep
your attention on the billiard balls, young man.
You don't seem to play a very good game. But,"
he continues pompously, "you haven't had much
time to learn. I suppose you commenced to play
billiards when you commenced to raise a mustache!"

This witticism at his opponent's expense producing a snicker from young Wilkes, makes Lawrence very angry, for he is extremely touchy as
to his youthful appearance, and particularly as to
his lately cultivated and highly valued mustache, of
which he is very proud, though it is not, to use a
slangy expression, a "marker" to the luxuriant
growth upon the doctor's lip, at which the neophyte has often gazed with envious eyes.

He returns, growing very red in the face, "We
won't discuss my mustache, doctor."

"No, there isn't *much* to discuss," gibes his tormentor.

"If you dare to criticise me personally, I'll make
it a personal matter with you!" says the young ban-
tam, growing very angry.

This the Doctor answers with a jeering "Ha!
ha!" and laughs: "Make it a personal matter with
me! Why, young Mr. Poppycock, you talk as if
you were really a man, and you're as puny as your
mustache!"

Now this slur on the insignia of his new manhood
makes the masculine Mr. Talbot very angry, and
some of his old feminine nature returning, he walks

up to his tormentor and soundly boxes his ears, an accomplishment he has learned as Miss Lilly Travers at a girls' boarding-school.

But the Doctor, having studied in a more masculine seminary, promptly draws back, and leading out from the shoulder, plants his " bunch of fives," after the manner of the prize ring, upon his opponent's " optic," and Mr. Lawrence Talbot, with a faint cry, " goes to grass " on the billiard table.

A moment after, staggering to his feet, very pale, but determined, he whispers : " You miserable bully ! You shall answer to me for this ! "

" In any way you please—" says the doctor eagerly. " Mr. Wilkes here will be my friend ! " A rôle which this gentleman is very anxious to play, and he expresses his willingness, while Lawrence leaving the two, with rage and fury in his heart, goes to his hotel.

Getting into his room, he looks at his eye and finds it a very bad one. Then, curiously enough, he commences to laugh : " Who would have thought it six weeks ago—that my own lovely Fred would have blacked his Lilly's eye ? "

He is engaged in doctoring his wounded optic, when suddenly he gives a groan of despair, and wonders what Bessie will think of all this—and how he can possibly make love—perhaps even be married, with such a fearful swelling on his face, for Doctor Fred has hit very squarely and very hard.

Here his solitude is broken in upon by the major. That gentleman has heard of the occurrence, and has come over to proffer his services, in his old-time Southern way, to his future son-in-law,

" Lawrence, my boy," he says, after hearing his
story, " that blow can only be washed out in blood."

" Yes," cries Lawrence, smarting with pain and
indignation. " He is bigger than I, but that'll make
him a better mark for a pistol."

" Spoken after my own heart ! " the major adds,
" I will step over and arrange matters for you very
quickly, unless this big fellow is white-livered ! "
Which he does, and shortly returning says : " To-
morrow at one o'clock. I have fixed it in the orange
trees behind Miss Connie's house. Nobody will
think we're going to fight there, and we're pretty
certain of not being interrupted."

Then he asks Lawrence the details of the affair,
which Lawrence tells him, wisely omitting the
shrewd suspicion that it was not billiards nor a
mustache that they were fighting about—but Mrs.
Stella Lovejoy.

To this the veteran remarks : " If you hadn't
called him out, my boy, you should never have had
little Bessie ! " and goes to telling him various anecdotes of his own duels in ante-bellum days, and continues :

" You're just like young Pinckney whom I winged
once—fiery, hot-blooded, and not bigger than a boy,
but plucky as old Nick himself ! "

Then he stops suddenly and ejaculates, " My God !
If anything happens to you ! " and the tears come
into his eyes, and he makes Lawrence very happy
and very miserable, by telling him how much he
knows his little Bessie loves him, and mutters : " We
must keep this from the little girl. Not a word to
her ! "

" Trust me for that ! " says Lawrence grimly.

With that the two gentlemen shake hands, the major remarking that he shall telegraph Bessie to remain in Jacksonville, which he hopes will keep the affair from his daughter's ears.

And Lawrence says: " Then I'd better write to her."

"Only a word or two," returns the father, " and don't write between the lines, for she's a perfect little witch at discovering hidden meanings," and astonishes Lawrence very greatly, and gives him quite a shock, for he continues: " Do you know, my little girl has sometimes said to me that your letters sound so much like your cousin Lilly's, that she would often think you had Lilly's brain in your body, only masculine and stronger, my boy ! "

So the major goes away, telling him he will drop in upon him in the evening, and recommending raw beef for the eye, and Lawrence, after making himself as comfortable as he can under the circumstances, sits down and writes a long, very tender, and yearning letter to his sweetheart in Jacksonville ; and then sighs and makes a short autographic last will and testament, leaving everything he has in this world to his dear little Bessie.

The evening brings the major, who takes dinner with Mr. Talbot in that gentleman's parlor, his eye preventing his appearance in a public dining-room.

But shortly after the meal is over the major says suddenly : " Oh Lord ! I forgot the pistols. I must take the barkers to the gun-maker's, to have them put in first-rate order for to-morrow. I'll go round and get them. I shall call for you at twelve o'clock to-morrow, my boy, and I think I will bring you out of this affair very nicely."

"How so?" asks Lawrence rising, for Horton has got up to go.

"Young Wilkes, the doctor's second, doesn't seem to know much about the delicate points of the duello, and I think I can obtain some nice advantages for you, of wind and sun," remarks this exponent of ancient fair play, after the manner of the code of honor, where any technical advantage that can be obtained by the second for his principal, is considered quite the proper thing among gentlemen.

But the next morning the mail from New York brings two letters to Doctor Frederick Cassadene, that change materially the major's prognostications of this eventful day.

The first is from the clerk of the Buckingham Hotel, which states distinctly and positively, that no young lady of the name of Lillian Travers has registered at their house during the last month; consequently she has not lived there, and has not left that hostelry for Europe.

The second is from the firm who had acted for some time as attorneys for Miss Travers. It is the following curious epistle:

"79½ NASSAU STREET, NEW YORK CITY,
April 7th, 1891.

DOCTOR FREDERICK CASSADENE,
     DEAR SIR:
     Your favor of April 2d at hand, and contents noted: In an-swer we would say that Miss Travers, during the last three weeks she was in New York, that is, from about the 6th of February to about the 23d of that month, withdrew all her papers from our office, and disposed of all her real estate in New York City. This

we know as we were called in to decide upon one or two of the titles to her realty, by clients who purchased the same.

Noting your apparent anxiety about the lady (to whom we know you are engaged) we have made some inquiries among the real estate dealers and stock brokers, through whom she transacted her business during her last stay in New York. She has apparently converted most of her fortune into Government bonds, and deposited them in the Central Safe Deposit Company, where she has taken her box in the name of herself and her cousin, Mr. Lawrence Talbot.

The records of all out-going steamers for the last week we have examined, and find that her name is on the passenger lists of none of them.

We have made this examination very carefully, very cautiously, and very thoroughly, knowing your interest in the lady, whose late actions in regard to her property were to say the least eccentric.

In case you should have reason to think that her mind is in any way affected, please notify us, so that we can communicate with our former client's relatives.

You need not fear to be entirely frank with us, as we have only the young lady's interests at heart, her father having been one of our oldest clients, and his daughter having endeared herself to us by many acts of personal kindness.

Awaiting your reply, we remain,
Yours most respectfully,
BROUGHTON & WILLIAMS.

If the first epistle astonished Doctor Cassadene, the second one horrifies him. He puts the facts together, and is more concerned than before; for this appalling chain of circumstances develops itself in his mind :

First, Miss Travers, for some reason or other, deposited an immense amount of securities in a box at the Central Safe Deposit Company, to which only she and Lawrence Talbot had access.

Second, That Miss Travers disappeared from the Ocklawaha boat on the night of February 28th, 1891. On that same trip Lawrence Talbot, who had surreptitiously taken passage on the same boat, left it in the middle of the night at Orange Creek Landing.

Third, Since that time Miss Travers has really never been heard of, though this same Lawrence Talbot has brought a letter, purporting to come from Miss Travers in New York, where Miss Travers has not been; therefore the letter is a forgery. From all this he concludes that Lawrence Talbot did murder his cousin, Lilly Travers, on the night of February 28th, and that he has kept the secret of her demise from her relatives and friends, by forged letters purporting to come from his victim, and that he had every motive for the act.   For his cousin, believing in his honesty and manhood, had for some reason or other, left open to him her safe deposit box, he perhaps having some small sum in it, so that, Lilly Travers dead, all her wealth, securities, and bonds were as free to this young man, as if they were his own.

"He must have used them as his own," concludes the doctor, for Lawrence's presents to Bessie have been the talk of St. Augustine, and this young gentleman has thrown his money away very recklessly and extravagantly on all occasions.

Looking over the evidence before him, Cassadene sighs: "My Heaven! poor, poor Lilly!" and then mutters to himself, dashing away a tear: "This infernal monster shall pay for his dastard work! I'll hang the scoundrel as an assassin—not shoot him as I would a gentleman!"

16

CHAPTER XVIII.

THE HORRIBLE METAMORPHOSIS OF DOCTOR FREDERICK CASSADENE.

THESE examinations, deductions, and inferences have taken Dr. Cassadene until eleven o'clock. Forgetful of the duel that is to take place at one, and his peculiar relationship in this regard to the gentleman whom he is to meet, he mutters to himself: " I'll give the fiend no chance to escape! I'll confront him with his crime! I'll gloat over the cruel scoundrel's agony and terror. I'll give him the same mercy as he gave my poor murdered Lilly, who would have again loved me, if he had but let her!"

So he strides over to the Cordova, and without sending up his card, knowing very well the number of Lawrence's room, steps up, and raps on the door of that gentleman's apartment.

He is ushered in by John, who has a very dark and serious face upon him this morning, though his teeth and eyes are excitedly white. This worthy seems somewhat frightened at beholding the warlike doctor.

" I wish to see Lawrence Talbot!" says Cassadene shortly. " He's in his parlor, isn't he?" and before John can stop him, he steps through the bedroom: for this suite of apartments, like most of the tower rooms in the Cordova, is curiously arranged, the entrance being through the bedroom and the parlor being the immediate corner room, having a

view of the Alameda and Cordova Street, from its
Moorish windows.

Here he is confronted by Lawrence, who has just
made an elaborate toilet, apparently for the approaching meeting.

This gentleman remarks : " If you have any communication to make in regard to the affair between
us, make it through your second to mine, Major
Horton."

" I have a few words to say to you," says the
Doctor, " that I don't think you would care to pass
between us through other parties, and after I have
spoken to you the sheriff's officer will do the rest."

At these words, a peculiar look comes into Lawrence Talbot's face. He ejaculates : " John, shut the
outer door ! "

" Oh, that doesn't frighten me ! " sneers Cassadene.
" There are a hundred people within call. You
can't get away—that's the only thing I want to
guard against."

" I'm not running ! " answers Talbot uneasily.
" Now give me your message."

" Very well, you miserable assassin ! " says the
Doctor sternly.

" Assassin of whom ? " gasps Lawrence, perhaps
some inkling of the extraordinary accusation that is
upon him, coming to him to make him pale and
nervous.

" The assassin of your cousin, Lilly Travers, whom
you foully murdered, together with her maid, Jane
Rouser, on the night of February 28, 1891, on the
Ocklawaha boat, to obtain her fortune, and in this
fiendish crime you were assisted by your man, your

accomplice John Robbins!   Ah! that brought you!"
cries the Doctor in triumph, for at his words Lawrence has grown very pale, and sunk into a chair,
and there is a murmured " Oh golly!   Oh Lawdy!
I'se 'cused of suicide!'" and a clashing together of
ivories, from " the accomplice, John Robbins," who
has gone into an ecstasy of mingled laughter and
terror, in the next room.

" What—makes—you—think that ?" stammers
Talbot after a moment.

" Think it—I know it!" cries the Doctor. " I can
prove it!   I can hang you, you cruel monster that
murdered that poor girl, who would have loved me
if you had but let her live!"

But this is interrupted by a fearful giggle from
Lawrence.

" Quiet, you—you young fiend!" hisses Cassadene.

" Give me your proofs!" whispers Lawrence. " I
would hate the man who had murdered Lilly Travers as much as you—yes—*much more !* "

" Very well!   Here they are—convincing ones.
Only don't try and come the sympathetic dodge—it
won't work on me.   I was on the boat that night!"
cries the Doctor.   " I saw you get off at Orange
Spring Landing—you and your accomplice John.
You had the same suits of clothes on in which you
left St. Augustine for New York."

" I admit I was on the boat," remarks Lawrence
candidly.   " I remember perfectly Miss Travers
threatening to knock you overboard, if you dared
put your hand upon her shoulder again."

" Ah, ha! you confess!"

"That much, certainly!"

"You went to New York, you pretended that you met Lilly Travers there. You forged letters in her handwriting to deceive her relatives and make them think she was alive. The strong box in the Central Safe Deposit Company was open to both you and her. You murdered her that you might get her securities and make yourself rich, the wealth you are now lavishing upon Miss Bessie Horton. Do you think she will love you after she knows you are the murderer of Lilly Travers? Ah! that touches you, you brute!" For this view of the case makes Lawrence shudder and grow deathly sick with apprehension. But Cassadene keeps on: "You miserable murderer! You wretched cowardly assassin! And you threw that beautiful girl overboard, to be the prey of the alligators and the reptiles of that swampy river! Monster!" Then the doctor, working himself up into a rage, almost seizes the supposed criminal by the throat.

He starts back astonished, however, as Lawrence gasps back at him : "I would cry vengeance on the murderer of Lilly Travers more loudly than you, because if Lilly Travers had been assassinated I would not exist!"

"Not exist?"

"Certainly not. The murderer would have killed *me!*" Then he says: "Fred," assuming as near as possible the old tones, "don't you know me, old boy? Don't you remember your fiancée Lilly Travers? Fickle one! Have you forgotten me in three weeks?"

And something in his manner and his tone strik-

ing the Doctor, he grows pale also, and murmurs:
"Good heavens! What do you mean?"

"I mean that you are not accusing me of murder
but suicide!"

"Suicide? Ha ha!—ho ho!—he he!" and the
Doctor jeers him.

"Yes, suicide!" cries Lawrence desperately.
"*For I am Lilly Travers!*"

"You, a man, assert that you're a woman!" Cassadene gasps.

"I can prove it!"

"You tell this bosh to me—a doctor?"

"Yes. Listen to me," and he rapidly gives Fred
the record of two or three interviews, that no one
but Lilly Travers could know.

But Cassadene turns this off with, "Bah! She has
told them to you. She trusted you as her cousin,
and you murdered her!"

"Not at all! I SIMPLY TRANSFORMED HER INTO
MYSELF!"

"What gibberish are you giving me?" cries the
Doctor. "Do you think you will escape by making
yourself out a lunatic?" Then he turns pale, for he
suddenly thinks he is in the presence of a madman
whose craze is murder.

"I am as sane as you are! Don't bandy words!"
begs Lawrence appealingly. "Listen to me, Fred,
and believe." Then to his accuser's astonishment,
he says: "You remember the casket I spoke to you
about purchasing, at Vedder's?"

"Yes," says Cassadene, shortly, as anxious to put
a stop to what he thinks absurd palaver.

"You remember how you deceived me by writing

that you were called to a case of snake-bite, when
you took that moonlight sail with Stella Lovejoy?"

"Yes!"

"You recollect the words you last spoke to Lilly
Travers when you parted from her at her aunt's
house; that you said within a month, despite myself, you would make me marry you?"

"Pooh!" cries the Doctor. "These revelations
you make to me, have been told you by your
murdered victim."

"Not at all—do you see this?" and Lawrence
produces from his neck a little vial containing the
two amber seeds that still play about each other
with the same vivacity and elfish life that they did
when he first looked at them, and he points to the
label:

FOR WOMEN WHO SUFFER. HA! HA! HA!

and then going on, he tells to the astonished Frederick Cassadene, old Hauser Oglethorpe's wondrous
story of the "Tree of Sexual Change," and how,
driven to desperation by the Doctor's untruth to
him, to drown the agony of jealousy in his heart, he
had taken one of these marvelous seeds to become
a man, and that to keep his secret, he had given his
maid Jane another, and Jane was standing there in
the next room now, his valet, Jack Robbins; and
as he finishes, he holds out his hand and whispers:
"Freddie, old boy, do you believe?"

And Cassadene replies: "Believe? Nonsense!
Impossible! I am a doctor. Tell such a story to

the jury and they will put you in an insane asylum,
but never anywhere else. Keep the hand that
slaughtered my lost sweetheart away from me. I
am going to have you arrested!"

"That you shall not do!" cries Lawrence desperately. "I can prove by one of these seeds—by trans-
forming myself into a woman again, that though
now I am Lawrence Talbot, I once was Lilly
Travers."

"Very well!" ·scoffs the doctor. "Take it!
Swallow it in front of me, and when you become
Lilly Travers again, I will love you as of old, and I
will marry you!"

But Lawrence, starting back, gasps: "Marry you,
who make love to all women, and think as little of
breaking a girl's heart as you would of destroying a
microbe—marry you—NEVER! and for that reason
I'll never become a woman again! But you shall
not make this public! My God! What would
Bessie say? Her father would regard me as one accursed—she would look on me as weird—uncanny—
unnatural—she would not marry me. You shall
believe—by this!"

And opening the vial, Lawrence takes forth one
of the Obi-seeds of Hauser Oglethorpe.

"You will take it?" says Cassadene to Lawrence,
who is half minded, in his despair, to become a
woman again, for one short moment, to make this
man believe him:

But as he thinks this and shudders at it, looking
through the open curtains of the door to his bedroom, he sees the stalwart Ethiopian his maid Jane
has developed into, and motions, and the negro,

understanding, comes silently and slowly forth, and then, like the spring of a black snake, seizes Doctor Cassadene around the waist and throws that gentleman down, and has his knee upon his chest.

Before the astounded Frederick can open his mouth to give a shriek, Lawrence has fallen upon him, and squeezing his enemy's nostrils between his fingers, the doctor opens his mouth, gasping for breath, and in that one fatal moment Lawrence has tossed in between the white teeth of Frederick Cassadene, a seed that springs joyously on its way down his throat to make the " masher " of the Ponce de Leon the sex of which his victims have been, but will be so no more.

This being done, the two suddenly release him. He springs to his feet, and gives an affrighted cry, for the winged seed as it sprang down his throat, had given his tonsils an awful grip.

" Is it poison ? " he gasps, with a pale face.

" No," says Lawrence, " I have taken one, and so has Jane there and we are both alive. You will live too, but as one of the sex you adore. *A woman !* "

" A WOMAN!" shrieks the Doctor. " Fiends of enchantment ! This morning the beautiful Stella promised to marry me !" Then he says trying to be calm but trembling all over, " Pooh ! Rubbish.! Absurd ! Idiotic !" but finally utters a faint cry and mutters with affrighted eyes : " What has come to me ? What is passing through me ? I am not as I once was ! " and sinks into a chair and mumbles to himself and utters little female cries of dismay in a voice that gradually becomes soprano and finally sits collapsed for some five minutes.

This scene would be weird and awful and cruel were it not for the hideous laughter of the negro, who guffaws : " Golly ! S'pose we had been brought up for murd'rin' ourselves ! Dat ain't a possible crime, is it, Mr. Lawrence ?" and chuckles now and then, " What will de widder say to yo', Missus Doctor !" and other hideous samples of darkey wit and humor.

But there is a knocking at the door, and Lawrence says : " Open it ! I think we have nothing to fear from this *lady !* " and bows politely to Cassadene, who suddenly looks at him, and astonishes him by saying :

" What a handsome young man you are !" as the major enters the apartment.

This gentleman starts upon seeing the Doctor, and says : " This visit to the gentleman I represent is so out of time and place, that hearing of it from an employee of the hotel, I found your second, and brought Mr. Wilkes with me to take you away. I demand your withdrawal from this room until you meet my friend upon the field of honor. These pistols, I think, Mr. Wilkes, will settle the business," and he produces two good old-fashioned duelling pistols.

But here the Doctor rises from his seat, and says, nervously: " You are sure they are not loaded ! I don't like to look at pistols ! They always make me frightened. Their noise is quite shocking !" and Wilkes and the major stare at each other astonished.

" Why, you fire-eater !" cries the ex-Confederate. " Is the rage oozing out of the ends of your fingers ? You have come here to apologize, I suppose."

".I didn't come here for that, but I am·so nervous about pistols and such things ; please put them

away. I know they'll go off, and then I'll scream!"
says Frederick in feminine voice and mincing manner.

On this Wilkes exclaims : " Hang you, Cassadene!
You're a coward."

And the major cries : " Why, this swash-buckler
has changed his tone! Mr. Wilkes, for the sake of
your principal, prevent any further such unmanly
exhibitions—withdraw him! The gentleman I represent meets only men who are not poltroons."

But the Doctress only laughs the hideous laugh of
despair, and says: " I don't think it's polite of you,
major, to treat me in that way. You are generally
gallant to one of my sex!" And she simpers at
him and disgusts him, till he cries out : " By Gad,
sir, you're no gentleman!"

"No, I'm not!" gasps the Doctress hysterically.
"I'm—! Oh Powers of Magic! What am I?"

"You're a libel upon manhood," answers his
second in disgust.

"You see, sir!" says the major pointing to the
Doctor. "Take this creature who has disgraced
himself away! I feel sorry for your embarrassing
position. I beg you to withdraw."

But Wilkes is saved any trouble on this point, for
suddenly uttering a hideous yell of despair, Doctress
Frederika Cassadene goes into a fit of hysterics,
bolts from the apartment and disappears, followed
shortly after, by his second.

Then the major, turning to Lawrence, claps him
on the shoulder, and says : " My dear boy, I would
have brought you out of this affair all right; but
perhaps it is best it ended in this way; even cow-
ards' pistols are sometimes fatal to brave men!"

CHAPTER XIX.

"I'VE COME FOR THAT SEED!"

HERE Lawrence suddenly suggests : " Hadn't you better telegraph Bessie ? There is now nothing to keep her away from St. Augustine."

" Ah ! a little lonely, my Romeo," utters the major playfully. Then he adds : " Think of the loneliness that you will cause me when you take her from me ; " and the veteran's lips tremble and there are tears in his eyes, but brushing them away, he continues : " You are a boy after my own heart, Lawrence. Egad ! How that white-livered doctor quailed before you ! " For Lawrence's adherence to the code has somehow put him very high in the Southerner's good graces.

So they step down to the telegraph office and wire Miss Bessie that she can come back. Then the two drive out to the major's place on the San Sebastian, Lawrence feeling his nerves a little unstrung by the terrible interview he has gone through with the Doctor, thinking to himself : " I would have sooner faced his pistol than been compelled to trust him with my secret." A moment after he cogitates with a sigh of relief : " *She* dare never reveal it. Poor old Doctress Freddie ! I wonder what she is doing now. I believe I have taken her last chance with the girls away from her. I've downed her with the widow this time, certain."

Of this there can be no doubt, for Doctress Frederika Cassadene, after a hurried visit to her room at the Ponce de Leon, has suddenly fled from that hostelry and the town of St. Augustine, and has even forgotten to liquidate the hotel bill, and other small accounts of the late Frederick Cassadene, M.D.

As they drive up the gravel road to the ex-Confederate's house, there is the fluttering of a white dress on the veranda and the major ejaculates: "Great goodness! Bessie's here already." And as they spring out of the carriage he says sharply to his daughter: " You got my telegram ? "

" Yes, dear papa," replies the girl, giving him a kiss.

"Didn't I tell you not to return to-day? What brought you here ? "

" Your despatch, dear papa! It told me not to leave Jacksonville, so I immediately came on, to find out what was the matter," replies the young lady riantly ; and turning to Lawrence, she opens her blue eyes very wide and gasps : " But what *is* the matter? Have you been fighting ?"—for he still bears the scars of yesterday's encounter.

"No ; but he came very near encountering Cassadene in a duel to-day, my little daughter."

"For me?—Oh mercy !" cries Bessie, looking astonished and horrified.

" No," replies the major; "for his insulted mustache. But the white-livered doctor didn't dare stand before your sweetheart. My little Bessie, I congratulate you on gaining a husband who will love you and who will fight for you if need be."

Then the old gentleman turns away and leaves the lovers together, Miss Bessie looking very serious.

A moment after she suddenly says : "What was the real reason of your duel?" then uneasily exclaims: "Was it about a woman?" next, apparently frightened, stammers: "No, no; don't tell me."

"It was about a woman," answers Lawrence.

"Ah! don't tell me."

"It was about Lilly Travers," continues this young man in nonchalant prevarication.

"Ah!—he thought she loved you?" says Bessie.

"No; Cassadene thought I had been instrumental in preventing that young lady marrying him."

"And you were?"

"Very much! I was the chief obstacle to his leading Lilly Travers to the altar, and he knows it now." With this Lawrence gives a little laugh. This is echoed by the young lady; who says: "I am very glad you prevented Lilly marrying the Doctor. I think he is very insincere in his attentions to my sex. Look at poor Stella Lovejoy at the Ponce de Leon—how he has dallied with her."

"Well, I rather imagine this deal has fixed him with her also," says Lawrence, his ripple of laughter growing into a broad grin. Next he asks: "But Bess, how about the trousseau?"—and continues nervously: "Will it be ready in time?" For this young man, in the presence of his vivacious fiancée, grows very anxious for his coming happiness.

"Y-e-s," murmurs Miss Bess, getting rosy with blushes, and the two go into a conversation that only lovers engage in who have passed the Rubicon of courtship and whose wedding-day and wedding-bells and orange blossoms are very near to them.

But before this takes place, a very curious adventure happens to Mr. Talbot. Chancing to visit Jacksonville one day on some errand for his sweetheart, he stops at the St. James Hotel, and while there, word is brought to him that a lady wishes to see him in the parlor.   He carelessly steps in, and a tall, gaunt, masculine-looking woman with a hunted· look in her face, gathering her gown about her in an uneasy way, rises and glares at him, whispering: "Don't you know me?"

He almost staggers as he gasps: "Doctor Freddie!"

"Don't mention my late name, dear," she says, giving him what she imagines to be a captivating ogle. "I dare not go back to St. Augustine, but I waited around here, for I could not leave you. You looked so beautiful to me that awful day you made me a woman, that I have lingered about hoping to see your loved face once more before you foolishly wedded another and destroyed both our lives.   For the memory of our old love has come into my heart to make me, as a woman, love you as a man."

To this Lawrence replies nothing, though his face grows very white ; and she goes on again in the impulsive manner of woman's self-sacrifice, and says: "If you will marry me, I will make you the best wife in this world.   I will complain of nothing.   I will be your slave—your idolater—your worshipper, my own, my beautiful boy! You shall go to the club and I will not reproach you if you stay out till the morning hours.   You shall have the love of a wife, with the devotion of a slave.   You are all that is left for me now.   Think how I love you!" And she gives him loving glances that seem to him hideous coming from this gaunt and masculine creature.

He shudderingly mutters: "No ! no ! Impossible."

256 A FLORIDA ENCHANTMENT.

Then a cunning gleam comes into her eyes and she says : " Though you despise me, I will still do you a service. I will make you richer than you are. I once had a patient as a doctor in New York, a woman, immensely wealthy, who will give for that one sacred seed you carry with you a million dollars —perhaps more. Give it to me and I will take it to her, and you shall have half of what I receive for it." And she looks with longing eyes upon the place where she remembers Lawrence always carries the vial that bears the one last magic seed of Hauser Oglethorpe.

But he mutters hoarsely : " No ! no ! With that precious implement in your hand, you would never reach New York a woman. You would be a man before you left Jacksonville."

And then she falls upon him, and almost struggles with him, crying in despair : " I will have it. You have ruined my life forever. Were I but a man again, I could marry the widow—the beautiful Stella, who loves me—who is ready to give her beauty and her wealth to me. Give it to me—I will have it." And begs him and prays to him with wild words and wilder gestures as she would do to a god who held her life in his hand.

But he mutters hoarsely to her: " Never ! It is the talisman that shall prove me innocent, if I am ever accused of Lilly Travers' murder by some one who hates me as you do." And breaking away from her, Lawrence runs to the depot and takes the first train for St. Augustine, though it is a local and a very slow one.

So it comes to pass, a few days after, in the beau-

tiful church at St. Augustine, that looks to the outside traveller more like a Moorish mosque of Islam
than a Protestant church, Lawrence and Bessie, 'mid
the chimes of joyous wedding-bells and in the presence of the notables of the town and the few hotel
guests that are left (for the season is drawing very
near its close),—are wedded ; and dear old Connie,
kissing the bride says : " If Lilly were only here to
kiss you too ! " But the groom says to this, his
eyes flashing very brightly : " I will take Lilly's
place. This is Lilly's kiss ! "—and puts upon the
blushing red lips of his newly-made bride the salute
from the girl Bessie had loved so well and whom
she had lost forever, to gain a husband.

And shortly after this the two take the train for
the North, en route for Europe, the major promising
to follow after them—partly on business, partly on
pleasure; for he has made a sale of most of his
phosphate lands to one of those all-devouring English financial syndicates which spend a great deal of
money in America and receive comparatively little
back again, and he is going on to London to complete the details of the transaction and add a goodly
number of English pounds sterling to the American
dollars in his bank account.

In New York they stop at the Brevoort, Lawrence
having selected this very fashionable but very quiet
house for his residence before the departing steamer
shall bear them away to Europe; and in due time
they are driven to the Etruria that is at her dock
with steam up ready to point her prow to England.
The great ship's crowded decks are covered with the
varying throng of passengers that in the early spring

17

take this great Atlantic ferry to spend a few months in Europe and return once more to winter in New York. And in this crowd are other bridal couples— some of them, perhaps equally as happy as Lawrence and his fair young bride—but none more so.

Bessie stands on the deck bidding adieu to some Southern friends who have come to see them off, when Lawrence's man Jack, suddenly stepping to him with mysterious air and frightened face and jabbering teeth, whispers : " Dar's a lady waitin' fo' yo', sah, in yo' state-room, dat swear she won't go on sho' till she see yo', an' dat she'll make de mos' terr'ble hubbub an' row in de worl' an'll denounce yo' right heah an' will bust de deck up, ef yo' don't see her."

Then Lawrence knows his fate is upon him again and that Doctress Frederika Cassadené is waiting to see him ; and he goes down to find the same gaunt female who had fallen upon his neck in Jacksonville.

She whispers to him, her eyes red with despair : " I have come for that seed. I will never leave you until I get that seed. I have tried to be a doctress in New York, but no patients have come to me. You have driven me to a woman's desperation.. I will denounce you to your bride as a changeling, if you don't give me the one thing on earth that can make me happy."

But Lawrence, very pale, says again : " No ; that story would never be believed. Tell them ! You will be thought a lunatic : I keep this last seed for my own safety."

" But is it for your safety ? " cries the once Doctor Frederick. " Think what would happen to you

if your bride—the lovely but inquisitive Bessie—
ever got hold of it and guessed its wondrous power!
Don't you *know* she would eat? Do you think
woman could resist such temptation? And when
once it had passed her lips, would not happiness go
away from you?—for there would be no other seed
left to bring her back to womanhood and wifehood,
and you would be bereft forever."

At this awful suggestion Lawrence grows pale and
leaning against the stateroom door exclaims: "My
God! If she ever got it!"

There is the flutter of a beautiful travelling-dress
coming down the companion-way, and he hears Bessie's voice saying: "Where is Lawrence? I must
show him the lovely flowers that have been sent
us from far away Florida to make our wedding trip
happy."

And thinking what would come upon him in case
his lovely, but inquisitive and impulsive little bride,
ever grasped the dangerous fetich he has in his
hand, he plucks it from his neck, and pressing it into
the palm of the gaunt creature who is looking at him
with gloating hungry eyes, he whispers: "Take it!
Become a man again and wed the beautiful widow."

There is a rush of semi-masculine strides over
the gang-way, and the gaunt female flies with a hideous cry of joy toward the shore, even while on the
gang-plank—not daring to wait—pressing into her
mouth the last sacred Obi-seed of old Hauser Oglethorpe.

Then the Etruria, 'mid the saluting whistles of
surrounding steam tugs, puts her prow down North
River, towards Sandy Hook, and steams away upon

her voyage across a summer sea, bearing to happiness and love in different scenes from the old Florida orange groves, Lawrence Talbot, who will be a man forever, and his bride, Bessie, who will still remain to him forever a woman, and a joy.

FINIS.

EUROPEAN NOTICES

OF

Gunter's Last Great Novel

Miss Nobody

of Nowhere

OPINIONS OF

THE GREAT NOVEL,

Mr. Barnes

of New York.

ENGLAND.

"There is no reason for surprise at 'Mr. Barnes' being a *big hit*."—*The Referee*, London, March 25th.

"*Exciting and interesting*."—*The Graphic*.

"'Marina Paoli'—a giant character—just as strong as 'Fedora.'"—*Illustrated London News*.

"A capital story—most people have read it—I recommend it to all the others."
—JAMES PAYNE in *Illustrated London News*.

AMERICA.

"Told with the genius of Alexander Dumas, the Elder."—*Amusement Gazette*.

"Have you read 'MR. BARNES OF NEW YORK?' If no, go and read it at once, and thank me for suggesting it. . . . I want to be put on record as saying 'it is the best story of the day—the best I have read in ten years.'"—JOE HOWARD in *Boston Globe*.

But at that time Mr. Howard had not read

"Mr. Potter of Texas."

That Frenchman!

Now in the One-Hundred-and-Tenth Thousand.

By the Author of "Mr. Barnes of New York."

PAPER, 50 CENTS; CLOTH, $1.50.

"The work exhibits the wonderful resources of the author's mind and the richness of his imaginative powers. The characters are forcibly drawn, the details worked up with surprising exactness, and the plot unraveled with scrupulous care."—*San Francisco Post*, May 25, 1889.

How I Escaped.

By W. H. PARKINS.

EDITED BY ARCHIBALD CLAVERING GUNTER.

PAPER, 50 CENTS; CLOTH, $1.00.

"The best story of the war yet written."
—*Atlanta Constitution.*

"Mr. Gunter's books are more generally read than perhaps those of ANY OTHER LIVING WRITER."

—*The Times.*

London, Eng., Nov. 4, 1888.

Miss Nobody
of Nowhere

Gunter's Last and Most Successfu

Miss Nobody
of Nowhere

"Full of incident and excitement."—*NEW YORK HERALD.*

"The popularity of Mr. Gunter will now be grea than ever."—*TACOMA GLOBE.*

"A story that will kee a man away from hi meals."—*^MAHA BEE.* •